NOCTURNAL DESIRES

BOOK 9 OF THE WESTWOOD PACK

F.D. FAIR

Foundations Book Publishing
4209 Lakeland Drive, #398, Flowood, MS 39232
www.FoundationsBooks.net

Nocturnal Desires
Book 9
The Westwood Pack

ISBN: 978-1-64583-129-7

Copyright © 2024 by FD Fair
Cover by Dawné Dominique Copyright 2024
Book Formatting by Bella Roccaforte

Published in the United States of America
Worldwide Electronic & Digital Rights
Worldwide English Language Print Rights

Chapter One

Loukas—Eleven years ago

"Well, hello there," a silky voice purrs in my ear as I sit on the beach and soak up the sun.

My eyes fly open, finding the bright blue eyes of a stranger boring into mine.

"Hello," I respond, regaining my composure as I blink a few times and climb to my feet.

My eyes begin at her feet, her tanned toes painted pink, and follow her smooth legs up to her black bikini bottoms, tanned, flat stomach, to the perky breasts almost popping out of her string bikini top.

I'm already practically drooling at the sight before I get to her absolutely gorgeous face. Tight black curls flow over her shoulders and surround her. Long, dark eyelashes frame her oval eyes, providing a gentle contrast against her skin tone. Her nose is graceful and in proportion to her face, with contours that blend seamlessly with her other features. It's her red lips that catch my attention with a warm smile that is soft and inviting. Her eyes crinkle into the smile and seem to sparkle.

"I'm Antonia," she says, her smile widening to show off her

pearly white teeth.

Instead of answering, I open and close my mouth like a stunned fish. She has to be the most beautiful woman I've ever seen, and that's saying something. I am used to meeting other supernaturals who have an otherworldly glow and unnaturally good looks, but the woman standing before me is more than that. She's a goddess in human form.

A soft giggle snaps me back to reality.

"Sorry," I say, clearing my throat and offering my hand. "I'm Loukas."

As she slips her small hand into mine, a shock of electricity shoots between us. I look from our joined hands up to her eyes, searching for a reason.

She's not my mate—of that I'm sure. My owl is silent, watching patiently from behind my eyes. She may not be my mate, but there's a connection between us that I don't understand.

The next few weeks fly by with Antonia and I spending every moment together, stealing kisses—and more—whenever we can. I've fallen so hard and fast for this incredible woman that it's hard to believe she's real. I joke that it's like she's put a spell on me. She's a witch, of course, but we both know she wouldn't do that.

"I was thinking..." She interrupts my thoughts as we lay atop a cliff overlooking the ocean. The sounds of waves crashing into them and the gentle breeze rustling through the trees nearly put me to sleep.

I raise up to my elbows, reaching out to take her hand in mine before bringing it to my mouth and placing a soft kiss on the smooth skin on top.

"About what, my love?" I ask, and she giggles.

"Well..." She bites her lip in that sexy way that drives me crazy. "I was thinking that maybe you could come with me when I go home next week."

I won't lie and say the thought hasn't crossed my mind, but the thought of leaving my home fills me with anxiety.

"What if *you* stayed instead?" I challenge.

A look of anger flashes across her sweet face.

That's not right.

It's not anger. For a moment, I think I see something more sinister in Antonia's expression, but it's gone so quickly that I question if it was my imagination.

"Loukas," she pouts.

"Seriously, Tonia. You love it here too. Why don't you stay?"

"I have obligations back home."

"So do I," I respond. I know already that this is ramping up to be our first fight.

This conversation was inevitable from the beginning. We've been so good at not bringing up the fact that she is leaving soon, but her leaving was always a threat on our horizon.

"I know that," she heaves out the words, slips her hand from mine, and rises to her feet. "I am next in line to be high priestess. I have no choice but to go home."

"I'm next in line to be alpha," I remind her.

"You could abdicate," she suggests.

"I could tell you to do the same." I rise to my feet as well, turning toward the sea and taking a deep breath.

I don't want to lose her, but I can't leave my family. There's no point in fighting over something that we always knew would have to come between us. She can't abandon her coven, and I can't abandon my parliament.

I hear a soft sniff behind me, and all my frustration flees at the sound. I spin and find Antonia behind me, tears streaming down her face.

"I just want us to be together," she sobs.

"Hey," I say softly, stepping closer to her and taking her face in my hands. "That's what I want too. We'll figure it out."

"How?" she asks, looking up at me, her blue eyes shining with tears.

"I'm not sure yet. But we will." I pull her in, wrapping my arms around her. "Why don't you come and meet my parliament tonight? We have a week, so we should explore all our options."

I hadn't planned on introducing her to my family just yet. They aren't purists or anything like that, but everyone expects their next alpha to find a shifter mate.

I've known since I met her that Tonia is not my true mate. The mating bond isn't there, but everything feels so right I have no doubt she could be my chosen mate.

"Really?" She perks up at my suggestion, and I nod. A squeal of happiness leaves her, and she jumps into my arms.

Even with the fight forgotten, for now, something just doesn't feel right...

Even my owl is eyeing her warily for the first time.

I take her hand and lead her from the cliff to the path that leads to the secret opening in the rock wall. I'd prefer to warn my family first, but I am afraid of losing the temporary peace between us. The location of our village has been a well-kept secret for eons. Some of us only leave the safety of our parliament for food, but others leave daily for work or travel. None of us bring outsiders without permission.

The few times that outsiders have been granted permission it is the final step between the visitor and host becoming mates. That's what I intend as well. I'm bringing my mate back to meet my family. So why does it feel so wrong to bring her here?

I glance over at her as we walk hand in hand. She's talking, though I don't register her words as I wrestle with my anxiety. She's beaming with happiness, and I should be too.

I stop just before the opening and turn to her.

"You have to swear not to share the location of our parliament with anyone."

"Of course," she says softly, going up on her tiptoes and

pressing a soft kiss to my lips. Almost instantly, any doubts I have vanish, and I pull her through the pass without a second thought.

As we approach, I can hear the hustle and bustle of the village on the other side with my enhanced hearing. As we step through, silence sweeps across the village. Children stop playing, adults pause their conversations with their mouths hanging open in shock. The face I focus on is my father, Spiros, as he stomps toward us with his face twisted in anger.

"Loukas, who is your *guest*?"

The way he says the word has my gut churning with regret. I had told my father about Antonia, of course. I had asked about bringing her to meet our family. Each time, he asked the same question. "Is she your mate? No? Then you have your answer."

I take a large gulp and glance at Antonia. I've already come this far, and I know the one way to avoid this argument with my father is to introduce her as my mate.

"This is Antonia, she is my..." I try to force the word through my lips, but my body refuses to cooperate under my father's knowing stare.

"I'm his girlfriend," Antonia supplies. "It's very nice to meet you."

She reaches out to shake my father's hand. He looks down at it once before raising a brow at me, spinning on his heel, and walking away from us.

Well, shit.

"Did I do something wrong?" Tonia asks, sadness lacing her words.

"No, baby. You didn't."

Instead of leading her further into the village, knowing she won't be welcome, I lead her back the way we came to the beach.

"Aren't you going to introduce me to your family?" she asks, confusion and hurt painted across her sweet face. I step away, trying to get room to think, and run a hand through my hair.

5

I fucked up. I really, really fucked up.

As I pace, I steal glances at her. Can I make Antonia my mate? Can I live for the rest of my life with this woman? For the first time since meeting her, I begin to question everything. When it was just the two of us, falling for her so quickly seemed to make perfect sense. Now that I see the stakes, I can't believe I've let this get so far. Is she worth throwing away the relationship I have with my father?

"Listen, baby, I have to go talk to my father and smooth things over," I explain, rubbing her slim shoulders calmingly. "I'll meet you here tomorrow, okay?"

"I don't understand. I thought I was going to meet your family."

"You will," I promise. "They are very secretive, and I should have warned them before bringing an outsider to visit."

"An outsider?" Her tone is somewhere between confusion and offense.

"The only time we allow outsiders into our village is if we intend to take them as our mates," I explain. "I didn't declare that to my father before I brought you."

"But you *do* intend to take me as your mate, right?" she questions, and I hesitate. If she asked me that yesterday—hell, even earlier today—the answer would've been a resounding yes.

"Of course." The lie slips easily off my tongue, but she eyes me warily. "I just need to talk to my father first."

"Are you sure?" she asks, anger lacing her words.

"It's you and me, my love. Now and forever," I tell her, capturing her lips with mine. "I'll see you tomorrow. Right here."

"I love you," she says as I turn to walk away.

"Me too," I respond, the sentiment churning in my gut for some reason.

Quickly, I shift into my owl, letting him take the reins as I think over what to do.

We cannot mate that woman, he says adamantly.

What? Why? I ask, shocked by the strength of his resolve.

This is the first time he has expressed displeasure at the thought of mating Antonia.

Isn't it? Since I met her, I haven't felt him much at all. I guess I haven't shifted much either. I try to think back to the last time I flew and can't recall. Strange…

My wings falter a bit, and I lend my owl some of my strength to even us out.

Something's wrong. My owl projects the words into my mind seconds before I'm forced back into human form. I fall sixty feet out of the sky and land at the edge of the village with a loud thud.

Everything goes black.

As I come to, I am aware only of my father's voice booming across the room.

"What was he thinking? Bringing her here?"

"He was thinking that he's in love, and he wanted to give her a reason to stay." My mother's voice, much calmer, reminds him. "Spiros, do you want him to leave us?"

I try to move, but my muscles protest. Everything hurts.

"What? No. Of course, I don't. Why would you say that?" My father's tone is offended.

"Well, what did you think would happen? He would just bid her goodbye next week and forget she exists? They're probably both trying to convince each other to stay or go."

"Rita, she's not his mate," my father argues, as if that is all anyone needs to know about the situation.

He and my mother are true mates and believe that I should wait for my own true mate. At twenty years old, I've almost given up hope. At eighteen, I traveled for a year around Greece and even Europe. I've had no luck finding her.

"She could be if he chooses her."

I open my eyes to see my four foot tall mother standing toe to toe with my giant father, hands on her hips.

"Dad's right," I whisper, finding my throat dry. "I made a mistake bringing her here."

My mother rushes over to me, helping me to sit up. She slides her arms under mine and gently moves me to a sitting position.

"Thanks, Ma," I say. She gives me a soft kiss on the head before rushing toward the kitchen to make what I'm sure is a meal fit for a king. It doesn't matter that we are all adults now. When any of her three children are hurt, we are her babies again.

My father walks up and settles heavily into the chair beside the bed with a sigh.

"Son, what were you thinking? You brought her here without my permission. Worse, with my express warning against doing so."

"I know," I admit, looking down at my lap. "I honestly don't know what happened."

"What do you mean?"

I glance up, see the concern in his eyes, and decide to be honest.

"If you asked me this morning if I intended to take Antonia as my mate, I would've said yes. I would have said it was just a matter of figuring out the logistics. But—"

"But what? That's all I needed to hear, son." My dad beams, his anger at my betrayal forgotten. "Bring her back tomorrow. We will have a feast."

I want to leave it there. He's no longer upset with me, and I have what I want. That's not who I am though. It's not who he raised me to be.

"Something changed," I begin, searching for the words to explain. "When I went to call her my mate, I just couldn't. It's like the words got stuck in my throat. Even now, the thought of taking her as my mate has my gut churning."

The chair's legs scrape against the floor as my father stands.

"So, you brought a woman who makes you sick to your stomach to our home?" he asks through clenched teeth. "This indecision is unfitting of an alpha."

"I'm sorry," I whisper as he walks away.

"I'm sorry too," he whispers as he exits, pushing past my mother through the doorway. She looks confused and apologetic as she places the steaming tray of food on the bedside table.

"What does your owl think?" she asks.

"That's the weirdest thing. At first, he was just as enamored with her as I was. Now that I think about it, he's been absent more often than not lately. I can't even remember shifting before today. You saw how that went."

"Hmm..." She worries her bottom lip as she thinks. "But he cares for her as you do?"

I close my eyes and search for the feelings of my owl. He's a part of myself, but his thoughts are a mystery to me just now.

"I don't know..."

"Well, I'm sure you will figure it out." She hands me the tray, laden with lobster bisque, a fresh bun, and some of her herbal tea. I greedily eat and drink before falling asleep once more.

The next time I wake, it's to the sounds of screams ringing out through the village. I throw the blanket off and rise, my muscles still protesting as I slide on the pair of linen pants folded neatly beside my head.

"What's going on, Ma?" I ask once I find her. She's standing by the door with my youngest sister, Evangeline.

"I don't know," she whispers.

"Is Dad out there?"

She just nods her head, looking lost. They are both watching the door, their eyes wide with fear.

"It will be okay. Stay here and block the door after I leave," I tell them, throwing the door open and closing it quickly behind me.

The scene that greets me is horrific, and I almost wish that I'd slept through it. It is no longer the peaceful village I know and love. People, bloodied and ragged, flee, trying to find safety. Behind them, robed figures follow, magic flying effortlessly from their hands.

I hear my name screamed by a voice I know well. What the hell is she doing here?

"Loukas!"

I lurch forward, ready to race to her side but stop short. She sounds angry, not afraid. She's not worried, not trying to find me for safety.

"He's not here," my father answers, his deep voice echoing through the chaos.

I slink through the shadows of nearby homes, hiding myself from view.

"Where is he?" Tonia demands.

"Gone. Banished." My father's voice is strained.

Once I round a corner and they come into view, I see why. Tonia's hands are raised above her head, and my father hovers in the air in front of her. He thrashes in the hold of the invisible bonds surrounding him.

"Liar," she spits. "Loukas! Come out or your father dies."

I wait to see if she's bluffing. My father chose to conceal my presence here, and I trust his instinct even if I can't trust my own. I continue to watch in horror as robed figures steer some of my people toward the clearing and force them to the ground in front of Antonia.

Over the past weeks, I have seen her use her magic casually. I knew she was strong, but I had no idea she could be so cruel.

It's not until my father begins writhing in pain that I rush out of my hiding spot.

"I'm here. What's the meaning of this?"

"There you are, my love," she sneers, and it's like seeing

someone I've never met. "I had almost started to believe you were gone."

"What's going on? Why are you doing this?"

"You were going to choose these people, this place, over me?"

A feeling like a bucket of ice poured over my head overtakes me. I blink away the film from my eyes, finally seeing her clearly for the first time. Whatever we had—whoever I fell in love with—is gone now.

I shake my head, trying to understand this new reality.

"No, my love. I was going to ask you to stay." I take a step closer to her hesitantly, watching as her face lights up at my words. "I was going to ask you to become my...my mate."

"You were?" Her beautiful eyes, so unfamiliar now, are unreadable.

"Of course, my love. I told you. You and me forever. Always." As I reach my father, I glance over at him. For the first time in my life, I see fear in his eyes. "Please, just let him go."

I reach out my hands to her, hoping that she will come to me and release him. Instead, her face contorts once again, and she is the madwoman from moments ago again.

"I know you were going to leave me."

"No, baby. I promise I wasn't. I fell when I shifted earlier. I had to wait to heal before coming to you."

She studies me with distrust, and I know she must see the discoloring of my rapidly healing bruises because her face softens and she rushes to me, dropping my father in the process.

"My poor baby," she coos.

Reflexively, I flinch as her hands reach out to touch me. It isn't the right thing to do because a flash of anger crosses her face, and she pauses just in front of me.

"It's your choice, Loukas. If you come with me, the people in your village will live."

"Antonia..." I plead.

She can't be serious. The woman I was going to take as my chosen mate could not be threatening my entire world.

Without glancing backward, she raises her hand into a fist and cuts off the air going into my father's lungs. He clutches at his throat.

"Stop! Stop," I beg as I step forward. She raises a brow at me. "I will go with you."

"Good," she says, releasing my father. "As long as you stay, your village will be safe. But if you try to leave me again..."

She doesn't let the threat hang in the air long. Her hands raise a gust of wind around my father. It swirls and buffets him before snapping his neck in one quick movement.

"No!" I rush toward him, catching his limp body before it touches the ground. Agony, unlike anything I've ever known, overtakes me as I sob over him.

"Please, Dad. Wake up," I whisper, rocking his lifeless body back and forth. I will him to start breathing again. Even if it's only to yell at me one more time.

"Are you ready to come along, pet? Or should I go find one of your sisters?" Antonia threatens.

"I'm coming," I say, pulling her gaze away from the crowd gathered nearby.

I rest my father down gently on the ground and close his eyes.

"I love you, Dad," I whisper, as I place a soft kiss on his forehead.

Robed figures pull me to my feet and drag me behind Antonia as she leads the way through the village, back through the once-secret opening, and onto the beach.

I glance back in time to see my mother and sisters hugging each other around the body of my father. I stop myself from calling out to them, hesitant to draw any attention to my grieving family.

They don't call out for me.

Chapter Two

Pearl

Even though we have had five years of relative peace on the island, the rest of the world hasn't been so lucky. Droughts, floods, and hurricanes have ravaged every corner except ours. The natural disasters become more severe and frequent every year. It's causing widespread panic among the humans. Friends turning on friends, families betraying one another. One thing that humans are not is level-headed when faced with a crisis.

There are also the disasters that are more difficult to predict or prepare for. They're less natural and more magical. The world was shocked and traumatized by the attack that caused widespread miscarriages and infertility. Now, it seems the vengeful goddess is ramping up again.

Just yesterday, every piece of man-made material was expelled from bodies of water all around the world. As if the waves and tides had agreed upon it, they rejected each foreign object at once, forcing them to the surface and vomiting them onto every shore.

When I say everything, I truly mean everything.

Ships that sank so long ago that no one remembered they were there now sit on the sand, drying in the harsh sun. Most boats are no longer welcome on the water, and submarines are not even safe to dock. The only exception seems to be simpler boats. If it is made from wood and without a motor, the goddess may allow the boat to pass and collect fish for a while. Once they take what they need, they are quickly ushered onto the shore.

Though human scientists have been trying to come up with reasonable explanations, it's becoming clear that supernaturals will not be able to remain in the shadows for long. One scientist claimed that climate change could have caused infertility. High levels of pollution in bodies of water were evaporated, stored in clouds, and eventually returned as rain. Rainwater, no longer clean, contaminated everything on the planet. Another group of scientists claimed it was a hormone issue caused by additives in the meat supply. There are some naïve enough to take these explanations as facts, but most are not so easily convinced.

For now, at least, I am still welcome in the seas.

These days, I spend most of my time swimming around the world. I can travel faster than most, but it means that I am often away and alone. I check in with the Westwood pack often, bringing them news of the outside. After all, their island is my home now too.

The seas, newly emptied of the landmarks I have come to know, are now unfamiliar. I marvel at how clear the waters are and how quickly the aquatic animals are reproducing and developing. Even though the creatures of the seas seem to be thriving, I can foresee them suffering the opposite fate of the humans on land soon. Overpopulation can be just as devastating as infertility.

Cities that were once crowded are falling quiet. Humans continue to die at an average rate, but there hasn't been a single birth to replace them.

No matter where I travel or how long I am away, I always end up back in the same spot.

Once again, I find myself in the Mediterranean Sea, watching the sun rise across the coast of Greece, floating on a patch of thick seaweed, and waiting to catch a glimpse of *him*.

I never consciously decide to end up here, but something pulls me toward the shore—toward him. Somehow, I always return to this place and wait to make sure he's still there and safe. When I do spot him, it's a relief to see his olive skin shimmering in the dawn light. He dives in, his bright pink swim trunks catching my eye and making me smile. He disappears beneath the water for a moment and resurfaces. His dark brown hair is slicked down and beads of water drip down his neck.

I dive under when he does to continue observing him. It feels wrong to watch him like this, but I do not fear being discovered. Because the sea is my natural home, I can see and hear underwater much better than he ever could.

Each morning, he dives into the water, sinking himself low enough to find the crustaceans who live there. Each morning, he catches two lobsters with his bare hands. Today, like each day before, two lobsters swim forward to meet him and accept their fate.

I have vowed not to follow him. I have promised myself I would not allow this strange obsession to go any further. I have convinced myself that watching him like this is enough.

He could be human or supernatural. He could be evil or kind. I do not know anything about him other than the fact that I am drawn to him in a way I've never felt before.

Today, though, I cannot simply watch as he swims to the surface and walks out of the sea. As he steps onto the shore and shakes some water from his glistening hair, my iridescent tail makes the choice I cannot and pushes me forward.

I know this is a bad idea. I know that I need to turn back toward the open water, but my body seems to have other ideas.

As the sand rises to meet the open air, my tail shifts into legs, and I follow him out of the ocean.

The hot sand burns the soles of my feet in seconds, and an unexpected squeak of discomfort slips from between my lips. He glances behind him, and I quickly jump behind a large bush, hoping it can hide me. A moment later, I peek above the bush and watch the muscles in his body bunch and contract as he turns each way, looking for the source of the noise...looking for me...

By some miracle, he doesn't see me. He turns back toward the path carved into a forested area full of olive, eucalyptus, and fruit trees.

I slip between the trees, carving my own path. I regret it instantly as the branches scratch against my bare skin and open shallow wounds. I ignore them as I try to keep up with him.

His feet glide silently over the forest floor, easily avoiding the branches and twigs. When added to the graceful way he carries himself and his respect for nature, that makes me think that he *has* to be supernatural.

He can't be a sea nymph unless he has incredible control of his shifting. He's not a vampire because he's out in the sun, his olive skin glistening like a Greek god. Could he be some kind of shifter?

As I wonder, he veers off the trail toward a rock face. I halt my steps, unsure how he plans on climbing the thirty foot rock wall while carrying the two lobsters when I see him pull back a curtain of vines and slip inside a crevice.

I give him a few moments before tiptoeing up to the same place and slowly peeling back the vines to peek inside. There is a pathway through the rocks that is maybe only two feet wide. As I step in, I breathe a sigh of relief at the change in temperature. The beach is scorching hot, and the humidity of the forest was oppressive. Here, the cool rocks give off the perfect temperature.

I walk for what feels like forever through the stone, the only sound coming from the drip of water somewhere deep within the cave. When I see a sliver of sunlight, I slow my pace before cautiously approaching the opening. My body hugs the sides of the cave, and I tuck my aquamarine hair to the side as I peek through, catching a glimpse of a small village hidden within the forest.

The modest-sized huts are built out of wood with thatch roofs. I see men, women, and children wandering the area, going about their day. Some carry baskets filled with clothes or food. A flash of pink steals my attention, and my eyes follow my mystery man as he greets each person he passes with a wave, a smile, or a ruffle of hair for the children.

I'm just about to make my move when a large owl hoots and lands in front of him, shifting into a man in the blink of an eye. An owl shifter? I'll bet he's beautiful. I close my eyes and imagine a beautiful brown owl with bright yellow eyes peering straight into my soul.

I linger there, watching the interactions until he is out of my sight. Something about this village, the way the people interact with one another, reminds me of my own village. The one that was lost so long ago when the hunters came.

There were once hundreds of us, spread out along coastal villages throughout the world. Each community was hidden but known well to those who call them home. Now, we find ourselves scattered. I've found some of my people and led them into the safety of Supernatural Island.

Some wanted to call it Westwood Island, others Moon Island. The options became endless as each supernatural faction wanted to lay claim to the patch of dirt we now call home. Ultimately, though, we decided it was safest to table that decision for now.

For me and my family, we couldn't care less about what they name the island. We are just happy to have a place to call home.

When Breanne "popped out"—her own charming phrase— their first child, Nora, a glimmer of hope spread throughout the island. She wasn't protected during the first attack from the vengeful goddess, so it should've been impossible for her to conceive and give birth.

Somehow, Artemis, the sneaky goddess who has adopted the island as her own, was able to work around it. According to Bree, Artemis invited her mother, Demeter, the goddess of fertility—among other things—to the island. Demeter gave her blessing to Breanne, allowing her to carry not only Nora but, a few short years later, Erik as well. There were crowds of women who weren't present during the attack hoping to be blessed, but Demeter warned them that it would not be a regular occurrence. She owed Artemis, and Artie chose Breanne to receive the honor.

However, Artemis *was* able to convince Demeter to add her magic to the barrier protecting the island. If I know Artemis—which I'd like to think I do since the meddling goddess makes regular appearances now—it was for more than just protection.

I'm sure she's hoping that Demeter's magic will somehow convince her granddaughter, Rayne, to have a child, or even make it happen by accident. I shiver at that thought. As much as I love Rayne—and I do—the thought of a little Drake or Rayne running around is alarming.

I know that I cannot slip into this village of shifters without being caught, so I make my way back to the beach, vowing that one day I will gather my courage and speak to him.

I glance back one last time before the village's light disappears, feeling like I'm leaving a piece of myself behind. The feeling makes me wonder if he could be my mate. Sea nymphs, like shifters, can recognize our mates instantly. Before that, though, we often feel a pull toward them—like the tides pulling us near.

As I jump back into the water, I shift effortlessly into my aquatic form. My tail camouflages neatly with the blue, green, and turquoise colors of the Mediterranean Sea

I swim effortlessly through the sea into the colder waters with a single question in my mind.

Am I ready to meet my mate?

"Pearl," Mizu, my cousin, calls out, halting my trek back to the island for my weekly check-in. "Pearl, we found more."

"Where?" I demand, not needing to ask what, or who, he found.

"Off the southeast coast of Australia." Without pause, I spin in the opposite direction, heading for where I believe Australia to be.

"How many?" I ask him as he easily keeps pace with me, each of us gliding effortlessly through the water.

"I've seen six myself. Caspian says he's seen eight."

"Did you make contact?"

I glance over at him and see him shake his head.

"They're skittish. The only ones I've seen are females. As soon as I get close enough for them to spot me, they swim away."

I pick up my pace, a feeling of urgency sliding up my veins. If there is a group of female sea nymphs alone, something must have happened to the males among them. They must be terrified. The women of my species are just as strong as any man, but we aren't violent by nature.

Our magic is meant to heal. It goes against everything we are to inflict pain on another, which makes defense unlikely. Even before the infertility crisis, women were sparse, averaging five men to one woman in each village. Even now, my sister and I are the only female sea nymphs on Supernatural Island. The others are all men, most of those being in my family. The idea that there is a group of women out there probably has both Mizu and Caspian excited.

"Show me where you saw them last," I demand as we approach the island, and Mizu veers off toward the lights of a small city glistening through the waves.

"This is where Caspian and I saw them."

I glance around, find a large rock protruding from the ocean floor, and lie down, getting comfortable.

"You can go," I tell him, and he opens his mouth to protest. I pinch the bridge of my nose. "This is the largest group of females I've heard of in decades. We don't know where the men are or why they aren't being protected like they should. They'll respond better if it's just me."

He glances at the shoreline, a look of longing on his face. Like all supernatural creatures, he would be considered handsome by most. His algae-green hair is long and flows freely behind him. His eyes, almost the same color as his hair, seem to glow in contrast to his pale skin.

"I'll bring them to the island," I promise, feeling a bit of sympathy for the man.

He's ten years my senior, in his early forties, and still without a mate. Before we were taken by the hunters and then rescued by the Westwood pack, my kind believed taking a mate of a different species to be impossible. We had been so removed from the rest of the world that we didn't know it was an option, much less one that could result in offspring.

We obviously know better now, but Mizu has continued to search without finding a suitable mate.

He gives the coast one last look before dipping his head in acknowledgment and swimming off as I get comfortable, ready for the long wait.

Chapter Three

Loukas

"Thank you for your sacrifice," I whisper to the two lobsters sitting in my hands because a sacrifice is exactly what it is.

I was a little boy when my father first took me to this part of the ocean and showed me how to provide for my mother and sisters. It has never taken any effort. Each day, lobsters would swim right into my waiting hands as if they knew how much we needed them. Just enough to provide for my little family—once four lobsters, now two.

We weren't destitute, but our village only takes what we need from nature. My father was the alpha of our parliament, and he sought to lead by example. Every other member was watching us for cues, so we took what we needed—never more, never less.

Even as I think about my father and what happened to him, my throat clogs with emotion. The thought sets off a spiral I've been trying to avoid. Tomorrow is the day I return to my prison...

A small squeak reaches my ears, and I spin, trying to locate the source of the sound. I find nothing and assume I must have startled a small animal.

I turn back and walk the familiar path through the trees to our hidden village, my mind turning once again to my father. What I wouldn't give to have him here with me, to hear his voice one more time. To apologize for what I did.

I shake my head to clear the thought. Regret is easy, but there's little it can accomplish now. Meeting Antonia was the beginning of the end for me and my family, and I never saw it coming.

After a few years of living under her thumb in Northern Ontario, Canada, I convinced her to allow me to visit Greece. I had won some favor by giving her a son and being "such a good little pet," so she even allowed me to bring our son, Zach, to meet his grandmother.

We were given one week of bliss. Seven full days with my family in the place I belong. One week of not having to look over my shoulder and worry about everything I say or do.

The weather was a definite improvement as well.

Now, eleven years later, I am allowed to visit my family in Corfu for six weeks each year. I'm no longer allowed to bring my son, the only mar on an otherwise perfect trip.

As soon as Zach's magic came in, Antonia made it clear I was no longer needed in his life. He's ten now, and he's incredible. I know he's safe, but I only get to watch him from afar now—never getting close enough to even say hello. From what I can tell, he's smart and caring despite his mother's influence. Even though I'm no longer permitted to see him, I hope the lessons I tried to instill in him stick. I pray that he doesn't end up cruel like his mother.

I was permitted to bring my daughter, who is now six, with me this time. She's become so happy and free during the previous weeks, and she and my mother have really hit it off. If it wasn't for Zach, I would take Amelia now and run away with her. She deserves a better life than her mother will ever offer her. Especially since she hasn't shown any signs of magic yet.

Daily, the fear grows that she's a shifter like me. I scoff at that thought. I'm afraid of my beautiful daughter shifting into a majestic owl instead of being gifted with magic. It's a concern I wouldn't have even considered eleven years ago.

I know Antonia will not stand for it. In her mind, her bloodline is the most dominant. She was well aware that I was a shifter and chose to have children with me, but having a shifter child would be considered an offense to her. If Amelia can't do magic, she'll be of no use to her mother.

If I knew of a safe place to send her, I would do it. It can't be here with my family. Antonia knows about them and would hunt every single person who tried to harbor her daughter. To Antonia, her family are her possessions. Amelia, Zach, and I are not people in her mind. We're hers to do what she pleases, whether that's to kiss and hug or punch and kick.

Not for the first time, terror grips my chest. When Antonia doesn't need something anymore, she throws it out. She doesn't set things free. If Amelia doesn't show signs of magic, there will be nothing I can do to protect her. Even I am approaching the end of my usefulness now that I cannot give her any more children.

It wasn't so bad in the beginning, when we first got to her home in Northern Canada. The weather was drastically different from what I was used to, but it held its own beauty too. Antonia's mother was the high priestess then and ruled everyone, including her daughter, with an iron fist...

The hair on the back of my neck stands up, and I stop to assess the feeling of being watched. I shake my head and continue walking. There's no one in this area stupid enough to attack my village now. Not with the warriors we have, not with the protection of the Daughters of Eris.

The eerie feeling doesn't leave me as I slip through the opening in the crack, but I brush it off. I didn't see anyone at the beach, and my owl—though he is subdued by Antonia's magic—would warn me of danger.

I greet the villagers as I walk by. None of them hold a grudge against me for what I did all those years ago, but they should. Instead of the warm smiles and pats on the back I receive, I should be rejected and denied entry. That's not the way of my people though. To outsiders, we are fierce and unforgiving. To our own...

"Hey, Loukas!" Bruce, one of the village elders, waves as I walk by. His long gray hair blends in easily with his bushy beard, and his warm brown eyes tip up at the corners.

I give him a nod in greeting. My people may have forgiven me for what I did, but I never will. Still, I try to be polite and interact with them as much as possible. I can never forget how I was the sole reason for the death of their alpha and so many of their loved ones.

"Ya-Ya, watch me." I hear my little Amelia calling to my mother. As I round the corner of my family home, I see her jump from the tallest branch of the olive tree planted in the front yard and land gracefully on her feet. A frown slips onto my face before I can stop it.

With each day she spends in the village, she shows more signs of being a shifter. Despite her being so young, I have a sneaking suspicion that she will shift soon. I will never give voice to that thought for fear of it coming true.

"That's beautiful, my little cherry blossom. Why not try the Eucalyptus next?" My mother coos, and Amelia's eyes light up as she rushes toward me, closer to the largest tree in the area.

I slip both lobsters into one hand and catch her by the waist as she runs past.

"Whoa, there. Not so fast, Pumpkin. I think the olive tree is high enough for now."

"But Dadddd..."

I chuckle at how grown up she sounds with her whine.

"'But Dad' nothing. Now, come on. Let's help your Ya-Ya prepare brunch."

24

"Don't worry, blossom. You can climb it tomorrow before you leave," my mother lowers her voice and brushes Amelia's hair behind her ear.

"Hey! I heard that."

My mother pins me with a look.

"You were meant to. Now run along, blossom, get the water from the well."

"Yes, Ya-Ya," Amelia says, immediately hoping to do her chore. Her long brown hair flows like feathers in the wind behind her, and her little feet bounce off the ground like she's about to take off. She looks free, like she should.

"You know she's going to shift soon." My mother's voice is matter-of-fact as she links her arm with mine.

I sigh, feeling defeated by her saying the words I have been avoiding myself.

"I know."

"What if she stays here? Where she's safe," my mother offers *again*.

"If I could get away with it, I would. Antonia is still holding out hope that her daughter will become the high priestess after her."

"But she doesn't—"

"I know that. You know that. I'm honestly afraid of what Antonia will do when she finds out. Besides, she shouldn't shift until puberty hits. That's at least another four or five years."

My mother turns back to look at my little girl struggling to carry the bucket, water droplets spilling over the sides.

"You don't have four to five years. I'd say four to five months... if you're lucky."

"What?" I ask, my mouth dropping open in shock. "How do you know?"

"My owl told me so. Doesn't yours sense it?" she asks, concern lining her eyes. "Amelia's owl is close to the surface already."

For what feels like the millionth time, I'm ashamed to tell my mother I haven't shifted since I left this village eleven years ago. I've never wanted to burden her. As far as she knows, my children and I are as free as we can be under Antonia's rule.

"He's made rumblings, but I chalked it up to wishful thinking on his part." The words that slip off my tongue aren't exactly a lie, but they're not exactly the truth either. My owl doesn't speak to me anymore. He is only able to break through the fog that surrounds him in times of true danger, and that has only happened a handful of times when Antonia has felt the need to *punish* me.

After a wonderful lobster bisque lunch with fresh rolls, my mother, Amelia, and I head for our daily walk. My mom says it's to help the food digest, but I think it's a way to keep herself busy. Each day, another member of our parliament stops us during our walk to ask her for help or guidance, and she loves every second of it.

When my father died, my younger sister's mate became the alpha of our parliament. Cassia never wanted to lead. Like me, she grew up watching our parents. Unlike the rest of the village, though, we saw behind the scenes.

We saw the late nights our mother spent worrying over something she had no control over. Cassia never wanted the stress of leadership, but she had no choice once our father was murdered and I was taken away. She still defers as much as possible to our mother, and I think they both prefer it to stay that way.

* * *

I wake to light streaming through the small window of my childhood bedroom and dread is already filling my stomach. I still hop out of bed, dress, and give two of my favorite girls a kiss on the head before making my way back to the beach for the last time this year.

I savor the quiet walk by myself, trying to take in the sights and smells of home. As the sand meets the water, I glance around. I'm not sure what I am searching for, but it feels like something is missing.

I take my time as I submerge myself in the warm water, swimming to a spot off the shore and soaking in the feeling of salt water on my skin before I dive down and collect my two lobsters.

By the time I return to the village, I catch a glimpse of my little girl leaping from one of the highest branches of the Eucalyptus tree. The one I specifically told her not to climb.

"Did you see, Daddy? Did you see?" She squeals after landing gracefully on her feet and runs toward me.

She leaps as she gets close, and I wrap my arms around her, a lobster in each hand.

"Did you see how high I jumped?"

"I did, sugar plum, and your landing was perfect. But what did I say?" I ask as she slides down until her feet touch the ground once more.

"That it was dangerous," she says meekly.

"And?"

"And that I should stick with the lower trees for now."

When her eyes dip to the ground, I immediately feel guilty. I never want to be the one to get her in trouble—she gets enough of that from her mother. I set the lobsters down on the ground, crouch low, and raise her chin so she meets my eyes.

"You're not in trouble," I assure her. "What you just did was very dangerous, and I don't know what I would do if something happened to you."

A small tear slips down her tanned cheek, and my heart cracks even more. I gather her up and squeeze her to me.

We're still sitting like that when a portal opens in the middle of the village, right behind Amelia. Despite knowing exactly who it is—or maybe because I know who it is—I instinctively push my baby girl behind me as the devil herself steps through.

"Miss me, pet?" Antonia asks, stepping forward and placing a soft kiss on my lips. Years of practice have me returning the kiss rather than recoiling the way every fiber of my being wants to.

"Of course, my love," I respond, keeping my voice even and calm. I can even manage to push a little emotion into them. I have to make it believable after all.

Gasps come from behind me, and I peek around Antonia to find out why. The sight makes me gasp too.

"Zach," I whisper my son's name and instinctively take a step toward him.

"Hi, Da—" Before he can finish the word, Antonia stomps a foot toward him. He flinches before correcting himself. "Hi, Loukas."

Tears mist my eyes, but not because he has stopped calling me dad. I hadn't heard his sweet voice in so long, I was having a hard time remembering what it sounded like. It's been too long. His young voice has grown deeper. He doesn't sound like a teenager yet, but he doesn't have a child's voice anymore either.

"Peanut?" My mom, Rita, calls, not bothering to hide the shake in her voice. She hasn't seen her grandson in years. I hold out my arm to keep her back when she reaches me. Zach lurches forward at the sight of her only to be slapped backward by Antonia's magic.

"Hi, Miss Rita," Zach says, clearing his throat and searching the crowd. I see when he finds her, some of the sadness that was floating in his eyes disappears. "Hi, Melia."

"Amelia," Antonia corrects.

"Sorry. Hi, Amelia."

"Hi," she says from behind me. I can feel that she is vibrating with the need to rush to her big brother, but she knows better. Just another thing to add to the growing list of things that she should not have to suffer through at six years old.

"My love," I call out, passing Amelia's hand to my mother and stepping forward. "I thought you and I might reminisce for a little while since you're here."

"What do you have in mind?" She purrs, placing her hand on my chest.

I lean over and whisper dirty things in her ear. Things I know she wants to hear. Things that will get her away from here and allow our children to visit without her watchful eye.

She nods, allowing me to lead her through the crevice in the stone. I glance back just in time to see Zach launching himself at my mother. As they fall to the ground, I see my mother peppering his head with kisses. I may not be able to do much to protect my children from their mother, but I can give them this little bit of time. Whatever I have to go through to make that possible doesn't matter.

For the next few hours, I keep Antonia busy, her thoughts full of nothing but what our two bodies can do. I haven't even finished dressing when she speaks.

"I'm taking a mate," she announces simply.

I stand there dumbfounded, my shorts not quite all the way up. I cannot process how she wants me to respond, and I cannot help but fear where this change will leave me in her schemes. I know she didn't take me as a mate already because I am a shifter and she is expected to mate with another witch to strengthen her bloodline, but it's been years since she spoke of it.

"Are you jealous, my pet?" she asks playfully, reaching over and rubbing a long red fingernail down my chest. "Don't worry, I will still make time for you. Zach will, understandably, need to spend more time with him."

"Him? You want this mate of yours to replace me as Zach's father?" The words slip out of my mouth before I'm able to stop them. Despite knowing I'll pay for them later, I don't care. How dare she?

"Zach has magic. He's not yours; he's mine. I can choose whomever I want to be his father."

"But..."

"Loukas. You are a pet. No more. No less. You're lucky I let you have the freedom you do."

She gets up and begins to dress, her body visibly shaking with rage. Shit.

I want to yell and scream at her. If I'm just a pet, why didn't she just leave me here in peace? Why did she need to kill my father? Why keep me for eleven years? Why did she make me give her children? Did she only want to break my heart again when she took them from me?

Despite all this, I keep my voice calm.

"I'm sorry, my love. You caught me off guard, and I don't want to share you." I reach for her hand, hoping to allay some of her anger before we return to our children. "I was jealous, and I lashed out."

"I knew you would be." She giggles and turns to me with a devious smile. "But don't worry, you'll still have me."

"But so will *he*," I growl, pulling her closer and kissing her hard, hoping that she mistakes the anger of my kiss for passion.

By the time we make it back to the village, it's getting dark. I hope I've given the kids and my mother enough time together. It's going to have to be enough because I don't have any more reasons to keep Antonia away.

I whistle a tune on the way back, making sure it is loud enough for those in the village to hear our approach. When we slip through the crevice, I smile.

Zach and Amelia are standing near the place the portal opened, looking like they haven't moved an inch while we were gone. My mother stands closer to her home, tears streaming down her face.

Thank the goddess, they heard my whistling and knew what to

do. Despite knowing they are tears of joy, I hate to see tears on my mother's cheeks. They are useful now, though, as I hope Antonia mistakes them for grief and anger. It makes it look like Amelia and Zach obeyed their mother the entire time.

"Let's go home, pet," Antonia says, opening a portal and using her magic to usher me and the kids through. She doesn't allow me to say goodbye to my family. I only hope that her taking a mate means that I can spend more time here, not less.

All thoughts of that are gone the second I am thrust through the portal and restrained with her magic. The tendrils squeeze around my throat, cutting off my air supply. I can hear what sounds like Amelia shouting in the background but am helpless to do anything as everything goes black.

Chapter Four

Pearl

It's been almost two weeks. Twelve days since I settled in to watch for the other sea nymphs. Twelve days of staring at the sea floor, eating in the sea, living in the sea. Normally, I would love every second, but all I've been able to think about is olive skin, deep brown eyes, and muscles. So many muscles.

I glance back toward Greece and frown, confused. I expect to feel a now-familiar pull. Instead, I feel nothing.

No. Wait. That's not entirely true.

I do feel a pull, but it's faint. So faint, in fact, that I wouldn't have realized it was there if I weren't looking for it. Granted, the distance could make the connection weaker, but it feels even further than before.

I flick my tail behind me, unconsciously swimming toward the faint pull when a splash draws my attention toward the shore. As I glance around, I realize that darkness has fallen while I was distracted. The usual clear blue color of the ocean is now a deep blue, making it hard to see any distance. The only light is that from the moon above and the glittering lights from the buildings further down the coast. I wouldn't be able to see at all if it weren't for the nictitating membrane that rests over my eyes while I'm shifted. They are the only reason I can see the flash of light pink hair swimming toward me.

I allow the tide to push me into her line of sight, ensuring that she sees me, and I hold my hands up, hopefully showing her I mean no harm. As she approaches, I feel tingles on the back of my neck, a warning that there is danger behind me. I don't turn, careful to avoid quick movements and knowing that the main threat is in front of me.

As she gets closer, I study her. Her innocent appearance makes it seem like she's no threat to me. The pale pink hair waving behind her is so long that it almost reaches the end of her tail, the two seeming to blend into one another. One look in her bright eyes, however, warns me against underestimating her. Her gaze bores a hole into my soul, and her heart-shaped mouth is set in a firm line.

This woman is dangerous, and she knows it.

"So, you're the nymph who's stalking us?" Her voice is musical, like the rest of our kind, but there's no mistaking the hardness in her tone.

"'Stalking' is a strong word," I rebut, keeping my tone light and my body ready for defense. I'm sure that the only reason they've decided to talk with me before attacking is because I'm a woman. If Mizu or Caspian were here, it would be a different story.

"You've spent two weeks out here waiting for us. What would you call it?" She snarks back and a hint of a smile graces my lips at her attitude.

She reminds me a bit of Rayne, so I try to channel my friend's nonchalant tone.

"I have no idea what you're talking about. I was swimming along, minding my own business, when I saw this rock here and fell in love."

"You fell in love with a rock?" Her brows raise, and I give her my best smile.

"Have you seen it? It's beautiful. A smooth surface that's just perfect for taking a nap." She glances from me to the rock and back again. "Go ahead. Try it."

I take advantage of her distraction, coiling my tail and shooting backward. I grab the spear from the hands of the woman who had been sneaking up behind me. I flip over her and secure my arm around her neck before "Pink" even notices.

"Don't move," I whisper in my captive's ear. Her body begins quaking in fear, making me feel guilty. If I didn't do this, though, they would have struck at me from both directions.

Pink turns to see her companion restrained and charges at me, baring her pointed teeth.

Well, two can play that game. I growl at her too, making sure to show her my teeth are longer and sharper.

"Stop where you are," I hiss.

Thankfully, she does. I don't want to hurt these women. I have every intention of inviting them back to the island with me, but I am not willing to let them hurt me either.

"What do you want?" she asks, her eyes darting between her friend's face and my arm wrapped around her throat.

"I just want to talk."

She snorts. "It doesn't really look like that."

"You gave me no choice. I knew that..." I pause, "What's your name?"

"Genevieve," the terrified girl in my arms whispers.

I nod.

"I knew that Genevieve was sneaking up behind me, and I couldn't allow myself to be attacked on both sides."

"We weren't going to hurt you..." Genevieve says, her voice betraying her fear.

Pink's eyes soften at the sound, and she dips her chin in agreement.

"We weren't."

"Then why sneak up behind me?"

She hesitates, and I squeeze my arm a little tighter around Genevieve's neck. I try to channel Rayne again. I feel terrible about threatening this girl, but I need answers.

"I can keep this up all night, but I'm not sure about Genevieve here."

Pink pauses a moment longer before she answers.

"We were suspicious of you because we're being hunted."

"What do you mean?"

"It's not my place to tell you."

"Then whose place is it?" I ask.

"Narissa. Our pod mother. We can take you to her, but you need to let Gen go."

I watch her, searching for signs of deception.

"I'm Pearl," I say, still keeping my hold on Genevieve.

"Kristle."

"Well, Kristle. If I let Gen go, are you going to attack me?" I ask. She shakes her head. "Okay, then."

Slowly, I release Genevieve's neck, and she swims to safety behind Kristle. Once I finally get a good look at her, a pang of regret flows through me.

She's young. Maybe only seventeen, with long navy hair, a round face, and big dark blue eyes. Her tail does not yet have full coloring, evidence that she hasn't yet grown out of the near-translucent hues of youth. Her tail starts a bright sky blue by her waist and grows darker as it nears the fins.

Kristle checks Genevieve over quickly before turning back to me.

"This way," she commands.

Without waiting for me to answer, they turn and swim back

toward the shore. Genevieve pokes her head out of the water first to make sure the coast is clear before she sprints toward land.

"You need to make sure there's no one out there before you step out," Kristle warns me.

"Why? Won't they just think we're skinny dipping?" I ask. It is the excuse I've always used when caught by humans, and it has always worked.

She shakes her head, a sullen look overtaking her fierce face.

"Not here."

Without another word, she raises just her eyes above the water before racing to the sand.

There's something I don't understand going on here, so I follow their lead. I check above water, unsure what I am searching for, before I join them. There must be a reason they're so cautious.

Kristle is still slipping her long dress over her head when I arrive, so Gen hands me another. I thank her and step into it. When she hands me a pair of flip-flops, I must look at her like she grew two heads. Wearing clothes, I understand. But shoes...

"Trust me," she says, placing them on the ground in front of me and handing both Kristle and me a spear. I slip my feet into the sandals, glaring at Gen and Kristle the entire time. Are they playing some kind of joke on me? They're lucky these shoes are open-toed, or they would just have to deal with it.

"Okay, what is going on?" I ask, unable to keep quiet any longer.

"We will explain when we get to Narissa," Kristle explains, her blue eyes pleading with me to shut my mouth. The sound of male voices nearby surprises me, and I turn toward them. "Maybe I won't have a chance to." She steps forward, taking the lead as Gen and I follow.

"Any luck tonight, girls?" As we pass by the group of five, one of the men calls out to us.

"Nope," Kristle responds, flashing them a brilliant smile. "Thought I saw a splash, but it was just a fish."

"Are you sure?" Another man asks this question. He looks to be the youngest of the group but is still in his late twenties.

"We're sure," she responds, her voice hard even though the smile is still on her face. The boy's shoulders slump. "Maybe you'll have better luck."

"Be safe," Genevieve calls back to them as we resume walking.

"Wha—" I begin, but they both shush me immediately. Kristle cuts her eyes to the men behind us without turning and pulls me forward.

Okay. This is getting scary now.

We weave through the path leading us to a small parking lot and paved road. We do not see a single soul as we make our way toward their home, and none of us say a word. I start to worry again when a sprawling neighborhood comes into view, but then I remember that I have a spear in my hand and can protect myself.

Being alone in a strange place is concerning, but I am no longer helpless. After the years I spent in the facility, I decided I was done being a victim. I am not a natural fighter, but Breanne and Rayne have made sure I stand a chance against anyone who tries to hurt me.

After more than an hour of walking, the road winds back toward the water. We are so close now that I can hear the waves crashing against the shore. It's when Kristle walks up to a large house that backs onto the beach, that I cannot contain my frustration.

"We could have just—"

"Shh," she hisses. Her hand darts out, pointing to the sandy shoreline. At first, I don't see anything. The longer I look, the more people I see walking along the shore, each with a spear or a gun in hand.

Before I can understand what I've seen, I am ushered inside.

Genevieve hardly gets her foot in the door before she slams it closed behind her and secures the multiple locks.

"Who is this?"

I spin to follow the voice and find an older woman surrounded by five more waiting for us in the hallway. The one who spoke has the same pale pink hair as Kristle, and I can only assume they are close relations.

"I'm Pearl," I say, stepping forward with a dip of my chin to greet the woman who I can only assume is their pod mother.

"I'm Narissa," she states, a proud smile on her face after my greeting. "The two next to me are my sisters, Kelda and Marea." Each one gives a little wave as Narissa says their name. Kelda's hair is a deep red, and Marea's hair is a shade of red that is closer to orange.

"It is nice to meet you," I respond, once again dipping my chin slightly, showing them the respect they deserve as the matriarchs of this pod.

"Left to right, you have Autumn, Summer, and Spring."

It is common for sea nymphs to prize family above all else, and thorough introductions are expected. Still, I am thankful when Kristle steps up to whisper in my ear.

"Their hair helps. Autumn is mostly red; Spring is green, and Summer has the purple color."

"These sweet children are Cordelia and Coral."

Narissa places a hand lovingly on each girl's shoulder. They are teenagers, nearer to adults than children, but I know a matriarch's desire to let her young ones be young as long as possible. Cordelia's hair is a pretty blue color, but Coral's is a bright red that will be easy to remember.

"Of course, you already know Kristle, my daughter, and Genevieve, my niece." Narissa gestures to the women standing next to me. "My other niece, Winter, has just stepped out. She went to the store with her mate."

"Her mate?" I question, looking between the members of this small group. "I didn't think there were any males here."

Narissa eyes me warily for the first time since I walked into the house.

"Obviously, you were mistaken."

I take a small step forward, raising my hands once again.

"I mean no disrespect to you and no harm to your pod. I came to offer you a place of safety amongst my people."

Someone scoffs. I look around and guess it was Marea based on the skeptical look on her face.

"There is no safety," Narissa says simply. "Not anymore."

"There is. I can prove it."

"If it's true..." Kelda whispers, looking at Narissa.

"It's not." The matriarch sounds decided. "There is nowhere safe. There is only death and destruction in this world."

"While you are correct for the most part, my pod has found a safe haven, along with many other types of supernaturals."

"That is not a safe haven as long as there are other supernaturals," Narissa says adamantly, and I internally curse myself.

I hadn't planned on mentioning the other supernaturals yet because I know most sea nymphs don't socialize outside of our own kind. I've theorized that our lack of socialization with other species is the reason why true mate pairings amongst our kind are rare and our female birth rate is drastically lower than that of other species.

"Listen, like you, I was raised to be wary of other supernaturals and learned that being safe meant only socializing with our kind. But it wasn't a sea nymph who saved me from the hunters. It wasn't a sea nymph who healed me. It wasn't a sea nymph who gave me a home away from the carnage that the humans have brought upon themselves." I use my eyes to plead with the group. I can see a few with hope shining on their faces. Whether or not they believe me, I can tell they want what I am saying to be true.

"This is going to sound crazy. But there's this island."

"An island?" Narissa says, unbelief clear in her tone.

"Yes. It's called..." I pause, deciding against getting into the whole name thing. "You know what? It doesn't matter what it's called. What matters is that it's the home of all different types of supernaturals who live in harmony."

"Can we go?" Summer asks, turning to her pod mother. Autumn and Spring quickly follow suit.

"This may be our last chance, sister," Marea whispers the warning.

"What proof do you have?" Narissa asks, and I breathe out a sigh of relief that I seem to be getting through to them.

"Do you have a cell phone I can borrow?" I ask. If I can call Matt, he'll have a way to prove it to them.

"Why?" That single question, paired with the look on Narissa's face, tells me I have pushed them back into suspicion.

"I need to contact a friend of mine who is on the island. He can send you proof."

Narissa scoffs.

"So they can come and attack us? No. Absolutely not."

"They would never attack you. I trust this friend with my life. His mate saved me from the hunters."

Of course, I don't say that she also gave me to the hunters. Even though I know the choice was not her own, I doubt the women in front of me would understand that.

All eyes turn to Narissa, waiting for her verdict. Although they will not speak against her, the women of her pod have fearful hope in their eyes. I watch her closely and see the moment she realizes she lost.

"Fine." Narissa lets out a heavy sigh. "She can use one of the burner phones." The Seasons and Coral and Cordelia squeal in delight, the latter rush off through the house, presumably to grab the phone.

"You might as well come in then," Narissa says, turning and

walking deeper into the house. Not wanting to give her the chance to change her mind, I leave the safety of the entryway and follow her.

The house is open and extremely clean despite having so many people living in it. A large painting on the wall catches my eye as we walk through the living room. It's a very realistic painting of waves crashing out on the reef, capturing the perfect aquas, blues, and greens.

"Who painted that?" I ask, turning to Kristle.

She gets a sad look on her face as she turns to face the painting. "My uncle."

"What happened?" I ask.

"I'm sure my mother will tell you..." she says, clearly hesitant to recount the story.

I glance around and realize that everyone else has left us alone in the living room.

"Since you asked, my father, two uncles, and three of my cousins went out for a swim one night about six months ago. There were ships out on the water—this was before the sea decided to spit everyone back onto shore—so they thought nothing of it. One of my cousins, Sky, was caught in a fisherman's net while it was being reeled in. The others did everything they could to get him out before he broke the surface..."

She wipes a stray tear that trails down her cheek.

"They didn't get to him in time," I supply. I know just as well as any other sea nymph that untangling yourself from those nets can be impossible.

She shakes her head sullenly.

"My dad was able to convince the others to come back here and plan a rescue while his brother, my uncle, followed the ship. Later that night, we headed to the warehouse where they were holding Sky." Kristle shakes her head, lost in the memory. "They had him submerged in a tank and were taking all kinds of samples from him. They took so many scales off his tail that the water was red with his blood. His tail, which was normally a beautiful sky blue, was white and pink."

I suck in a breath at her description of the torture of one of my kind. Even having a single scale ripped off is excruciating. I cannot imagine having hundreds pulled away in such a short time.

"The warehouse was filled with people wearing white coats and surrounded by others carrying guns. There was little hope of us getting him out that night." She sniffs and wipes another tear from her eye. "We left. We promised to go back for him, but we didn't get the chance."

"The next day," Narissa picks up where Kristle left off, "men with guns surrounded our home." I glance behind her, expecting to see the rest of Kristle's family, but find no one.

"If they came the next day, how are you all still here?" I ask, feeling suspicious for the first time since arriving.

Narissa sighs, gesturing to the couch where the three of us take a seat.

"We quickly learned that they only believe men have the gene. We're still not sure why they think that, but they were not interested in us at all."

"The men, though..." Kristle says.

"Yes, they tried rounding up the men. We were able to make a diversion long enough to let all but Ash get away. They tested Ash by spraying him with water first." I can't hold in the laugh that escapes me. If a sea nymph shifted, every time they were sprayed with water, showers would be impossible, the rain would be problematic, and humidity may even be an issue. "Our reactions exactly. In hindsight, we should have kept our chuckles to ourselves. Next, they submerged him completely. First in fresh water and then in the sea. It was only his complete control over his shift that saved him."

"You mean he didn't shift?" I watch them shake their heads.

"At all?"

"It was something we thought was impossible. Perhaps the goddess took pity on him, but he was able to hold off his shift. Once they had nearly drowned him, they left us."

"And Sky?"

"By the time we returned to the warehouse, everyone was gone. Those demons and their equipment, and Sky too," Kristle answers.

"Where are the men now?"

"Out searching for Sky," Narissa says.

"And help," Kristle adds.

I shake my head.

"I don't understand...Why are those humans out there, then?"

The two share a look, and I know I'm not going to like their answer.

"They are hunting for us—"

"Parts of us," Kristle interrupts.

"They believe that our tails specifically have intense healing properties," Narissa finishes with a grimace.

"They are waiting for one of us to surface with a tail...so they can take it?"

"They believe they'll be able to use science to create a serum using our scales to reverse the infertility plaguing the world right now," Narissa explains.

"But it's something magical that caused the infertility, not scientific."

"What do you mean?" Narissa asks and with that, I launch into the story of what I know about the vengeful goddess. Even as I say the words, it sounds fantastical to my own ears.

"Wait." Kristle holds up her hand. "You're telling me that the gods and goddesses are real, like 'walk the earth' real?"

I nod. "Yes." Her mouth drops open in shock, obviously not expecting that answer.

Chapter Five

Pearl

"I don't know why you're surprised." Narissa's voice is calm, as if her eyes didn't bulge at my words only moments ago. "We suspected there was something magical behind recent events."

"Suspecting something magical is one thing. Knowing that the gods and goddesses walk the earth is something else entirely," Kristle snarks back.

I smile.

"Then I guess I shouldn't tell you that one of my friends living on the island I was telling you about is the granddaughter of one of those goddesses."

This time, Narissa is unable to contain her shock and, dare I say, excitement.

"Which one?"

"Artemis."

"She's supposed to be a virgin goddess," Kristle says. "How can she be a grandmother?"

"I asked the same thing, and she told me not to believe everything I heard. She asked if I would be able to abstain from sex for a millennium."

"Well, when you put it that way..." Narissa smirks while Kristle looks over at her mother, horrified.

"So, this friend you want to call..."

"Matt," I supply.

"Can he be trusted?" Narissa asks, searching my eyes for answers. "I hope you understand my reluctance. I want to believe everything that you're saying, but I need to think about the safety of my pod first."

I nod. "As you should. I assure you no one on our island means you or your pod any harm."

Kristle and her mother share a long look, communicating with each other seemingly without words. After a few tense moments, Narissa hands me an older smartphone.

"I'm putting my trust in you. Break that trust, and I break you." Her voice is as dark as the threat, but I am not scared. I have no intention of betraying her or the other women I've met here.

"Thank you," I say solemnly, taking the phone and dialing the only phone number I have memorized.

"Hello?"

"Bree."

"Pearl?" Her beautiful voice rises an octave in excitement. "Where are you?"

"Somewhere in Australia, I think." I look at the women sitting across from me to verify.

"Melbourne," Kristle supplies quietly.

"Melbourne?" Breanne says, and I can envision her little nose wrinkling in confusion. "You were supposed to come home two weeks ago. We were ready to come find you when Mizu arrived to tell us that you were tracking more of your kind. Is that why you're calling? Did you find more?"

"Bree," I interrupt her before she can continue. "Yes, I did find more sea nymphs, and that's why I'm calling. I need to talk to Matt actually." I grimace, knowing what's coming next.

"I see how it is. You're just using me for my mate."

"You've been spending far too much time with Skarlyt and Rayne, I think," I chide her newfound jealousy.

"At least they spend time with me." She tosses back the response, and I sigh.

"You're right. When I get home, I promise that you and I will have a full day—twenty-four hours—of girl time."

"Forty-eight or no deal," she counters automatically.

I let out a little chuckle and readily agree.

"Deal."

"Matt," she calls out her mate's name behind her. "It's Pearl." There's rustling as they pass the phone between them.

"Pearl? Everything okay?"

"Besides your mate somehow being jealous of both of us?"

"Hey!" Breanne exclaims in the background, causing Matt to chuckle.

"Listen, I found more sea nymphs. I want to bring them home with me, but I need to prove to them that the island is what I've said it is. They've been through a lot lately."

"Haven't we all?" He sighs. "Okay, turn it on video chat."

I pull the phone away from my face and only see a black screen. I'm not out of water enough to have learned the ins and outs of modern technology. I hear a sigh on the other end of the phone.

"Press the button on the side of the phone. It will make the screen come up, then press the button that looks like a speaker."

I follow his instructions and instantly hear the difference.

"Okay. Now what?" I ask.

"Is there a button that looks something like a video camera?"

I search the screen of the phone. "No?"

"Okay, give me a second." I hear him walk over to his computer, his fingers flying over the keys. "Who's there with you?"

"Narissa, the pod mother, and her daughter," I supply.

"Nice to meet you both. What I'm about to do is going to seem invasive, but I promise that you have nothing to fear from me," he says, and the two women share a look of concern. A few clicks of his fingers later, the TV settled in the corner of the room turns on and his face pops up.

"How did he do that?" Kristle asks, more curious than concerned.

"Let's just say I'm good with technology," Matt responds. His blonde hair is styled messily as usual, and his bright blue eyes are sparkling. "Nice to meet you both."

"We're here too!" Bree's face peeks out from behind him, holding a smiling Erik.

"Look at you, little man! You've gotten so big!" I coo at him, leaning closer to the screen.

"Say hi to Aunty Pearl," Bree says, grabbing Erik's pudgy hand and making him wave. "Tell her you wouldn't look so much bigger if she visited more often."

"Where are my girls?" I ask, not realizing how much I missed them until now.

"They're getting ready for bed," Matt says. Before he can say anything else, I hear the sound of little feet flying across the floor toward the camera.

"Is that Aunty Pearl?" Makayla asks, pushing her dad aside so that she can see me on the screen.

"It is!" Nora says, climbing up onto her sister to get a better look. "Are you coming over?"

I shake my head and feel tears cloud my eyes.

"Not today. I hope I'll be there soon."

"Can we send Aunty Opal to get her so she can come sing me a song before bedtime?" Nora asks her mother.

"Aunty Pearl, I've been training with Rayne." Makayla cuts off her mother's response.

I glance at Breanne, not wanting to ruin Makayla's mood but also unsure if Rayne is a good influence for any child.

"That's great! Did your momma decide that was a good idea?"

Bree nods and mouths, "Nightmares."

I dip my chin, acknowledging her words before turning my gaze back to Mak.

"You've been having dreams again?" I ask. She shares a dark look with her mother.

"Some."

"I'll be home soon, and we'll do another healing session," I promise her. The two women across from me gasp.

"You heal them?" Narissa asks, and I nod.

"They're my family."

"All right, girls. Say goodnight to Aunty Pearl and get into bed," Breanne says, causing both girls to pout.

"I promise I'll be home soon, but I need to talk to your dad for a minute."

"Will you sing me a song after you're done talking to Daddy?" Nora asks, and I smile.

"When she's done talking to Daddy, I'll bring the phone into your room," Breanne says, ushering the girls out of the room without giving me the option to say no.

"Now that the excitement is done for the night, why don't I show you a little about our island here?" Matt says, the screen switching from his face to an aerial view of the island. The camera zooming in on different villages spread throughout, ending with a beautiful shot of the sun rising behind the academy. "Any questions?"

"Yeah. How do you have children?" Kristle blurts, her mother elbowing her in the side.

It's so complicated that I cannot answer, but Matt has no problem with it.

"Before the attacks, we were shielded by Artie—that's Artemis—so that the infertility didn't reach us. When she created this island..."

"Created?" Narissa asks.

"Yes, our earth witches were working hard to create it, but Artemis took over because they were—in her words— 'taking too long.' She blessed the island with her magic, and eventually her mother, Demeter, added to it as well. It's still difficult, but the people here have a better chance of having children."

"So, if we choose to call your island our home, it's possible for us to have children?" Kristle asks, still sounding unbelieving.

Matt and I share a look, and I hope he treads carefully here.

"I won't lie to you. It's possible but not probable," he explains. "Those that weren't shielded from the first attack are still having fertility issues. Some get pregnant, only to lose the baby."

I glance at Narissa and Kristle, seeing the concern in their eyes.

"Thank you, Matt. I think these two have some questions. I'll call you back later."

"Aren't you forgetting something?" he asks with a smirk, the TV turning off and his voice coming through the phone once more. "I believe you have a song to sing."

"Right," I say, taking the phone off speaker and holding it up to my ear.

"Aunty Pearl?" Nora's small voice comes through the phone.

"Which song would you like, sweetheart?" I send Narissa and Kristle an apologetic look and hope they will be patient.

"The one about the ocean waves," she says.

I immediately begin singing one of the lullabies of my people. I sing to her of the tides of time and how the waters are ever-flowing and ever-changing.

"And...she's out like a light," Bree whispers into the phone. "That was the easiest bedtime we've had in weeks."

"Anytime, Bree. I'll call soon."

"You better." She hangs up before I can say anything else, and I turn back toward Kristle and Narissa.

"We're welcome there?" Narissa jumps into her questions immediately and is obviously skeptical.

"Everyone is welcome there. It's meant to be a safe place for all supernaturals."

"Mom..." Kristle says, looking at her with a wary hope shining in her eyes.

"Can you take Kristle with you to the island first? Then, if Kristle believes it is safe, I'll send the rest."

"Yes, of course. It's only about a day's swim...but I have people I could call. Friends who could teleport us there and back within minutes."

"Witches?" Narissa hisses.

"Yes, but they're trustworthy, I promise." I rush to allay her fears. "We can go somewhere other than your home to call them if that would make you feel better."

"No," Kristle interrupts. "We don't want to risk drawing any attention."

"Call them," Narissa agrees with a growl in her voice, "but return tomorrow by sundown or we will hunt for you."

I pick the phone back up, send a picture of myself in the living room to Breanne, and ask her to forward it to Skar or Opal. Within moments, Skar, the black-haired menace, is flashing into the living room. Both Narissa and Kristle bare their teeth and fall into a fighting stance.

"Oh, hello," Skarlyt says. "Somebody said you could use a pickup."

Regardless of how she stumbles into a room, Skarlyt always makes it seem like she's meant to be there.

"Kristle and Narissa, this is Skarlyt Moon. High Priestess of the Coven of the Moon."

"Nice to meet you both. Oh, wow. I love your hair!" Skarlyt exclaims. She ignores their tense stances and lifts a strand of Kristle's hair in awe.

"Skarlyt," I scold. When she turns to me, her face is a picture of innocence.

"What?"

"We've talked about personal space before," I remind her. "Especially with sea nymphs."

"Kristle didn't mind," Skarlyt claims. "Right?"

"Well..." For a moment, Kristle seems to have forgotten her suspicion. It seems she can't determine how to respond to Skarlyt.

"See, I told you she didn't mind," she says, completely unaware of the flabbergasted sea nymph next to her.

I heave out a breath.

"Let's just go."

"Come with me if you want to live," Skarlyt says, making her voice deeper and pushing her hands out toward both Kristle and me.

"Oh, I love *Casper*." Kristle giggles, looking young for the first time since I met her.

"Return my daughter in one piece," Narissa warns.

"Tomorrow night," I agree. "If, for whatever reason, we will be delayed, I'll call you on that phone."

"Buckle up, buttercups. It's going to be a bumpy ride." Skarlyt giggles, making Kristle's eyes go wide with fear. I'm about to tell her that she was just kidding, but don't get the chance as we disappear from the living room, landing in the small village we have claimed for ourselves.

"Pearl!" My younger sister, Aqua, rushes toward me. I let go of Skar's hand just in time to wrap my arms around her, giving her a soft kiss on the head. Even at twenty-two, she still greets me the way she did when she was a little girl.

"Hi, pip-squeak," I say, hugging her back fiercely.

She steps back, wrinkling her nose in distaste at my nickname for her.

"When are you going to stop calling me that?"

"Never," I tell her, booping her on the nose. "Kristle, I'd like you to meet my baby sister, Aqua. Aqua, this is my new friend Kristle."

"Nice to meet you," Kristle says, giving a small bow that is customary among sea nymphs.

"No need to bow to me. Pearl is the closest thing to a pod mother we have," Aqua explains, waving her off and jutting out her hand to shake.

"Pod mother?" Skarlyt interrupts, looking at me with betrayal written all over her face. "When were you going to tell me? This whole time, I've been talking to your father about decision making. No wonder he always tells me he will get back to me. He probably has to talk to you about it first!"

"It's not like that," I begin, earning a scoff from both Kristle and Aqua. "Okay, it is kind of like that. It's practically unheard of to have a pod mother as young as I am. I shouldn't become a leader for many, many more years."

"But you *are* the leader?" Skarlyt probes, and I dip my chin in acknowledgment.

Pods are led by matriarchs—the oldest woman in the pod who is willing to accept the responsibility. However, I am only the eldest in my pod because of the disasters we have suffered. For now, I am happy to let my father shoulder some of the responsibilities.

Skarlyt seems personally offended by the fact that I never told her I was in charge. Her diatribe includes hurt that she's been the "only woman" in all these meetings with stinky alphas, but we both know that's not true. The alpha couples here share their power, and the women are often more aggressive than the men.

It's clear to me that she's really just upset there was something she didn't know. Skarlyt is a lot of things: in charge, curious, intelligent, and foolhardy. She isn't often unaware, so it probably stings.

"Skarlyt," I say firmly, interrupting her.

"What?"

"I know you're upset, but I only have twenty-four hours to show Kristle around before I have to bring her back."

"Okay, but this isn't over," she warns, popping away. She's probably going to complain to Phoebe. And probably Rayne. And Drusilla.

In fact, I'll probably be cornered by everyone on the island about this by tomorrow night.

Ugh. I scrape my hand down my face.

"All right..." I begin at the same time Kristle lets out a huge yawn.

Even though it's first thing in the morning here, it is nighttime back in Australia. She's probably tired. "How about a quick swim around the island and then you can sleep for a bit before I give you the full tour?" I ask, altering my plans.

She agrees and Aqua, Kristle, and I head out to swim. We pass the rest of our small pod as we go, but I forego overwhelming her with introductions. Still, she looks them over curiously.

Each man we pass has to pick his jaw up off the floor as we pass, but it's when we get to Mizu that it gets really interesting. Before we are close enough to speak to my cousin, Kristle and he pause, not breaking eye contact.

I glance between them, watching as my cousin squeezes his hands into fists to stop his shaking. It's not until Kristle takes the initial step forward that he practically runs the final ten steps to her.

"Hi," she says breathily.

I grasp Aqua's arm, pulling her away. If I didn't know any better—which I do—I would say that Kristle just found her mate and her reason for staying on the island.

"Are they—?" Aqua asks, raising her eyebrows meaningfully.

"I think so," I respond.

"So does that mean her pod will come and live here?"

I glance back at Kristle and Mizu, watching as they make their way toward the water.

"I hope so."

Knowing that Mizu will show Kristle all she needs to see of the island and convince her to stay, I link my arm with Aqua's and make my way to our home.

It's been too long since I've seen my father. If what Skarlyt says is true, he probably has a few things to discuss with me.

Chapter Six

Loukas

It's been two weeks since we returned to the coven. Two weeks of pain. Two weeks of not seeing my children. Two weeks of being chained in this room.

My wrists have become chafed and raw from the leather straps that suspend me from the ceiling. Antonia didn't mistake my anger for passion in that kiss. If she did, she must believe I did something else to earn this punishment.

She would never willingly take care of Amelia on her own for this long.

Just the thought of my Pumpkin with that woman—even though she's her mother—sends chills down my spine. My mother said she could shift at any time, but I hope it hasn't happened yet.

No. If she had, I would have heard Antonia cursing me from here.

"Good morning, pet," Antonia calls out as she opens the heavy basement door, bringing with her the first sliver of light I've seen in days.

"Is it?" I ask, my voice hoarse from disuse. For the first two days, I pleaded with her to stop. I begged her to tell me what I did to warrant this punishment. She would respond only with dark laughs. I stopped begging.

Then came my screams as she had her brother brand me over and over as hers. It didn't take long to realize she was getting off on my pain. Since then, I've kept my mouth shut and let her—or her brother—do whatever they want. It is difficult, but they don't deserve the satisfaction of hearing me suffer.

"It is. I trust you've learned your lesson by now," she says matter-of-factly as she steps in front of me. Her makeup is perfectly done, and her long black hair hangs loosely down her shoulders and chest.

"It would help if I knew what lesson I was supposed to be learning," I snap back. Gone is the man I pretended to be for eleven years. I played my role perfectly to keep myself and my children safe. In his place is an alpha male who will do whatever it takes to get the three of us free from this monster.

She clicks her tongue at me, shaking her head.

"You think I'm stupid, Loukas? You think I don't know you were distracting me so our son could have his head filled with pretty fantasies by your mother?" She grips my chin with her hand, and her long, red fingernails dig into my cheeks.

Of all the reasons I had imagined for this punishment, that was not one of them. The fact that she even thinks of my mother as a threat is a shock.

"It's taken me this long to deprogram him, to pull that woman's nonsense from his mind." She pushes my face to the side as she uncuffs one of my wrists. "That's the only reason I am letting you out of your cage—because I was able to deprogram him. Do you understand?"

I brace myself, but it's no use. My legs were hovering above the ground, so I fall in a heap on the concrete floor when she releases me.

"Make yourself presentable before you come out," she hisses, throwing a towel and the keys at me before walking away.

I glare daggers at her back as she walks away. For a moment, I consider walking out of the basement just like this. Caked in blood, feces, and dirt. My clothes are in tatters, hanging off me. Then her precious coven can see what kind of person she is. The thought of either of my children seeing me like this, of knowing that their mother is the type of monster capable of doing this to another person, gives me pause.

Painstakingly, I unlock my feet with the set of keys, pick up the towel, and attempt to stand. Even with shifter healing, a body can only take so much damage and walk away. Besides, other than water and a meal here or there, I haven't had anything to sustain myself. Beyond that, I'm sure Antonia put something in the food to keep me weak and suppress my healing. My owl, who had come out a little during the time that we were gone, is now back to being completely silent.

After trying to stand multiple times, I decide to crawl my way to the bathroom. I feel a little strength return as the shower comes into view and rise up enough to turn the water on. I send a prayer of thanks to the designer of this bathroom who had the forethought to install a walk-in shower.

I don't bother removing my clothes just yet. Instead, I sit back on the ground, lifting my face to the water and gulping down as much as I can stomach.

A hiss leaves me as I peel the scraps of fabric that used to be my shirt off my body. The wounds inflicted on me by her brother and his friends are still raw. She didn't do any of the torturing herself. She only sat back and laughed as her minions beat me to a pulp and then used my body any way she wanted while I was too weak to fight back.

I shudder at the thought of her naked body touching mine ever again. I am disgusted with her for daring to use my body's natural reaction to a naked woman against me. I don't think she realizes that she's ruined whatever normality we had. If these past two weeks hadn't happened, I would still be playing the role of her side piece. I would've been compliant. Never completely willing, but I wouldn't have fought back.

In truth, she did me a favor. I no longer need to be the man she deems unworthy of being her mate but is unwilling to give up. Never again.

The water I gulped down comes back up, spewing over the floor of the shower and I find the strength to lift myself onto the bench seat in the corner so that the vomit doesn't make me even more filthy than I already am.

By the time I've washed myself so much that my skin is raw, the smell of something hot and delicious wafts through the room. I shut off the shower, wrap the towel around my waist, and slowly walk back into the room. There, sitting on the table, is a large plate of pancakes, bacon, and eggs.

I try to rush, but my muscles protest. I grip the pile of clothes sitting on the chair and look around, not seeing anyone and not remembering hearing a door open or close. I might have been too focused on getting myself clean to notice.

My mouth waters at the sight of the food, but I know that I need to take it slowly. After pulling on the clothes, I take a bite of food, chewing thoroughly and letting it settle for a moment before repeating.

As I slowly savor the food, the taste and warmth filling my belly, I can't help but wonder about Antonia's motives. She's kept me captive and subjected me to unimaginable pain, but now she's provided a meal and some semblance of freedom. Her explanation about deprogramming Zach and her concern about my mother's influence on him leaves me conflicted. Could that really be the reason she kept me down here for so long? Or is it possible that she wanted to try to break me even more than she already has?

As I eat, my mind races with thoughts of escape and reuniting with my children. I know that I can't let this continue any longer.

I've always feared for my parliament. I stayed and played my role to protect them. Now, I know that I also need to look out for myself and my children. Despite my worry over the rest of my family, I'm determined to find a way out of this situation. For now, I need to regain my strength and heal my body. The wounds inflicted upon me are still fresh, and I need to be strong if I hope to break free.

I take a deep breath, trying to summon the strength and resolve to confront her and find a way to escape this nightmare. It won't be easy, but I'm determined to do whatever it takes to protect my children and end this torment once and for all.

As I exit my underground prison, my heart pounds in anticipation. Two long weeks have passed since I last saw the sun or either of my children. Zach, I had grown accustomed to not seeing, but not my Amelia. I am used to seeing her every day. Just the thought of seeing her today has excitement bubbling up inside me.

The door groans in protest as I push it open, and a sliver of golden light pierces through the crack. I have to shield my eyes with my hand. My eyes are no longer accustomed to the sun after spending so long in darkness.

With a deep breath, I step out into the world I have missed so dearly. The transition is almost overwhelming. The air feels warm and inviting against my skin, and I stop for a moment, allowing the sensation to wash over me. With my eyes closed, my other senses kick into overdrive. The sound of birds chirping and the rustling of leaves in the gentle breeze is loud in my ears.

Slowly, I open my eyes, allowing them to adjust to the brilliant sunlight. The sky stretches out endlessly above me, an unbroken expanse of blue that seems to go on forever. The sun itself hangs in the sky like a radiant jewel, casting its golden glow over everything in its path.

I take a few hesitant steps forward, my eyes scanning the landscape before me. The world has changed in the eight weeks I have been away. I spent six in Corfu—an entirely different climate—and two hidden in that basement. The trees that were barren when I saw them last are now adorned with lush green leaves, and the flowers that were mere buds are now in full bloom, their colors a riot of reds, blues, and yellows.

I can feel the sun's warmth seeping into my bones, chasing away the chill of the underground. It is as if the sun itself is welcoming me back, its rays caressing my skin like a long-lost friend.

I raise my arms to the sky, basking in the glory of the sun's embrace. It is a feeling of pure euphoria, but not as euphoric as the sound I hear next.

"Daddy!" My head snaps in her direction, and I catch a glimpse of her long, chestnut hair flowing behind her.

I force my feet to move as quickly as they can as we race toward each other, only to be stopped by a blast of air just before our bodies collide.

"Daddy!" Amelia cries, reaching out her hand toward mine. Tears begin flowing down her beautiful little face.

"It's okay, Pumpkin." I say the words, not knowing if they are true or not, and search out the cause of our separation. As I look around, I see many of the coven members nearby staring in shock, mouths dropped open. There are more than a few that host smirks on their faces though.

"We talked about this, Amelia," Antonia scolds our daughter as she steps into view.

"But—" Amelia begins, earning a glare from her mother. My little girl flinches away from the look, and my stomach sinks. That single action tells me everything I need to know about what happened over the past two weeks.

I look over my little girl, paying more attention this time.

Though she looked as perfect as always at first glance, I can see the toll that spending two weeks with her monster of a mother has exacted when I look closer. Gone are her full cheeks. They are now hollow with weight loss. Big, black bags rest under her eyes, and I'm sure I'd find bruises beneath her long-sleeved shirt and pants.

I turn my glare toward Antonia.

"What is the meaning of this?"

She ignores my question for a moment, walking over to Amelia and stroking her hair with a cruel smile.

"It seems your usefulness is coming to an end, pet."

"My usefulness?"

"You were such a good babysitter while I needed you. Just a few minutes ago, my little Amelia was able to prove once and for all that she *does* have magic. She grew flowers all on her own."

I feel both shock and relief as I study Antonia's face.

"I didn't—" Amelia begins to deny it but is cut off quickly by Zach.

"She did. I saw her," he declares. His face is a hard mask, daring anyone to disagree. As I stare at my son, I note the changes in him too. Just like Amelia, it's clear he has lost weight and missed a few nights of sleep. Unlike his sister, there is a hardness to him that wasn't there before.

As he moves to stand protectively between his mother and sister, I understand it all. I know where the flowers came from. Amelia is an owl. I know it, my mother knows it, and my son knows it too.

I lock eyes with my son and give him a nod of thanks for protecting her when I couldn't. He's done his best, but I know he doesn't realize the problem he's now created. When Amelia shifts —and she will—Antonia will find out that this was all a lie.

I give my children one last look before turning to their mother.

"And what are you going to do with me?"

"I was going to kill you."

"No!" Both of my children cry out in my defense.

"But then I thought it might be nice to have some extra help around here. You wouldn't be able to interact with *my* children, of course, but it seems it would upset them to watch you die." She pauses and glances at Zach as he holds a sobbing Amelia. "For now, anyway."

With that, she waves her hand, pushing me back so I fall on the ground, and I watch in horror as she ushers my children away from me.

I have no choice now. Despite the threat to my village, I have to plan an escape for the three of us. Zach has bought us some time, but he can only do so much. I only wish that I could get a warning to my mother and tell her to get out of Greece before Antonia's wrath heads their way.

Chapter Seven

Pearl

I was right. In the time I've been gone, my father has accumulated a long list of issues to discuss with me. He already has suggestions for each decision, and I completely agree with his choices. I hate that he feels like he needs my approval. For most of my life, my father was the one in charge. My mother died when Aqua was born, and I was only eight. There was another woman in our pod who had just turned twenty who took over the role of pod mother.

When I was freed from the hunters and finally reunited with my family, she was gone. My father later explained that he and a small number of our pod refused to leave our pre-planned meeting location, knowing that was the first place I would look if I were to escape. Since he refused to give up hope that I would find my way back to him, the few women there were—none of whom were willing to step up into the leadership role—left along with most of the men. When I returned, my pod was a fraction of the size it once was.

Now that I'm back, though, even the original members of my pod have begun looking to me for guidance and answers. I hate it. I know my place is at the head of my pod, and I want to do them justice. Still, I don't feel quite equal to the task.

It's the main reason I truly hope Kristle and her family join us here. Perhaps Narissa will seamlessly step into the role of pod mother with our people as well.

The possibility fills me with both hope and anxiety. If I'm honest, as much as I long to be free of the responsibility, I just don't know what type of leader Narissa is yet. I need to know before I give her control over my family—we've been through enough. From the small interactions I've had with her, I doubt she would be as willing to defer to my father as I have been.

"Pearl?" Mizu calls out as he steps through the front door.

"In here." I raise my voice so that it carries from the sunroom at the back of the house overlooking the ocean.

I turn and watch as Mizu and Kristle walk through the door hand in hand and smile at the sight. My cousin has never looked so happy, and Kristle is practically glowing.

"Hey, guys. What's up?"

"Well, I just talked to my mom. She is understandably excited about our mating..." She turns her head and looks at my cousin like he hangs the moon each night. He leans over to kiss her on the forehead.

"They want to come here," Mizu finishes for her, "but were hoping to talk about some logistics before."

"Step into my office." I chuckle, gesturing to the couch opposite me. "Congratulations on your mating," I begin as they sit down, still clasping each other's hands. They look completely at ease with each other already.

It sends a small pang through me, and I search inside me for the pull that I became accustomed to. It flickers weakly, and I make a mental note that I need to return to Greece soon to see if my hunch is correct about my mystery man.

"Thank you," Kristle says. When she turns to me, her face

instantly switches from in love to all business. "In exchange for us coming here and strengthening your numbers, my mother would like your assistance."

I raise a brow. "In exchange?"

Kristle nods, a knowing smirk on her face. Narissa definitely told her what to say.

"By my account, we are the ones providing you with a safe haven—not the other way around."

"You're right. However, like your cousin here, having the rest of us come increases the chances of your men finding mates and strengthening your pod."

"I'll be sure to factor that into my decision." I smile, knowing full well that if they're asking me for help, I would've given it without this back and forth. "What is it you want in return?"

Mizu looks at me like I'm crazy. He does not recognize this little game Kristle and I are playing with one another.

"My father, uncles, and cousins are all swimming the sea. We don't know where they are, and my mother and I are requesting your help in locating them."

"Why didn't you say something before?" I ask, leaning forward. When they told me that they were gone, I assumed they had a way to contact them, a meetup location, something, anything. But knowing that their loved ones are out there somewhere, possibly hurt, maybe captured...I can't sit by and do nothing about that.

"We weren't sure we could trust you," Kristle says quietly, knowing exactly where my line of thinking just went.

"Trust or not. Your pod is out there. What kind of leader lets their family—"

"Hey!" Kristle yells, getting to her feet. "We had no other choice. It was a decision made by the entire pod that they would follow Sky and look for help along the way."

"How long have they been missing?" I grind out the words, not willing to let go of my anger. These people aren't even part of my pod and already I feel a connection to them. It may be because of Mizu mating into their pod, but the thought of these men lost and alone in the seas makes me sick.

"Eight months." Shame coats her words. Good. She should be ashamed. If that were my father out there, I'd be tearing the world apart to know he's safe. These women are a little too unconcerned for my comfort.

"Eight months?" I grunt in frustration before I stand up, walk over to the phone, and dial Skarlyt.

"Hello?" she answers sweetly.

"Emergency. Get to my house now." I leave no room for argument and hang up the phone.

"Now Pearl—" Mizu begins.

I point my finger into his face.

"Don't you 'now Pearl' me.' If that was you or Dad out there, I'd be losing my mind. I never would've let you go on your own. We would've found allies..."

"There were no allies. We only had ourselves, and we couldn't leave Sky alone."

"Then you *all* should have gone," I snap back.

She lowers her head, and a tear slips free. The sight makes me feel awful, but I know I am right.

"Who do I have to kill?" Rayne asks the second she materializes in front of me, letting go of Skar's hand.

"No one," I tell her, looking over at Kristle. "Yet..."

Rayne, being the bloodthirsty vampire she is, pouts at that news.

"I need Skarlyt to teleport Kristle home."

"But—" Kristle begins, stepping forward to defend herself. I hold up a hand to pause her.

"To get items that belong to her family to help you do a locator spell. Apparently," I look pointedly over at Kristle. "Some members of her pod are missing. Between your magic and my knowledge of the seas, I am hoping we can find them quickly."

"And then we kill some people?" Rayne asks excitedly.

"Probably," I admit. If we find out her family has been captured, we are going to need Rayne and her many knives.

I walk out of the house, needing the solace of the ocean. I leave Kristle to call her mom and explain. It's clear Kristle is upset too, and part of me knows I am being too hard on her. Still, there is a furious rise in my gullet that I cannot ignore. How could Narissa let this happen?

These are her people—her pod—and she just rolled over and let humans split them up?

I rush toward the water like I'm ablaze. Is this the protective impulse Alaric is always describing?

This is not what I intended to do today. I wanted to get Narissa and her pod here safely before making my way back to Greece to find my mystery man. As I look out at the ocean, watching the waves crashing on the shore of our beautiful beach, I feel turmoil rather than the usual calmness the sight supplies.

I close my eyes, listening to the rhythmic ebb and flow of the waves, a calming melody that resonates deep within me. The gentle lapping of water against the beach whispers the secrets of the sea, and the distant calls of seagulls overhead add a touch of serenity to the symphony. The wind, with its soft sighs and occasional gusts, carries the scent of salt and adventure.

Normally, I relish the feeling, listening to the song of the ocean as if she's a wise and ancient storyteller. Today, all I feel is a churning in my gut. There's a light pulsing of urgency, pushing me to find *him*. Now, the demands of my position hold me back.

I look back at our little village full of small beach cabins. Some are finished to perfection, sitting high up on stilts with steps leading directly into the water. Others are still under construction, as our community is still growing every day.

I turn back to the ocean, my eyes drawn to a place far past the horizon. If I swam straight in that direction, I would find my way back to Greece.

Not for the first time, I wish that I wasn't the eldest woman in my pod. That our laws allowed our men to be leaders.

I let the last of my anger flow from me with a deep breath. I'm still appalled at the thought that Narissa has gone eight months without knowing where her mate is. If she had told me last night that they'd lost all contact, we could have started the search then. Almost an entire day has passed us by, and I know from experience that one day could mean the difference between life and death.

I heave out another heavy sigh, not wanting my anger to ramp up again until I can hear her reasoning and deal with the issue. There is nothing I can do about what has passed. I had hoped that Narissa could replace me as pod mother, but after this...

How can I trust her to watch over *my* family?

I sit on the sand, dip my toes in the cold water, and wait for Skarlyt and Kristle to do what they need to. I trust they will come and find me when they have something.

* * *

"Pearl?" My eyes snap open, a familiar voice calling from behind me.

"Yes," I respond without turning. I am not ready to face her just yet, but it doesn't stop her approach. I hear her soft footfalls on the sand getting closer until she reaches my location.

"I know you think I was wrong—" Narissa begins.

"Because you *were* wrong," I snap, turning to see her nod at me before turning to face the ocean.

"Perhaps I was." My mouth drops open in shock at the admission. "I was given an impossible choice between keeping my mate safe and sending help for my nephew."

When she puts it like that, I can begin to understand what she did.

"Why did you wait eight months to go find them?"

She turns to me, tears shining in her eyes. "Because I didn't know where to begin. I worried that if we left Australia, they would come home to find us missing."

"Why not have him call you? Check in sometimes?"

"In hindsight, we should have arranged something like that. By the time the thought crossed my mind, he was gone, and I didn't know where to find him."

I nod my head, the rest of my anger fading when I see the pain on her face.

"I still don't agree with your choice, but I do understand it."

"I also have to tell you that you were right."

I smile and point to myself. "Me? Right?"

She chuckles and waves me off.

"Yes. You were right about your friends. That witch Skarlyt was able to get their location. They're all in the same area off the coast of Greece."

"Greece." I nod in understanding and rush back to my home with Narissa at my heels. It can't be a coincidence that both my duty and my heart take me in the same direction. This has to be some kind of divine intervention. "Thank you, Artie," I whisper to the wind. I know that if anyone was meddling on my behalf, it was her.

"They're on the move," Skarlyt says as I step through the door.

It is my house, but it no longer looks like it is. I live a minimalist lifestyle. I spend so much time in the water that I do not need as many material things on land. My living room, which once housed a singular couch and coffee table, has been converted into one of Skarlyt's workshops. The room is unrecognizable with all of

Skarlyt's things spread around, including a large table covered in maps, jars full of ingredients, and a cauldron with a fire already under it. If she needs it for her spells, she has it here.

I've seen her do this to places before, but I can't help but wonder how long it will take for my home to go back to normal.

"Where to?" I ask, and all eyes turn to me.

"They are still off the coast of Greece," Skarlyt responds. "But they are going deep in the ocean. It's almost like they're following a boat."

"That means we need to go now." I look around the group, surprised to find it much larger than the one I left earlier. When I land on Mizu and Kristle, they nod in response.

"Here," Rayne says, walking over to me and placing a phone in my hands.

"It won't work underwater."

"It will," Drusilla interrupts me. She comes to stand next to her best friend. "Matt made it for you. Opal said you might need it, but she won't tell us why."

"That's alarming," I admit as I study the phone. It looks like a cell phone, sure, but not one from this decade. "How does it work?"

"It's completely waterproof and can get a signal even underwater." I hear Matt's voice and find it coming from another phone that is held aloft by Phoebe.

"Really?" I ask excitedly.

"Yes. There is a depth limit of one thousand feet. As long as you're above that, you should be good."

"Thank you," I say, not only to Matt but to the large group of people filling my living room.

"You're a member of our pack, Pearl," Alaric says, stepping up beside Phoebe and putting his arm around her.

"You are our family," Sarah adds.

"Damn right, she's family," Breanne's voice comes through the speaker of the phone. The touching moment is broken as we all laugh.

"I also made this," Sarah says, stepping up with a backpack. "It's lightweight, completely waterproof, and is spelled to hold way more than it looks like it can."

"That way, you can bring clothes with you if you need them," Alaric, adds.

Phoebe steps forward, offering me the phone in her hand.

"I haven't been able to get you a high-quality camera on that thing yet," Matt warns through the speaker. "If you can find a well-known spot for us to come to you, that would be helpful."

"Okay," I tell everyone, placing the phone inside the bag. Sarah was right, there's more than enough room for me to pack the clothes I'll need to cover the six people I plan to bring with me. "Kristle, Mizu, get Caspian, Autumn, Spring, and Summer. I will meet you at the beach."

They nod, immediately rushing out the door and leaving me alone with my friends.

"Thank you," I begin, emotion threatening to creep up my throat. I have never felt so supported as I do now. "Thank you for everything."

Drusilla rushes to me and wraps me in a hug.

"You never have to thank us, Pearl. Your war is our war."

"She's right," Andres adds, the giant dragon shifter coming into view just behind his mate's slight frame. "None of us are okay knowing that a supernatural is being held captive by humans."

I step back and dip my chin in acknowledgment before walking out the door.

"Come back or I'll hunt you down," Rayne calls out to me. I chuckle, waving her off with what she always refers to as a "one-finger salute."

I find the group waiting for me on the beach. As I approach,

Mizu takes the bag from me and shoves some more clothes into it before strapping it onto his own back.

"You know where we're heading?" I ask.

Kristle nods, already moving toward the deeper water. Tensions are high, and no one speaks as we swim.

Hours later, we arrive at the spot the locator spell indicated to find it empty.

"All right. Fan out," I command. "Each person swims ten minutes in that direction and comes back if they don't find the boat. If you don't come back, we will assume you found it and will follow you."

It doesn't take long for us to spread out enough that we are all swimming in opposite directions. I wait a few extra minutes, but everyone except Summer returns.

"It looks like we are going this way," I tell everyone, swimming in the direction Summer went, hoping and praying that she didn't just get sidetracked. I don't know her or the other Seasons, but I needed people to help and wanted to bring some people Narissa's pod would recognize.

I see glittering through the water to the right and make a sharp turn, gliding through the water toward it. I slow down as I approach the forms coming into focus before us, but Kristle speeds by me, wrapping her arms around a man with pale blue hair.

By the way Mizu is hanging back, completely unconcerned about his mate in the arms of another man, I'm going to assume that is her father.

When Spring and Autumn rush toward the other men, it's confirmed.

"You should not have come," Kristle's father tells her.

"We have help now," she responds. He turns, finally seeing the three of us watching their interaction. He completely dismisses me, turning instead to his daughter for direction.

"What's the plan?"

Instead of answering, Kristle turns to me, dipping her head in submission. It's clear this move shocks her father as much as it shocks me.

I follow her lead and swim closer.

"I need to know the details of what's going on."

"And you are?" he sneers.

"Pearl. I am the pod mother of your daughter's mate," I snap back.

"Mate?" he asks, and Kristle leaves his side, swimming closer to me and tucking herself into Mizu's side.

"This is Mizu," she says, beaming as she looks up at him. "I met my mate."

"Well, then. I'm Taron." His aggressive tone disappears. Instead, there is something akin to pride in his voice as he dips his chin in my direction. "Above, there is a massive wooden boat containing at least one hundred well-armed humans. They are holding my nephew Sky hostage."

I glance up at the silhouette of a massive boat.

"Where do they dock?"

He shakes his head.

"They've docked a few times, but never at the same place twice. By some stroke of luck, the goddess has allowed them to be at sea for the past month straight."

"She has let them sail here that long? Have they been fishing? Diving?"

Taron shakes his head.

"How do they get food?"

"Smaller supply ships come and drop off supplies once a week." Another man with pale green hair adds this piece of information.

We spend the next week watching, waiting, and gathering as much information as we can. Just like Taron said, there is an army of well-armed soldiers on the boat. They wear uniforms, but they look more like mercenaries than military.

Nymphs are not bellicose people. We don't like to fight. As time passes, though, and nothing on the ship changes, it becomes clear we may have no choice. I know my friends on the island would be happy to help me, but they can't do much while the ship is adrift in the ocean.

While we wait, the members of Narissa's pod celebrate their reunion. Taron and Mizu, luckily, get along incredibly well. The members of my pod who accompanied me are happy to meet more nymphs and learn about them.

The joy of finding these missing men and uniting our pods—at least temporarily—is obviously strained by the presence of the ship above. It's a constant reminder of Sky's suffering and our inability to confront the humans directly.

I feel the shift in the sea when their next supply ship is approaching. This ship has a motor propelling it and disturbs the quiet peace underwater.

We notice its presence long before the humans above could see it on the horizon.

Taron and the others confirm it is the same vessel that has brought deliveries several times. It's small, carrying only two humans and supplies for the larger ship. Not as hopeless an encounter as the larger ship where Sky is trapped. Not as hard to sink.

"Okay," I call out, finally seeing our way forward. "Here's the plan."

Chapter Eight

Pearl

With the plan in place to starve them out by sinking their shipments before they arrive, I leave the group and head to shore to check in with everyone back home. Even a magic cell phone sounds muffled underwater.

Instead of heading to the nearest shore, my tail takes me to a familiar beach. It's early morning, so I find a large rock and hide behind it, waiting for a glimpse of *him*.

I wait. And I wait. And I wait some more.

Countless people come and dive into the ocean, but none are the man I'm waiting for.

When the sun hits its peak, I decide he's not coming and slip out of the water, grab my clothes and phone out of the bag, and dress quickly. Powering on the phone, I dial Breanne.

"Pearl?" She answers on the first ring.

"Hey."

"Is everything okay?"

I immediately jump into details of what we're doing.

"Do you need reinforcements?"

"Not yet," I tell her. My head turns at the sound of a snapping twig. A man walking down the trail toward the hidden village catches my eye. He isn't my mystery man, but I am curious all the same. "I'll call you right back."

I hang up the phone and power it off before I can hear her complaints. I'm sure she'll call the phone back a dozen times, but this feels more important. I need stealth, and the phone ringing continuously would ruin that.

I search inside myself for that little tug. Just like I noticed before, it's not pulsing and pulling me inland, toward the village I know is hidden there. Instead, it seems to be further away. It's possible I was wrong about him being my mate. Or maybe he's just not here...

Taking the route deeper within the trees, I keep my steps light and follow the man at a safe distance. I use the villagers welcoming him home as a distraction to slip further inside than before. I snag a hat off the ground, wrapping up my blue hair to hide beneath it. I can blend in for a little while—but not with my hair glowing like a beacon.

As I slink through the shadows, I keep my eyes and ears peeled for my mystery man. I see no sign of him until—There. A pair of fluorescent pink shorts hangs on a line outside of a large house. I creep up to the window, hoping for a glimpse of him. If he's in there, though, it means that the pull isn't leading me to him after all.

"Ma, we've talked about this." A feminine voice comes through the open window. "Loukas is a grown man. He knows what he's doing."

"That's hogwash, and you know it. He wouldn't be in this situation if it weren't for *her*."

The way she says it tells me all I need to know. Whoever *she* is, these women do not like her.

"Yes, I know that," the original voice concedes, "but he would leave if it was that bad."

"*She* knows where we are. He knows she would come here and kill us all. Or would you prefer she kills the two little ones instead?"

"You don't know that she would kill anyone."

"Has it been so long that you've forgotten? Have you forgotten how she got her hooks into him in the first place? How she murdered your father?"

"Of course not."

"Maybe you're blind to the fact that my cherry blossom was only skin and bones when she arrived. Maybe you did not see that Loukas has new scars on his body that weren't there before. Scars that a shifter shouldn't have."

"There is nothing we can do," the original voice says, this time sounding sad and resigned.

I lift myself, peeking through the window. The second I see the large family portrait hanging on the wall, I know I'm at the right place. His gorgeous face is smiling, looking over at three women who I assume are his mother and sisters.

"We have to try. She's going to kill him if Amelia shifts."

"Why would she kill him if she shifts?"

"Because she won't suffer herself to have a shifter for a daughter, and he will put himself between that monster and my cherry blossom. She will kill him."

My blood runs cold at the woman's, who I now assume is his mother, words. If Loukas is who I think he is to me and what she is saying is true, he's in danger. A lot of danger.

"Maybe we can get there in time, sneak into Northern Ontario, and smuggle Amelia out before she shifts." The second voice does not even try to sound hopeful at this suggestion. "The Daughters of Eris would never need to know."

"You know there's no way for us to do that," his mother chides, and I get an idea.

They may not be able to smuggle anyone out of anywhere, but

I can. I quickly snag the pink shorts from the line and make my way back to the beach.

I send a text with a low-resolution picture of where I am and immediately call Breanne.

"Thank the gods you're okay."

"I need you to send someone to get me."

"Why? What's happened?" she asks, though I can hear that she's put me on speakerphone.

"Nothing with the sea nymphs. But..." I pause, unsure of how to explain what's going on. I look out at the ocean and feel conflicted once again. My heart is telling me that I need to focus on Loukas, but my head is telling me that the sea nymphs need to be my priority.

"But what?"

"How did it feel when you first saw Matt? Before you two spoke?" I ask.

"Like there was this little thread inside me that was constantly trying to pull us together. Why?"

"Because that's how I feel..."

"You met your mate?" she asks excitedly.

"Maybe... But he's in trouble."

"What kind of trouble?"

"If what I just heard is true, the kind that you don't come back from. The kind that I'm going to need Rayne's help with..."

"And now you don't know what to do because you don't want to leave your pod behind," she states. There is no question in there. She already knows how I'm feeling, and that's why she's my best friend.

"Yeah..."

"Okay. Sebastyn is on his way to get you. Come here, and we'll figure it out."

Sebastyn pops up before I can even respond.

"Beautiful beach you got here, Pearl. Are you sure you want to come home?" He chuckles, looking around. I hear Breanne cursing him out for even asking that question before I hang up the phone.

"I'm sure. Can you take me to Bree's?"

"Sure thing," he says, taking my outstretched hand and popping us into Breanne and Matt's office at the academy. Breanne is pacing back and forth, muttering obscenities while Matt sits at his desk, smirking at his mate.

"Don't give her options about whether or not she can come home," Breanne begins, jutting out her finger at Sebastyn.

"It's okay, Bree. I would never leave you," I placate her, walking up and wrapping my arms around her shoulders. She hugs me back fiercely. I wink at Sebastyn, who takes the opportunity to vanish. Smart man. I wouldn't want to be on Breanne's bad side either.

"Now tell us about this dilemma. All I got from Bree was that you think you met your mate and he's in trouble," Matt interrupts our hug, getting right down to business. It's one of the things I love about him and what makes the two of them work so well. Breanne is action first, questions later; Matt likes to have a solid plan in place.

"I'm not sure where to begin," I admit, but then it just starts flowing out of me. I start with the pull to the island, watching him each day, then how I felt the tug inside me dull and pull me some-where else. If I look at the map of where our island is floating now, Canada is exactly where I'm being pulled to.

As soon as I mention the Daughters of Eris, Matt sucks in a breath.

"What?" I stop my tale, knowing I have reached the crucial part. "What do you know?"

"The Daughters of Eris are a coven located a few hours north of Parry Sound—at least that's where we think they are. No one I know has ever actually met any of them, but they were near enough for us to hear whispers."

"Whispers about what?"

"Evil." He doesn't say anything else. Just that one word and goosebumps pebble my skin. "We need Skarlyt."

He stands up and heads over to his phone, leaving me with Breanne.

"Have you heard of these people?"

She shakes her head. "Nope. I was with the Hunters for a very long time, and all their news was old news."

I nod, not needing her to explain any further. She was taken by hunters as a child and spent years in their clutches.

"They are just witches, right?" I ask. "What does he mean by evil?"

"Just that," Skarlyt jumps into the conversation the moment she enters the room. "Those women and the Sons of Ares are the worst sort of magical beings you've ever met."

"If they're so evil, wouldn't they be mages?" Bree asks.

Skarlyt nods. "Yes, that's what I would call them. They pray to Ares and Eris. Even though the names suggest they are two separate covens, they are not. Why are we talking about them?"

Both Matt and Breanne look over at me expectantly.

"Because I think I met my mate, and I think he's being held captive by them."

"Your mate is a witch?" Skar asks, her blue eyes sparkling with excitement.

I shake my head. "I think he's an owl shifter."

Her brows furrow in response.

"What's an owl shifter doing with the Daughters of Eris?" Skarlyt's mind catches up with her excitement for me. "What is your *mate* doing with the Daughters of Eris?"

"I asked that question too," Matt pipes in.

For the second time in an hour, I launch into the tale of how I met Loukas—or saw him—and what I overheard from his mother and sister.

"If they have him there and this woman—who I can only assume is the high priestess—killed his father, I'd say what you heard isn't even the half of it."

"What do you mean?" I ask.

Skarlyt sighs, looking scared for the first time since I met her.

"The Daughters of Eris and Sons of Ares are purists. They do not play well with other supernaturals. If they have this Loukas among them, they have him for a reason. We definitely need to get him and the kids they mentioned out of there."

"Do you know where their coven is located?"

"I have an idea," Skarlyt admits. "It's a big area, but—lucky you—it's surrounded by water."

"Do you have another one of these phones?" I ask, turning to Matt.

"I do. Why?"

"Because I need to give this one to Narissa and send her to monitor what's happening with the sea nymphs while I go to Northern Ontario."

"Wait a minute," Bree protests. "You can't go alone."

"I have to. I can get in through the water undetected and gather intel. Besides, that's why I asked for the other phone—so that I can call in the cavalry if needed."

"This one has a better camera," Matt says, handing over a more modern-looking phone. "It doesn't have as deep a range, but you'll be in lakes more than the ocean. I think you'll be fine."

"Can you swim in freshwater?" Skarlyt asks.

"I can. If I'm injured, I won't be able to heal as quickly as I can in salt water."

"Take Rayne with you," Breanne suggests.

"There is no way I will go undetected if I take her with me. And she can't stay under the water like me."

"Then take another mer—" Breanne begins, and I make a face,

knowing she is about to call us mermaids. "Take another sea nymph with you."

"I can't. Their main focus needs to be rescuing Narissa's pod. It's where my focus should be too," I admit.

Breanne comes and places her hand on my shoulder.

"Your focus needs to be on your mate. The rest of your pod will understand."

I look up into her eyes and dip my chin in agreement, though I have a feeling they will not understand as well as she thinks they will. Bree doesn't know sea nymphs like I do. The ones here on the island with me—my pod—have adapted to the way of life on the island, with the rest of our friends and family. The ones in Narissa's pod haven't had that opportunity yet.

"Can you take me to the pod?" I ask Skarlyt.

She nods, reaching out for me.

"We will organize two teams here," Matt pipes in before we disappear. "We'll be ready to help with both rescue missions."

I give him a nod of thanks.

"Good luck," Skarlyt whispers as she drops me in front of the home we gave Narissa to stay in.

I let out a heavy sigh, not wanting to have this conversation. After all the grief I gave her about choosing to let her pod members go missing for months, now I feel as if I'm doing something even worse...being selfish.

I knock on the door twice before it swings open, revealing Narissa. Her smile fades into a frown as soon as she sees me.

"What's happened?"

"Everyone is okay, but I need to talk to you," I tell her, and she steps back, allowing me to enter her home.

I take a seat at her dining room table and wait until she sits across from me.

"Pearl? You're scaring me."

"We found your pod, and they are safe." I heave out another sigh. "I need you to take my place in rescuing Sky."

"What? Why?" she asks, knowing this is not easy for me. As the pod mother, I should be leading the charge. By giving up that position, I'm opening myself up to being replaced by her within my own pod. It's a possibility that relieved me before, but now I am not so sure.

"Because I think I found my mate."

"In my pod?" Her eyes sparkle with hope, but the longer I stay silent, the more her brows furrow.

"No. He's a shifter, and he's in trouble."

"But—" I know what she's going to say.

I didn't get the impression that her pod is full of purists, but mating outside our species is not exactly welcomed—especially for the pod mother.

"It was a surprise for me too." I save her the effort of finding the words to say. "But the signs are all there. If I don't go to him now, I may lose the chance forever."

"What do you mean?"

And once again, for the third time today, I launch into the tale. Her eyebrows crease more with every word.

"I see." She doesn't offer any other word of congratulation or concern, proving my suspicion that not all in the pod will understand.

"So, will you go?"

"Yes."

"Good," I respond, handing her the phone and texting Sebastyn to come pick her up in an hour and to take her back to the spot where he picked me up. "When Sebastyn drops you off, you'll have to swim straight out for about thirty minutes and make a hard right. You'll want to stay deep underwater, but you'll find your pod there."

She waves me off. "My mate is with them; I won't have a problem finding them once I am in the right area."

I nod, walking out of the door without saying goodbye. I make time to find my father and sister before I leave. The story is getting familiar as I repeat it to everyone.

Unlike the conflicting emotions shown by everyone else so far, Aqua and my dad were excited for me, ready to celebrate as soon as I can bring him to safety.

As soon as I was done saying goodbye to them, I called Skarlyt. They both offered to come with me. Of course, it would be smart to have someone with me, but this feels like something I need to do alone.

Without warning, Skarlyt transports us to a frost-covered beach and unfolds a map as I get my bearings.

"This is the area where they're rumored to be." She points to our current location on the map and circles a long finger over the small patches of water surrounding it. "All these lakes are connected."

I take the map from her, studying it one final time before folding it up and placing it into my bag.

"Be safe," she says, throwing her arms around me. "We will be waiting for your call."

I thank her and return the hug before walking into the freezing water and allowing the shift to overtake me. It takes a few minutes for my body to adjust to the cold and lack of salt in the water, but once it does, I start to swim.

Luckily, the sun is just setting as I circle the largest group of islands. I stop and investigate each light I see on the shore, hoping that I will find this coven behind them.

By the time the sun is dawning overhead, I've been swimming for almost ten hours and able to eliminate many of the landmasses on this side of the map as possible hideouts. I am trying to decide if I should rest a while when I see it.

A large cluster of lights on the edge of a seemingly abandoned lake. The closer I get, the stronger the thread inside me pulses.

It makes me wonder if he can feel it too.

Does he know I'm out here? Does he know I am searching for him?

Chapter Nine

Loukas

It's been a week since Antonia let me out of that basement. A week of watching my children from afar. Seven days of watching my daughter be belittled, broken down, and beaten while I am unable to say or do anything about it.

The only thing that helps me sleep at night is knowing that Zach is there with her, protecting her when I can't. It's too much to put on his shoulders. He should be allowed to be a kid, but instead he has to step into the shoes of a man and protect his little sister. It makes me proud and sad at the same time.

The amount of physical abuse he's taken in her stead is maddening. Each time, I hold myself back from rushing in. It's killing me to watch, but I know that Antonia wants me to react. She wants me to give her a reason to kill me, and I can't allow that to happen. I can't leave my children here alone with her.

My stomach rumbles, reminding me that I haven't had a good meal in over a week. That is another change from my life before the basement. I'd always been fed well, partaking in meals with Amelia; now, I am no longer welcome and have to fend for myself.

I've been able to make do scavenging in the forest. I even got lucky and caught a rabbit two days ago, but it isn't enough to sustain me.

The hunger and pains in my stomach have me feeling weaker. The only benefit is that it has my owl feeling stronger every day. If it keeps going the way it has been, I may actually be able to shift by the end of this week.

Meat, he begs.

"I know, buddy. I know," I say out loud, climbing out of the hunting shack that I've been given as my home and grabbing a fishing pole. The goal for the day is to catch enough fish to replace the protein I need. If I get lucky, maybe I can find a few extra to save for the next few days.

"Where do you think you're going?" A male voice calls out as I reach the shore.

I turn to find Anthony, Antonia's brother, staring at me with a sneer.

"To catch some fish," I respond, holding up the fishing pole and giving it a little jiggle as if he didn't already see it.

"Did Tonia say you could go fishing?"

I scoff at his question. "I have to ask permission to go fishing now?"

"You are no longer a *guest* here."

I let out a hard laugh.

"I was never a guest here. Unless she plans on explaining to my children that she let me starve to death, I'm going fishing."

Before he can respond, I turn on my heel, pushing the wooden rowboat off the shore and hopping in.

"You have one hour," Anthony yells as I row away.

"I have as long as it takes to catch enough food for myself," I call back, knowing full well that he's just trying to flex his authority now that his sister has given him permission to treat me the way he's always wanted to.

I row the boat to the middle of the lake and cast out my line using the worms I was able to gather up last night. A small splash off to the right catches my attention, and I quickly reel in my line to cast it in that direction. Immediately, the line begins to bob, and I yank it, spin the reel, but the line doesn't move.

"Whoa this must be a big one," I grunt as I use all my strength to keep myself inside the boat and holding the pole. I plant my feet on the sides of the small wooden boat, leaning back as the fish on the hook at the end of my line begins to pull both me and the boat.

As it pulls me toward one of the small islands, the fish lets go of the line, but the boat doesn't still. The momentum continues carrying me forward until it pushes up on the shore. If the fish can do this, I am not sure I want to catch it after all.

I look down at the rocky shore in confusion. I begin to reel in my line once more, and it glides like butter, wrapping around the spool over and over. As it does, I search the water for whatever has pulled me so far. I turn in time to see a flash of bright blue rising out of the water.

My hand opens, dropping the pole as the blue turns to the peach-colored flesh of a beautiful woman.

Mate, my owl hoots excitedly in my head. We both watch in awe as the beautiful woman rises from the water like a goddess.

"Hi," she says. Her voice is musical. Her bright hair and the fact that she's rising from the water tell me she can be nothing other than a sea nymph.

"Mate," I say, taking a step toward her.

"Mate," she confirms, quickening her steps until she's flinging herself into my arms, her lips merging with mine. I snake my arms around her waist, pulling her naked body closer to mine. I love the feeling of her smooth, chilled skin against my hands and deepen the kiss. I slide my hands under her ass, lifting her as she wraps her legs around my waist. I turn, carrying her to the soft grass.

Hunger pains cause my steps to falter, and she breaks the kiss, looking at me with concern.

"You are hungry," she says. A statement—not a question. I nod sullenly, hating to look weak in front of my newly found mate. I had lost hope of ever finding her after meeting Antonia and everything that has happened since.

She drops her legs to the ground.

"Will you make us a fire?" Without waiting for an answer, she jumps back into the water, and I see a bright blue tail flicking through the dark water.

I want to protest. I should be taking care of her. I should be strong enough to feed her, not the other way around. As fast as that thought pops into my head, I push it away. This woman is my mate. My equal. It's our job to take care of each other. Besides, she's probably much better at catching fish than me.

I get to work gathering birch bark, sticks, and fallen logs. I make a ring of rocks, set the wood in the center, and begin shredding the birch bark. After pulling out my flint and steel, I strike it once, the sparks easily catching. After a couple of gentle breaths, the birch bark lights, going up in a whoosh.

Now that I have a moment to think, I look around. Are we far enough away that no one from the coven will find us?

My gorgeous mate is back in minutes, carrying three large fish. She hands them to me before pulling a long dress over her head. I curse internally, wanting nothing more than to stand here and ogle my naked mate. I suppose being close to a fire naked isn't such a good idea. I set the fish down and grab a couple of long sticks I can use to cook the fish on.

A minute of silence rests between us. The only sound is the crackling of the wood from the fire, and then she speaks.

"I'm Pearl."

I turn to look at her, her musical voice once again causing goosebumps to pebble my flesh. I finally allow myself to take in her appearance. Her blue eyes sparkle with the flickering of firelight, her pale skin glows, and my eyes drop down to her full lips which curve into a smile.

"Sorry," I begin, my eyes darting back up to hers. "I'm Loukas."

The aroma of the cooking fish causes my stomach to growl loudly.

She looks down at my stomach and back up to my eyes, concern shining in them.

"Why..." She stops and bites her lip in contemplation, obviously not wanting to offend me.

"Why am I so hungry?" I supply, and she nods.

I let out a sigh and look back at the fire for a moment, not exactly sure how to answer it. I know that she's my mate; my owl knows she's my mate. After everything in my past, though, there's a chance she could reject me.

Hell, I might reject me. After all, I've spent years living with the woman who killed my father. I have allowed the mother of my children to become the villain in our story.

Her hand on my arm startles me, and I look up to meet her eyes.

"It's okay if you don't want to tell me."

I search her eyes, finding nothing but honesty in them.

"I do want to tell you, it's just that..." I let out a soft chuckle. "I guess I don't want to tell you, but only because I don't want you to look at me any differently than you are right now."

"I won—" she begins, but I shake my head.

"You will, and that's okay. You deserve to know everything before you decide if you want me as your mate."

She places her free hand on my cheek.

"I've seen the goddesses work in pairing mates a lot over the last five years. I trust Artie picked the perfect mate for me."

"Artie?"

She nods apologetically.

"That's a story for another time. Artie as in Artemis—the Moon Goddess." She waves off my confused look, and I realize there is no use pushing it. She's not going to tell me what that means...yet.

"Mine's a pretty long story."

"We have a while; the fish are still cooking." She gestures to the fish crackling over the fire.

I nod and begin the story of my life, cringing when I get to the point where Antonia kills my father, smiling when I tell her about Zach and Amelia, and staring into the fire when I tell her about the past month.

"She's keeping you and your children captive?" Pearl asks, anger coating her words. I flinch as she reaches out a hand and places it on my shoulder.

I look up from the ground, and her eyes soften. Her gaze is full of anger and something else I can't quite put my finger on, but she's definitely not looking at me with the hatred that I expected.

"I think I could leave now, and she wouldn't care," I say, glancing back in the direction of the coven.

"But you couldn't leave your children, could you?" Pearl asks, and I shake my head.

"No, I don't think I could." I think about what she's said for a moment and then nod my head "No. I *know* that I wouldn't be able to leave them behind with that monster."

"If you would, then you're not the man I hoped you were." My eyes widen at her admission. I had expected her to reject me because of my past. I had no hope that she would care enough about me and my children to accept me.

"You still want to be my mate?"

She once again places her free hand on the side of my face, looking deep into my eyes.

"Did you think that I wouldn't want you because of everything that's happened in your life? Because of what that monster has done to you?"

I look into her eyes, see the honesty there, and realize that I'm expecting her to react as Antonia would. I'm expecting her to throw a fit that there was another woman ever in my life. I am expecting her to be the monster that I've lived with for over a decade.

Like Pearl said, maybe I should trust in the goddess that she didn't pair me with someone who isn't my perfect match. I nod my head, a little ashamed and my answer.

"I haven't had the greatest experience with women."

She lets out a little chuckle "I can see that, but I promise you that I am nothing like *her*."

I study her face. Like Antonia, she's beautiful. Unlike Antonia, her eyes shine with kindness. It is a look that Antonia could never perfect even in the beginning. Even when she pretended to be something or someone different, she never had that shine, that glow.

"Why don't I tell you about my life?"

I nod my head eagerly, wanting nothing more than to hear every single detail about this amazing woman.

She smiles as she tells me about her family and her pod, especially about her younger sister. Then her eyes darken, and she looks away.

"One day, while we were exploring on land—further inland than we usually travel—a hunter came upon us." My brows furrow in confusion.

"A hunter? Like a human hunting for deer?"

She looks up at me, her mouth dropped open in shock. "A Supernatural Hunter. You've never encountered one?"

I shake my head.

"Lucky," she says with a sigh. "Supernatural Hunters are a special kind of human. Or I guess they're more supernatural than human."

"But they hunt supernaturals?" I ask in confusion.

She nods. "They do. There are five bloodlines of hunters all tracing back to the Norse gods. The way Artie explained it, they were supposed to be the protectors of the supernatural world. They were gifted qualities to make the task possible, and it was the women who were specifically tasked with this. As time went on, the men took over and twisted their purpose. Instead of protecting, they began eradicating and capturing supernaturals."

"Wait. You said the way 'Artie explained it.' Is this the same Artie you mentioned earlier? Like, as in Artemis?" That shouldn't be what I focus on, but it sticks out of her statement like a sore thumb.

She smiles. "I'll get to that part, but to be able to finish this story: yes. Artie is Artemis, as in the Moon Goddess. Yes, I have met her in the flesh."

"Met her in the flesh?"

"Yes, but that's another story entirely. So anyway, we encountered a hunter. Apparently, they had taken an interest in my sister Aqua and wanted her for their experiments, I couldn't let that happen," she says, her face filling with determination. I don't need her to finish to know what happened next.

"Luckily, the hunter was a vampire."

"Wait a second. A vampire chose to be a hunter and kill her own kind?" I ask in disbelief.

"If you let me finish you would know," she says, though it's with a soft smile telling me she's not really angry.

I nod for her to continue. "As I was saying. Luckily, the hunter was a vampire. And since you asked, no she did not choose to be a hunter, she was forced. She was taken captive as a child and tortured for years before being forced to capture her own kind. Her name is Bree, you'll meet her someday and maybe she'll tell you her story." I open my mouth to interrupt with another round of questions, but she raises a brow at me, and I snap it shut. "So, when Bree came for my sister, her heart wasn't in it. She gave us the opening to get Aqua out of there with my father and cousins but not without a sacrifice."

This time I can't hold my tongue. "A sacrifice—meaning you?"

She dips her chin in agreement, and a stray tear slides down her face.

"I gave myself up thinking that they would just kill me. I made peace with that. As long as Aqua and my father were free, I would give my life willingly."

"But they didn't kill you."

"No, they didn't. Instead, I was taken to their laboratory and studied. For years, they poked and prodded me, making me go months without water. Any kind of torture you can imagine, they did it. Until one day, another group of supernaturals came, stormed the facility, and freed us all. You would not believe me if I told you how many supes were in that place, but let's just say it was a lot."

"I can imagine."

"Take whatever number you're imagining and triple it."

My mouth drops open in shock. I was imagining it in the high hundreds. If there were as many as she says...

"That's..." I'm at a loss for words.

"During that raid on the facility, they learned of five more spread out over Canada. While they were planning though, I left and searched for my family. We always had a handful of safe locations planned at any given time. If we were ever separated, we would go to each and leave a message for one another before staying put."

"That's smart."

"Once I found them, I wasn't ready to separate, but I knew that I needed to help free the rest of the supernaturals. It was there that I found Bree again."

"Bree? As in the vampire that captured you to begin with?"

She nods. "Yes, turns out Rayne—who is the granddaughter of Artie and ex-hunter." I open and close my mouth like a fish. "I know it's a lot to process. Rayne is also a lot to process. So, Rayne, her mate Drake, and her friend Matt were staying at the facility to monitor the hunters. At the same time, the hunters had sent Bree in to see what was going on. While there, Matt met Bree—turns out they're mates—and Bree is the best friend of Drake's sister and Rayne's bestie, Drusilla, who was captured when they were kids."

"There's so much to unpack in that."

"I know. Believe me, I know. It will get easier to keep it straight once you meet them. Anyway, with the help of Artie, the West-wood pack and the Coven of the Moon were able to create a super-natural island—don't ask what it's named. Trust me, it's a whole thing." The way she rolls her eyes has me filling that away for later in case I want to annoy her. It's so cute. "The island is safe, and full of more supernatural races than we can count—which I should probably tell you includes dragons—"

"Dragons?" I feel my mouth drop open in shock. "You mean real dragons?"

"Mmhm. Andres, the King of Dragons, is the mate to Drusilla —the sister of Drake who I told you about earlier." She says the names like I'm going to remember them tomorrow. As much as I'm hanging on to her every word, it would be impossible for me to remember every name and who their relations are.

"Oh, the fish are done," she interrupts her own tale. "Let's eat first before your stomach starts to eat itself."

My mouth is hanging open, my shock completely evident as I dig into my fish. Everything she's said so far is running rampant in my head as I glance from my fish to her and back again. I am half in love with this woman already just from the way her eyes light up when she's passionate, the way her nose wrinkles and eyes roll when she's annoyed, and how much she obviously loves her friends and family.

Chapter Ten

Pearl

I watch the man beside me, *Loukas*, as he devours his fish and pick at my own. He's the same man I was watching all those weeks ago, I'm sure of it, but he's also *different*. His full cheeks are sunken, and the bones in his shoulders are more pronounced.

Even his hair has lost some of its luster. Even if I hadn't overheard his family's concerns, even if he hadn't told me about Antonia, I *would* have known just by looking at him that he's in some kind of trouble.

I cannot lie; the fact that he has children with that monster shook me to my core. But I wasn't lying when I told Loukas that I trust in the goddess to have paired me with my perfect match. Artie is a lot of things especially when she gets in her moods, but pairing fated mates is one thing she prides herself on.

Sure, both Skarlyt and Lennox argue that she got it wrong with their first mates, but Artie explained that sometimes things have to go a little wrong to get it right. If it weren't for the two of them being rejected, they would not have met each other. Although I am not sure I truly believe that she had that planned out the entire time, I do believe she made up for that small mistake in the end. She's a goddess, but she can only do so much. She can't help human influence as the two halves of the soul grow. Perhaps when they were born, their souls were perfect matches. Maybe it was their experiences within the world that warped their previous mates into someone unworthy of them.

Loukas' stomach growls once more as he sucks the meat off the tiny bones of the fish, proving that he was hungrier than I expected. Just how long has it been since this man has eaten?

Gently, I take the fish carcass from his hand and replace it with my half-eaten fish, allowing him to finish it. He looks up at me with wide eyes, using the sleeve of his shirt to wipe his mouth, embarrassment flashing in his eyes.

"It's okay," I tell him tenderly.

"Sorry. I guess I got a little carried away," he says sheepishly.

I wave my hand and gesture at the fish. "You eat, and I'll keep telling you my story."

My heart breaks at the sight of him, and I am desperate to do anything to take his mind off his suffering.

"You mentioned the king of dragons...my mother used to tell me stories of how they ruled the supernatural world," he says between bites.

I dip my chin in agreement. "The way Andres tells it; his father was an amazing ruler. Your mother was right, they were able to keep the peace within the supernatural world for centuries. When the hunters I told you about earlier crossed the ocean, it forced everyone into hiding."

"Sometimes hiding is the only safe option."

I wave my hand once more, gesturing to his fish.

"Anyway, for the past five years, a large group of us on the island have been working tirelessly to make the island a safe haven for *all* supernaturals. No matter what faction or if you're a hybrid—"

He scoffs. "Hybrids don't—"

I bite my lip, a small smile tugging the corners of my mouth.

"They exist too?"

I nod. "They do. They are very, very rare, but I know a few personally. Most of them have one side that is stronger than the other, but a few have the magic of both parents that are equally matched."

"Incredible," he says, his eyes wide.

"But the big thing we've been working on is a supernatural network like a 911 system."

"911?"

"I had the same reaction. It's like emergency services for supernaturals around the world. We have teams that monitor it twenty-four-seven. If there is someone in danger, they only need to send a message and picture of where they are and the team teleports to them, bringing them back to the island."

"The witches on your island teleport?"

"Yeah... Why? How do the Daughters of Eris get around?" I ask.

"They use portals." He shrugs before going back to the original subject. "That 911 thing is amazing though. Seriously. I wish it was more well known."

"We've been working on that. It's gaining traction, but Matt is trying to figure out how to reach those who are more remote without cell phone service."

"So, in order to access it, you have to have cell phone service?" His question is one of the main things we've been trying to work on. There are groups like the jaguar pride in the middle of the Amazon jungle who, despite constantly being asked to come live on the island, choose to remain deep in the rainforest. The only way they can contact us is through a satellite phone.

"Unfortunately. Right now, Matt's working on a way to place a spell on cell phones that allows them to access the supernatural network through magic rather than cell phone service."

"But then how do you get them out to everyone?"

"And that right there is the big question," I tell him as he slowly finishes his fish. "They're working on it and if anyone can figure it out, it's Matt."

"What about more sea nymphs? More like you?"

I heave out a sigh before telling him about finding Kristle and her pod, then moving into the fact that Sky is currently captured.

"Shouldn't you be there with them?" he asks.

"This was more important," I tell him, the look of shock not leaving his face. "You're more important."

"But... How..."

I let out a slow breath knowing that I have no choice but to tell him about my stalkerish ways. "Well... Uh.... I kinda used to watch you."

"Watch me?" The corner of his mouth tips up into a smirk.

I nod. "I kept feeling this tug inside me here." I place my hand over my heart. "It led me to a small island in Greece."

"Corfu," he whispers.

"It was there that I saw you for the first time, diving down to get lobsters. After that, I watched you every day for weeks until I was called away. I didn't want to talk to you in case you were already mated." I look down at the ground, a little embarrassed that I watched him without speaking to him.

I look up as he places his hands on either side of my face.

"Oh, *agapi mou*, I wish you would've approached me. I've been waiting my entire life for you. Anyone that came before you was forgotten the second I got a glimpse of those turquoise eyes."

I don't give him the chance to say anything else, I lean forward, capturing his lips with mine, taking his gasp and momentary shock as the chance to slip my tongue into his mouth. His shock doesn't last long, and he reaches forward, pulling me toward him. I slide my legs on either side of his hips, straddling his lap as our tongues tangle together.

My dress rides up my legs as he pulls me closer, my bare center pressing up against the denim of his jeans, and a moan escapes me as the friction hits my clit. Next thing I know, I'm flipped onto my back and Loukas is pulling my dress up over my head, roaming my body with his eyes before moving back up to my lips.

He doesn't waste time, though, and begins exploring my body from my lips and neck, down to my breasts. I give him a little encouragement and arch my back, allowing him better access and showing my desire for him to feast on my breast—he doesn't disappoint. He takes each nipple into his mouth in turn, nipping and sucking, lavishing them both with the same amount of attention, while snaking his hand over my abdomen and down to my core. He strokes my clit with a delicious slowness and draws a deep moan from me.

After he has lavished my breasts with more than enough attention, he ceases his fingers' delicious teasing and follows the trail his hand took earlier with his mouth, kissing, licking, and nipping his way down.

Can someone die from too much pleasure? Because even though I'm having a love-hate relationship with the slowness of his movements, the amount of pleasure coursing through my entire body is making me feel like I may spontaneously combust.

After what feels like hours, but is only seconds, his mouth arrives at my wetness. He pauses for a moment, locking his eyes with mine and allowing me to see how dilated his pupils are with lust, then he lowers his mouth and devours me.

Oh, god. I run my fingers through his hair, moaning loudly in pure bliss.

It doesn't take long for my climax to find me, and amid my delirious pleasure I scream out, "Loukas!"

"My turn," I growl, gripping the bottom of his shirt and pulling it up over his head. I pause for a moment at the sight of his scars, running my fingers over them gently. I sit up and place soft kisses on each one. He looks down at me, his eyes still blazing with lust, but also with something like thanks. I vow to find each and every one of the scars that monster gave him and claim it for my own.

My fingers make their way to his waist, unzipping his jeans and pushing them down. He kicks his pants off and slowly slides his body up mine, lining his beautiful, thick cock up to my entrance, and plunges inside of me in one quick thrust.

Holy hell! This is amazing. I've never felt so full in my life. After a brief pause, he grasps my hips, raising them off the forest floor, and powers into me with hard, deep thrusts. Once he's found his rhythm, I plant my feet and begin moving in time with him, like we're partners who have been dancing together for years.

I am loathe to admit that it doesn't take me long to reach my peak once again—I wish I could bottle up this feeling of euphoria and keep it forever. If the way Loukas' muscles are tensing and relaxing is any indication, he is getting close too.

My gums begin to ache, and my teeth feel too big for my mouth. I let out a strangled moan, and he looks down at me, halting his movements.

"Pearl," he pleads breathlessly. "We can't. Not yet."

I open my mouth to ask why but he continues. "I don't want us to mark each other with..."

"With Antonia still in the picture," I finish for him, and he nods sullenly.

"I'm sorry—" I place my finger on his lips to stop his apology.

"Don't be," I tell him, pulling his face back to mine in a passionate kiss spurring him to begin his movements once more. With each thrust in, he hits that perfect spot inside me. It takes more willpower than I care to admit as my orgasm overtakes me once more to refrain from marking him as I scream out my release.

He follows me over the edge with a grunt only seconds later.

"That was..."

"Amazing? Incredible?" he supplies.

"Mind-blowing," I agree, pressing a soft kiss to his lips.

"Loukas!" A male voice shouts, the sounds faint carrying over the water. We both turn in that direction.

"Shit. I have to go," Loukas says, standing up quickly and pulling his clothes back on. I follow suit, pulling my dress over my head.

"I'll come with you," I announce, ready to stand and fight for my mate.

Loukas spins.

"As much as I would love for you to be with me, I don't want you to get hurt. I'll make a plan to get Zach and Amelia out of there with me."

I nod, agreeing that we need a plan and knowing that we can't leave his children behind. "Tomorrow?"

"I'll meet you at the water's edge tomorrow, and we will see what we can both come up with," he says, placing a soft kiss on my lips once more.

"Loukas!" The voice shouts once more, closer this time.

"I'll see you tomorrow."

"Tomorrow," I agree. I help him push the boat back out into the water and watch as he rows away. I stand, watching until he's a small speck on the horizon before pulling off my dress, shoving it into my bag, and hopping back in the water. My shift overtakes me quickly. I feel almost whole for the first time in my life, like a hole inside me I didn't even know was there has been filled just by meeting my mate.

I swim to the small island where Skarlyt dropped me off before pulling the phone out of my bag and calling her.

"Pearl?"

"Can you meet me at the spot you picked me up?"

"Is everything okay?" she asks, her voice sleepy.

"Yes. No. I don't know. I think I need your help."

"I'll be there in a minute," Skar says before hanging up the phone.

While waiting for Skarlyt, I throw a pair of jeans and a T-shirt on and sit down on a large rock, thinking over the events of the day. I've met my mate and, even though it doesn't seem possible, his life is even more complicated than my own.

"Brrr...I do *not* miss this cold!"

I spin on the spot to find Skarlyt dressed in her black silk pj's.

"It's not even that cold," I tell her.

She waves her hand. "That's because you're a shifter, you run hot."

"Actually, I'm a *sea nymph*."

"Potato Po-ta-to. You still shift into something. The fact that you shift into an aquatic animal just means you're even more used to the cold."

I shake my head and smile at my friend. She and I could sit here and argue all day about semantics, but I have more important things to do.

"You're right."

Her mouth drops open, probably not expecting me to give up so easily. The two of us have had hour-long debates in the past, and she was definitely gearing up for one.

"Okay. What's wrong?" she asks, stepping up and placing a hand on my forehead like she's checking for a fever. "Are you sick?"

I slap her hand away. "No, I'm not sick. I just think we have more important things to do than spend the next hour discussing the cold and why I don't feel it as much as you."

"Puh-lease," she scoffs. "We could've gone for at least two hours."

I nod. "Of course. But I was hoping you could help me with

something instead." I wait for her acknowledgement before continuing. "Is there a way to stop someone from being tracked with a locator spell?"

Her face goes from playful to serious in the blink of an eye.

"What do you mean?"

"Is there something you can spell so that the person holding it can't be tracked by other witches? Kind of like the barrier spell does for the island so that people can't find it."

"I'm sure there is something I could do." She looks lost in solving the problem already. "Why?"

"Because I was right, Loukas—"

"Your mate?"

I nod. "He's in trouble."

"And for him to escape the Daughters of Eris, he needs one of these anti-tracking things."

"I actually need three."

"Three? Why?"

"Because we can't leave without his children," I tell her, jutting my chin out.

"His what?" she asks, shaking her head. "You know what? It doesn't matter. Let's go."

With that, she grabs my hand and the two of us land in the middle of her workshop back on the island.

"I'll work, you talk," she says, pointing an accusing finger at me while rushing to grab books off the shelves. As she does, I spill the tea—so to speak. I tell her most—but not all—of what Loukas told me.

"Let me get this straight. This Antonia chick, the High Priestess of the Daughters of Eris, and Loukas, your mate, have two children together, and she's been keeping them there by threatening to kill his family?" I nod. "And she killed his father?"

"That about sums it up, yes."

"Damn," she says, staring off into space. "I always thought I had cornered the market of crazy exes kidnapping you."

She shrugs, and I smile and wait for her laughter to die out.

"So, can you do it? I'd like to go back and be close by in case he needs me."

All laughter drains from her face at my words, and she walks over to me, wrapping me in a hug.

"I can. Why don't you go get a few hours of sleep while I get them ready? Then I'll teleport you back there as soon as they're done."

"But..." I go to protest, but she steps back, holding up her hand.

"You need rest if you're going to be able to help them. Sleeping in my spare room is going to be a lot more comfortable than sleeping on the forest floor or a rocky beach. Besides, I'm going to call Sebastyn and Sarah to come over and help me. It won't take long for us to do this together."

Agreeing with her logic, I nod and turn toward the hallway leading to her spare room. I do not need any directions. I've spent more than my fair share of nights in her spare room when we've had our girl nights, and I didn't want to go home alone.

What I suspect is more than a few hours later, I am gently shaken awake.

I sit up with a start. "Skarlyt?"

A scoff greets me.

"Is that how you greet your bestie?" Breanne asks in a tone of mock hurt.

"Sorry, Bree. I was expecting Skarlyt," I tell her, pulling her in for a hug.

"Now that's the reception I was expecting," she says giddily. "Come on, get up, get dressed. I heard you have a mate to save."

Her words spur me into action, reminding me that I do have a mate and his children to save. I throw the covers off me.

"I brought you some clothes, and you have enough time for a quick shower. We'll meet you in the workroom."

"You're the best!"

"I know," she says with a smirk before she heads out the door, leaving me to get ready, which I do in record time. I hate the idea of washing the scent of Loukas off me, but I am hopeful that I'll be able to replace it over and over again for the rest of our lives.

"Here she is!" Skarlyt exclaims as I walk into the workroom. Fortunately, it's only Skar, Bree, Seb, and Sarah in there waiting for me. I honestly expected the room to be full.

"How long did I sleep?"

"Four hours," Sarah answers.

"That's better than letting me sleep the day away," I tell them, walking around the counter to see what they've been working on. "What do we have?"

Skarlyt gets all giddy, rubbing her hands together.

"Well, I had to get my baby bro to help with the spell, and Sarah helped with the design."

"Hey. I helped with the supplies," Bree says jutting out her bottom lip.

"Yes, yes. Opal called and said we needed to add an extra element, but she wouldn't tell us why."

"She never does," Sarah growls, though it's likely just out of annoyance that her best friend has to keep so many secrets from her.

"What extra element?"

"Well, these two necklaces with the black onyx stones are the anti-tracking necklaces. This one, the Azurite, has the anti-tracking spell but also a little extra. When the person who wears it is submerged in water, an air bubble will surround them."

"It works. I tested it half an hour ago," Bree confirms proudly.

"What would I need that for?" I ask.

"I'm sure you'll find out. Opal works in mysterious ways. She also put some other things in your bag—I didn't ask or look at what they were," Sebastyn adds.

"Please thank her for me and thank all of you."

"We're family. That's what family does," Bree says, pulling me in for a hug. "Now go get your mate."

I chuckle as Bree pushes me toward Skarlyt who is already holding my bag and the necklaces.

"I will. See you soon." I wave goodbye to Sarah, Sebastyn, and Bree as Skarlyt and I teleport back to the forest.

"Be careful, stay safe, and call if you need us," she says and pops away before I even have the chance to respond.

Guess she really doesn't like the cold.

Chapter Eleven

Loukas

"Were you trying to escape, my pet?" Antonia sneers as I arrive back at the clearing belonging to the coven courtesy of Anthony. Although I was already making my way here, he seemed to think I needed a little extra help in the form of magical restraints.

"Never, my love." I use the sweet voice I've perfected over the years.

"Then why were you out of sight?" she asks, stepping up to me and running a finger down my chest. Involuntary shivers wrack my body. Thankfully, Antonia must believe that it's from lust rather than revolution.

"I was hungry, so I went out to catch some fish. They weren't biting close to the coven. I probably went further than I should've but only to catch something to eat."

"And where is this fish?" she asks, searching my empty hands.

"I stopped on an inhabited island and cooked it."

"You were that hungry?" she asks, her eyebrow raised in question.

"That tends to happen when I'm not welcome to eat with the coven anymore." I'm unable to keep the growl from my voice as I speak. Antonia bursts out laughing at my words, and I cringe. I know that laugh. That's her "I'm going to punish you" laugh.

"Yes, I suppose that's true. I've always loved how resourceful you can be, my pet." Her hand caresses my face momentarily before she steps back into the arms of a tall, blonde man with pale skin and bright blue eyes. "Speaking of love, I'd like you to meet Roman. He is the High Priest of the Sons of Ares and my chosen mate."

I know that she wants me to react out of jealousy but seeing her in the arms of another man makes me feel nothing but relief that I am no longer needed to warm her bed.

"Nice to meet you," I tell him, formally tipping my head in his direction. The shock on Antonia's face makes me smile—on the inside of course. I have no idea why she's so obsessed with keeping me as hers when she already has someone else.

"You too," Roman says, pulling Antonia closer as if staking his claim on her.

She's all yours, buddy. She's more trouble than she's worth.

"Now, my pet, what should we do with you?" Antonia steps out of Roman's arms.

"What do you mean?"

"I mean, you broke the rules. You must be punished."

"Punished? For getting myself food?"

"No, of course not. Punished for trying to escape."

"I wasn't."

Antonia *tsks* at me.

"If my brother says you were trying to escape, then you were trying to escape."

I don't get another chance to protest as magical restraints are wrapped around my body, including my mouth, securing me to a tree. I struggle for a moment, but the second I see Zach's fearful eyes I stop. I do not want to upset him any further than he already is.

Antonia follows my line of sight, her brows furrowing when she finds nothing. Zach is quick enough to slip behind one of the other coven members and out of sight.

"I think keeping you here until morning should suffice. When the sun rises, the binds will release," Antonia says, spinning on her heel and heading away from me.

For the rest of the day, Anthony takes it upon himself to treat me like a special attraction. He is happy to play tour guide, bringing groups of people to see me helpless while I try to ignore them and rest as much as possible.

After hours of horrible sleep, I wake with a start as my body falls to the ground when the bindings suddenly release me.

"Ugh," I grunt, stretching my body out. Sleeping while magically restrained to a tree isn't good for the body. All my muscles are stiff, and there's a crick in my neck that definitely wasn't there before.

I sit up and look around, watching as the sun begins to rise over the horizon. I tilt my head to each side, doing my best to work out the pain there.

The first subtle light of the morning paints the sky in delicate shades of pink and orange, and the water's surface mirrors these ethereal colors, as if nature itself is an artist at work. With bated breath, I watch as the sun's golden disk emerges from the horizon, casting a radiant path of light across the tranquil water. A large splash causes ripples in the mirrored images on the water and, without my consent, my body begins to move to the water's edge. I know deep in my soul what—or who—caused that splash.

As I walk, my bare toes run against something slimy. I look down to find two large perch lying on the beach. I lean down and scoop them up, scanning the water for my gorgeous mate.

I catch a glimpse of blue amongst the dark water, and a smile graces my face, knowing that these fish are a gift from her. I pucker my lips and blow her a kiss before turning back toward my little shack to cook the fish, thankful that I get another protein-filled meal that I don't need to waste hours catching.

A full belly and a cold shower later, I take my time walking around the coven, looking at it with fresh eyes. I only see a few people roaming around, which makes one part of the escape plan easy. As I approach the cabin where they teach the children, I pull myself up and peek in the window.

I watch in horror as one of the middle-aged witches holds her hands up in front of Amelia as she strains against her magical restraints.

"I said do it."

My sweet daughter whimpers.

"She's trying, Miss," Zach says, stepping between the witch and his sister,

"She's not trying hard enough," their teacher, Sabrina, chides.

"Let her go," Zach says, clenching his teeth. His hands are balled into fists at his sides.

"No," Sabrina says, with an evil smirk I know all too well.

Amelia cries out and starts thrashing around. My knuckles turn white as I force myself to stay outside this building, knowing that any punishment Amelia gets will only be worse if I interfere. As fucked up as that fact is, it's the truth. To stop Amelia from getting hurt worse, I can't interfere.

Luckily, I don't have to do anything because, in the blink of an eye, black smoke begins to coil from Zach's hands to wrap around Sabrina's neck. The evil witch brings her hands to her throat, trying to grasp the magic without success. As she does, Amelia drops to the ground. A smile graces my lips at the lengths my son will go to protect his baby sister.

Rather than keeping his eye on his opponent though, he rushes to his sister's side as she lands in a heap behind him.

"Melia, are you okay?"

She nods sullenly, and I watch in horror as Sabrina catches her breath. An angry snarl comes from her mouth as she unleashes her magic on him. I need to teach him to never look away from an opponent, not until you're one thousand percent sure that the threat is gone.

"Zach!" Amelia screams.

"That's quite enough out of you!" Sabrina snaps.

"What is the meaning of this?" Antonia demands as she flings the door open. I crouch down lower, trying to remain hidden from her sight.

As soon as Sabrina sees Antonia enter the room, she drops Zach and turns her ire onto Amelia.

"That girl is a menace."

"A menace, you say?" Antonia asks, raising a perfectly plucked eyebrow.

Sabrina, braver than most would be in her position, nods.

"Perhaps if you let her see Loukas, she would be more agreeable," Zach says as he gets to his feet, causing Antonia to turn her sights on him rather than Sabrina or Amelia.

"And why would that be?"

I watch Zach's face as he's caught off guard by the question. He raises his chin as he answers honestly.

"Because she misses him. She spent time with him every single day, and now she hasn't seen him in weeks."

Now, it's Antonia's turn to be caught off guard by his answer. and I watch with rapt attention to see what she does next. Instead of lashing out, she surprises me by contemplating his answer for only a few moments before nodding slightly in agreement.

With the hope that Antonia will allow Amelia to spend time with me, I rush away from the window and back to the clearing where I normally spend my days and sit down to meditate and plan. If Antonia brings me Amelia, there's a chance that Zach could come with her and the three of us could leave this place today.

Ten minutes later, I'm actively plotting our escape when the most beautiful sound reaches my ears.

"Daddy!" I open my eyes to see my little girl running toward me, her long hair blowing behind her.

I stand quickly, my bare feet slapping against the grass as I rush toward her, closing the distance. She leaps into my arms, and I catch her, tears streaking down both our faces at being reunited. Even my owl is flapping his wings in excitement.

"You get two hours with her," Antonia says, and I look up, not caring if she sees the wetness on my cheeks.

"Thank you," I manage to croak out as I continue rubbing Amelia's back through her sobs.

"Don't thank me. Just make sure she knows how to behave when I return for her."

With that, she spins on her heel marching back toward the coven.

"Let me look at you, my beautiful girl," I say, pushing Amelia backward and running my hands over her face, growling at the sight of the dark bruises surrounding her throat, the bruising on her cheekbones, and the blood caking her hair.

"I missed you so much, Daddy!" she exclaims between hiccups, throwing herself back in my arms.

"I missed you too, Pumpkin," I tell her, gently lifting her and carrying her to the water. Once I set her down, I gently wash the blood out of her hair and notice a couple more fish waiting for me.

I scan the horizon for Pearl, wishing her into existence. If I can't get Amelia out of here today, perhaps she can. Even if I'm not with her.

"Come on, beautiful. Let's go cook these fish and have something to eat." The words are hardly out of my mouth before her stomach growls loudly, and she nods eagerly. "When was the last time you ate?"

She shrugs her bony shoulders. "Zach brought me some berries this morning."

"And before that?" I ask, holding her hand as the two of us walk toward my shack.

"Mommy said I get to eat when I can get my magic working. She says the hunger is supposed to mot...mov..." She struggles with the word.

"Motivate you?" I offer.

She nods, and a growl bubbles up in my throat. I sound more like a wolf shifter than an owl.

"I'm sorry, Daddy," she says softly. I stop, turning and kneeling in front of her.

"I'm not angry with you, Pumpkin. I'm angry with your mother for allowing you to be treated this way. If it was up to me, you, Zach, and I would be far, far away from here."

Her eyes shine with hope at the prospect of getting away from her mother. She may not be the reason that there are bruises on Amelia—no, she would make her underlings do the punishing—but it just cements that I need to get her out of here and soon.

After cooking both fish, which I feed to Amelia, we walk back to our special spot in the clearing.

"Look, Daddy! A mermaid!" She runs toward the water with a cheer, and I scan it once more. I do not see Pearl anywhere. As she's running, she falls to the ground, screaming in pain.

"Amelia!" I yell, rushing to her side, roaming my hands over her body, searching for the wound, and finding none.

Shifting, my owl supplies as I frantically search for the source of her pain.

"What?" I ask out loud rather than inside my head. Now that he says it, I can recognize that is exactly what is happening.

"Breathe, baby. Don't fight it."

"Hurts," Amelia whimpers, clutching at her chest.

"I know, baby. I know. It's just your owl coming out to meet me. You have to relax. Trust her and I to keep you safe."

Her eyes go wide in realization before nodding. Her shift is extremely painful and takes far longer than it should—probably from the lack of food—but soon enough, a small white owl is standing on the ground in front of me.

"You're so beautiful," I whisper, reaching out a hand to pet her feathers while she preens under my gaze, her little wings flapping.

"That's it, Pumpkin, flap your wings," I tell her, lifting her higher to help her with her first flight. Unlike newborn owls who need to start out in a large tree and glide down carefully, we are capable of flight as soon as we shift for the first time. Amelia is still so young, though, that I am sure she needs some help.

"I'm going to throw you into the air, and you will spread your wings. Stay away from the coven."

Her white fluffy head nods, and I throw her up, watching in amazement as she glides around the clearing, flapping her wings a few times to keep herself in flight.

"She's beautiful." I hear a musical voice call out from behind me, and I take my eyes off Amelia to see Pearl standing at the water's edge, watching my owlet's first flight.

"That she is," I respond, my eyes moving back to the gliding owl as my feet move slowly toward Pearl.

"Amelia?" I call, raising my arm, hating to cut her flight short. She understands perfectly, gliding shakily and landing on my arm.

As she lands, fear threatens to stop my heart. Amelia has shifted. It's time. I look from Amelia to Pearl and then back to the coven.

"I need you to take her away from here."

"What?" Pearl asks, meeting my eyes reluctantly, as if she didn't want to look away from the beautiful owl in my arms.

I look down at Amelia, tears threatening to fall from my eyes.

"She's not safe here. I need you to take her and not come back."

Pearl steps forward, putting her hand on my arm. Amelia flinches backward, further into my arms.

I hear voices getting closer, and I begin to panic.

"Please," I plead with Pearl, squeezing Amelia before thrusting her toward Pearl. "I need you to take her and keep her safe. If you can get my family away from Greece, they'll take responsibility for her. They can't stay there; that's the first place they'll look for her."

"Loukas," Pearl says, trying to keep a hold of the squirming owl in her arms. "I can't—"

"You have to go." I glance back, the voices getting closer. "Now."

Pearl looks down at Amelia and back before nodding solemnly.

I lean forward, capturing Pearl's lips with mine hoping that it isn't the last time I will taste her but making sure it counts if it is. We break apart, both panting, and I place a soft kiss on Amelia's head.

"You're going to be okay, Pumpkin." I turn to head off the coven members coming to retrieve Amelia.

"Wait," Pearl calls out, pushing two items into my hand. "Here. There are two necklaces. One for you, and one for Zach. They'll stop any witch from tracking you. That includes my witches." I take them both, watching as she secures a blue necklace around Amelia's neck. "Head south, toward Parry Sound. Find the Westwood pack. Ask for Aryn, tell him you need to see Alaric. They'll bring you to me."

"Thank you," I choke out, giving both of them another quick kiss. I watch as Pearl takes a part of my heart in her hands and jumps in the water, swimming away. A moment of panic hits me that Amelia will drown.

Mate will keep her safe, my owl assures me.

"I hope so," I whisper, my trust in Pearl overriding that particular panic.

It's Antonia, Zach, and Anthony who appear through the trees, and I allow the panicked look to remain on my face as I gear up to give the best performance of my life.

"Where's Amelia?" Queen bitch herself asks, looking around.

"She shifted and flew away," I say, letting the anxiety I feel fill my voice. Rather than having to look at Antonia's face, I pretend to search the skies for our daughter.

"Shifted?" Antonia asks, and I nod, continuing to look up. I don't need to see her face to know that she is confused by this development. "Impossible. She did magic."

I spin. "Well, she shifted into a beautiful brown owl about twenty minutes ago, so I'd say whatever magic you thought she did was not her." I don't tell her that Amelia's owl is white, so she has more of a chance of getting away. Even then, I'm taking a gamble. Right now, she is probably trying to calculate how feasible it is to hunt down every brown owl in a hundred miles.

She turns her head and glares at Zach, clearing her throat.

"You wouldn't know anything about that, would you?"

He shakes his head vehemently.

"No, ma'am." The words we both know are a lie slide off his tongue easily.

She *tsks* and shakes her head.

"Find her," she commands her brother, and I turn back around to continue my pretend search.

"And where do you think you are going?" I hear her snap, her magic lashing around me. "Did you think that you would get away with her disappearing?"

"I'm sure she'll come back," I wheeze out, the binds tightening with each word.

"For your sake, I hope she does."

With that, the invisible binding around my neck tightens cutting off my air supply and the world goes black.

Chapter Twelve

Pearl

Well, now I know why Opal wanted an air bubble added to this necklace, and I send a silent thank you to my friends as I swim as fast as I can while holding a squirming little owl.

"Hold on, Amelia. We will be somewhere safe in a minute," I tell her, and she squawks. "I don't know what you're saying, sweetheart."

The words are hardly out of my mouth before she shifts back, and a small girl with big brown eyes, olive skin, and long brown hair is staring back at me, her eyes wide with fear.

She shivers and I try to hug her closer to me, hoping to keep her warm through the cold water, especially since shifting back has left her naked. She tries to push away from me out of fear.

"I know you don't know who I am, but I promise you can trust me. I won't let anyone hurt you. Not anymore." With wide, fearful eyes, she nods at me.

Her shivers get more violent, and I curse, surfacing and searching for the nearest cabin thanking the gods when I spot one not far.

"Come on, sweetheart. Let's go get you warm and call in the reinforcements," I say, keeping my voice upbeat.

"O-kay," she says, her teeth chattering so hard I worry that one is going to break off. Skarlyt was right when she said that shifters run hot. Amelia is too young to be shifting at all, and I imagine her body is too weak to heal itself as fast as it should.

The swim to the cabin seems to take forever as I rub my arms up and down Amelia's back and arms, trying to warm her as she clings to me, trying to absorb some of my warmth.

Soon enough, my tail turns into legs, and I take off, running toward the house. There are no lights on, and no boat at the dock, making me believe that it's empty. I am proven right when I force the door open.

"Sit here while I start a fire," I say, setting her down, grabbing blankets off the back of the couch, and wrapping them around her before rushing over to the woodburning stove and quickly starting a fire. Once it's lit, I turn around, taking in the terrified little girl.

"I know you're scared," I begin, stepping toward her. When she flinches back, I raise my hands to show her that I truly don't mean her any harm. "I promise I will never hurt you," I say, crouching down in front of her.

She searches my eyes for what feels like forever before she nods.

"My mommy hurts me."

I pull her into my arms, hoping to all the gods that I'm not traumatizing her more.

"I know, sweetheart. I know. I promise I'm nothing like your mommy."

"I want my daddy." She sobs, and my heart breaks a little. I push her back so I can look into her eyes.

"I promise that I'm going to do everything I can to make sure you and your daddy are together again and away from that place."

"Zachy too?"

"Zach too," I tell her with conviction as I wrap my arms around this little girl who has already carved a place for herself inside my heart. "I'm going to call my friends so they can help us get your grand..."

"Ya-Ya," she supplies.

"Your Ya-Ya to safety." She nods, and I step back, rummaging through my backpack, grabbing the phone, and dialing Skarlyt.

"Pearl?"

"Hey," I respond, hearing a bunch of voices in the background. "Who are you with?"

"Seb, Sarah, Dru, Rayne, and Andres."

"Good. I'm going to send you a picture and I need you all to come." I don't give her a chance to respond. I hang up the phone and snap a picture out of the front door. I rummage through my bag once more and find a pair of fluffy, warm pajamas that are definitely too small for me.

"Thank you, Opal," I whisper, turning and handing them to Amelia. "My friend sent these for you. Why don't you go get changed in the bedroom there while we wait for my friends."

She looks from me to the clothes. Her hands rub over the soft fabric and tears swim in her eyes, but she gets up and walks to the bedroom, closing the door behind her. While she dresses, I take the opportunity to cover myself as well, pulling out some comfy yoga pants, a tank top, and a sweater.

I hear shuffling behind the door before she opens it, and I turn to find her with a genuine smile on her face as she rubs her hands over her legs.

"You look comfy."

She nods, her smile dropping from her face and her eyes widening on something over my shoulder.

"Well, hello, little one," Skarlyt says soothingly. Despite her tone, Amelia backs up, fear pouring off her in waves.

"It's okay. Skarlyt won't hurt you," I promise. Amelia's eyes slide to me and then back to Skarlyt, who halts her steps and raises her hands.

"Of course, I won't."

Amelia must not believe her, backing up until her back is up against the wall, her body vibrating with fear.

"You're scaring her Skarlyt. Here let me try," Rayne says, barreling through my friends.

"Rayne," I warn.

She spins on me.

"What? Kids love me."

I scoff. "Sure, they do."

She pokes a finger into my chest.

"They do. Just watch." She turns back toward Amelia. "It's okay, pretty girl. We won't hurt you."

Instead of being appeased, Amelia seems to vibrate even more in fear.

I take a step between Rayne and Amelia but rather than soothing her with my presence like I hoped I would, she shakes even harder.

"I think she's broken," Rayne whispers. I turn on her in shock, not believing that she just said that.

"She's not broken," A deep voice rumbles from behind me and we all move out of the way as Andres, the mountain of a man, pushes his way through our group.

I watch in awe as Amelia stops shaking.

"It's okay little one."

It only takes those four words, and Amelia launches herself into Andres' open arms, sobs wracking her body. He cradles her like a baby, her head nuzzling into his chest.

Within seconds, soft snores drift from her little body.

"What is that about?" I whisper, stepping closer and running a hand over her hair.

"She's an avian shifter who is terrified of women. She recognized me as an alpha of sorts," Andres responds, keeping his voice low.

"Oh, so the King of Dragons is better with kids than me now?" Rayne asks, not even trying to keep the snark out of her voice.

"Possibly," Andres responds simply. Rayne crosses her arms over her chest, muttering under her breath about being the granddaughter of a goddess and how that should be worth something.

"So, what now?" Sarah asks, her eyes roaming over Amelia's small face.

"We need to go to Greece. Loukas' parliament is there and that's the first place Antonia will look."

"So that's the monster's name? Antonia?" Rayne sneers while Drusilla steps up and puts her hand on her best friend's arm.

"Do you think we should take her to Aurora?" Dru asks, gesturing toward Amelia.

"I don't think we have the time."

"What's the plan when we get there?" Sebastyn asks, stepping closer to Andres and Amelia. If I had to hazard a guess, he was feeling the emotions pouring off Amelia more than the rest of us since he's an empath.

"I will go in and talk to them."

"Alone?" Rayne clarifies, and I nod.

"If we all go in guns blazing, it will be taken as a threat."

"What about the little one?" Sarah asks, and I look over to the sleeping child in Andres' arms and shake my head.

"She will stay with Andres until I figure out if it's safe or not."

"Safe?" Skarlyt asks a little louder, causing Amelia to whimper and a deep rumble to come from Andres' chest. "Sorry," she whispers. "Aren't they her family? Why wouldn't she be safe?"

"They are, and I don't know. It's just a feeling that I should go in and talk to them alone."

"I'll come with you," Rayne supplies, putting her hand on my shoulder in solidarity.

I turn to her. "No offense, Rayne. You know I love you, but you're not the most subtle person in the world."

She puts her hand on her chest as if I just wounded her greatly, and her mouth drops open in shock. I pin her with a "are you for real" look before turning back to Skarlyt.

"The best course of action is for all of us to go to the beach in Greece, and you wait while I speak to them."

"What if you need help?" Sarah asks, concern lining her features.

"I'll get you a signal somehow," I tell her, the words falling flat as they leave my mouth. Because if I'm being honest with myself, I have no idea how I would signal them if I needed help. Sure, I could scream and hope that Andres could hear me.

"How about Sarah and I bring Rayne to hide in the trees or something out of sight but able to see in case you need us?" Sebastyn supplies.

I turn, pointing a finger at Rayne. "The only way I'll agree to that is if you promise not to interfere unless I truly need help."

I wait with bated breath as she first mocks shock, then feigns innocence before finally agreeing with a nod.

"Okay then. That's the plan. Drusilla, Skarlyt, and Andres will wait on the beach with Amelia. Sebastyn, Sarah, and Rayne will find some place high up to hide—don't forget they're owl shifters so you need to make sure you stay out of sight. While I go in and talk to my mate's family." I wait for everyone to nod before both Rayne and I step up to Skarlyt. Sebastyn steps next to Andres and Amelia, and Sarah grabs onto Drusilla.

In the blink of an eye, our group is standing on a familiar beach in Greece. The air is far warmer than the cabin we just left, but, instead of the late afternoon sun shining in the sky, it's darkness with a sliver of a moon that greets us.

"Well, at least it will be easier for us to hide," Seb says.

"And harder for us to see," Sarah warns.

"Not for me." Rayne winks at her.

"Then I guess it's a good thing you talked them into letting you go with them, isn't it?"

"Yup," she responds, popping the *p* at the end.

"Okay, if you three want to hide off in the distance over there," I say, more to Seb and Sarah than Rayne, and point to the west side, where I know the village is.

They nod. Seb stands with his back to Rayne and gestures for her to hop on like a piggyback ride.

"Seriously?" she asks, but I can see the excitement in her eyes at the prospect of flying.

"It's the easiest way," Seb responds, and Rayne wastes no time hopping up onto his back, the three of them rising into the sky— Seb and Rayne a little slower than Sarah—but still rising, none-theless.

"You'll keep her safe?" I ask Andres, Drusilla, and Skarlyt.

"With our lives," Andres rumbles out.

With that, I turn and make my way along the path toward the village. The last two times I was careful to go unheard. This time I make sure my footsteps are loud enough to be heard by any sentries who may be standing guard.

I feel eyes on me as I enter the crack in the rock, but I don't turn around, keeping my gaze fully focused on the path before me.

By the time I come through the other side, a large group of people are waiting for me. I keep my hands at my sides, fists unclenched, hoping that I appear as non-threatening as possible.

"Why are you here?" A male voice booms through the crowd.

They are gathered in the middle of a clearing, surrounded by their homes. A sea of curious, wide eyes study me. They must've already been gathered for some reason because there is no way they could have gathered this quickly after just hearing me approach.

"I am looking for the family of Loukas." I don't raise my voice above my regular talking volume, knowing that every single one of these shifters can hear me perfectly fine.

"For what purpose?" A female voice calls out this time, and I watch as the younger woman I saw in the room with Loukas' mother steps forward.

"I have his daughter." I don't get a chance to explain any further before sharp spears are thrust forward, all pointing at me. Before anything else can happen, a brown-haired menace drops down from the sky, blurring from one person to the next, leaving them in heaps on the ground.

"Rayne," I shriek.

"What? I didn't kill them. They're just knocked out." As if to prove that point, she walks up and spins in front of me. "See, no blood."

My hand reaches up and slaps my forehead. "Not. The. Point."

"What is the meaning of this?" The male voice that called out when I first got here booms, walking closer to who I'm assuming is Loukas' sister and crossing his arms.

"Sorry about that. My friend can be a little..." I look over at Rayne searching for the word. "Protective."

"You come here, proudly announce that you have kidnapped my niece, and then dare to say this woman is protecting you when she attacks our warriors?"

"First of all, you should be thankful I just knocked them out. I am capable of much worse." Rayne hisses, displaying her teeth.

"Rayne," I whisper-shout. "Sorry. I never said I kidnapped Amelia. You didn't let me finish."

"Then what did you mean?" Loukas' sister questions.

"You're right. It was a poor choice of wording. Loukas asked me to take his daughter to safety and to warn you that Antonia will probably start looking for her here."

"Where is she, then?" Loukas' sister's voice is full of accusation, and I can tell she doesn't believe me.

"She's..." I begin, but before I can finish, a large dragon lands in front of me, the ground rumbling with the weight of him as a small girl launches herself from his back.

"Ya-Ya!"

An older woman, who I already believe to be Loukas' mom, rushes forward, catches the small girl mid-air, and squeezes her to her chest before peppering her head with kisses.

Immediately, the murmurs start.

"We're not safe while she's here."

"Send her back."

"The Daughters of Eris will kill us all."

It's the louder ones demanding that they trade Amelia back to Antonia to guarantee their safety that really start to piss me off. Luckily, I'm not the only one.

A mighty growl emanates from Andres' throat.

As one, the voices stop as fear permeates the air.

"My King," Loukas' mother cries out, throwing herself on the ground in front of him and taking Amelia with her—or trying to.

"Silly, Ya-Ya. That's not a king. That's Andres," Amelia giggles, running over to the giant dragon and wrapping—or trying to wrap—her little arms around his thick legs.

Loukas' mother takes in the sight of her granddaughter nuzzling into the king of dragons with wide eyes and mouth gaping open. Andres must see this too, because he shifts back, scooping Amelia up into his arms.

"Once that was my title," he rumbles. "But no more. The time of Kings and Queens is long over."

"Yes, my k... I mean Andres," Loukas' mother says with a bow.

"But let me be clear. Anyone who wishes harm on this child will answer to me." The growl in his voice is fierce and leaves no room for argument.

"And who are you?" Loukas' mom asks as she steps closer to me.

"Pearl," I respond. Amelia wiggles her way out of Andres' arms to stand next to her Ya-Ya.

"She's daddy's mate."

Now it's my turn to be shocked. I didn't tell her that I was Loukas' mate, I am sure he didn't have time to.

"Is she, now?" Loukas' mother asks, a smile tugging at the corners of her mouth. "I'm Rita. It's a pleasure to meet you." She reaches out a hand for me to shake which I meet eagerly.

"And you."

"Mother. This could be a trick," Loukas' sister says, stepping up and pulling her mother and niece back into the crowd. "Look how many people have descended upon us. How many more do you have hiding amongst the shadows?"

I raise my hands once more, hoping to appear non-threatening.

"It's true that I do have four more allies waiting."

"Bring them out." The words are hardly out of her mouth before Seb and Sarah lower themselves to the ground, and Skarlyt pops in with Drusilla. Drusilla immediately links arms with Rayne and pulls her toward Andres.

"Witches?" The male voice asks this, and my brows furrow as I only now realize that it has been his mate who has done the majority of the talking. I thought he was supposed to be the alpha.

"I understand your aversion to witches. Believe me, I do," I tell the crowd. "But these are not the same sort that you're used to dealing with. The entire reason we came here was to warn you and offer you protection."

"What kind of protection?" A voice calls out.

"We," I gesture to our group, "Live on an island filled with supernatural creatures. All factions live in harmony and peace with one another, safe from the wrath of the vengeful goddess and the humans."

"Impossible."

"No where is safe."

Skarlyt steps forward. "The island is safe for any and all who wish to have a safe haven. We have disagreements and we often find ourselves in danger when we try to help others, but we do not tolerate any violence on the island."

"We also have a school there, where all types of supernaturals from age four to twenty-four attend to learn," Sebastyn adds. Sarah is tucked into his side protectively as voices from the crowd begin to fill the air.

I can feel time slipping away from us, and I know we don't have the luxury of enticing each person here with the promise of our island home.

"Listen, you can make whatever decision you want," I interrupt whatever Sebastyn's next advertisement is going to be. "At the end of the day, Loukas asked me to come here and warn you. He wanted me to offer you a safe place to go now that Antonia is on the warpath looking for Amelia. As far as I'm concerned, I've done that. If you choose to stay here and wait for her, you can. I will be taking Amelia with me where she will be safe," I say the last words with a look at Rita who nods.

"I will come."

"Mother," Loukas' sister says, pleading with her mother.

"This is your brother's mate. He's asked her to protect us for a reason. I trust your brother. You should too."

"I trust Loukas. Of course, I do. How do we know she's really his mate?"

"I feel it in here," Rita says, placing a hand over her heart.

One by one, most of the parliament agree. All but a few agree to come with us to our home. They take a little time to pack up only what they need, vowing to return once the threat is over.

While the parliament is busy, Rita tracks me down.

"Where is Loukas?"

"Hopefully, he and Zach have escaped and are making their way to my allies."

She searches my eyes, her eyes misting up with what I hope are tears of relief, and throws her arms around me.

"Thank the gods."

Chapter Thirteen

Loukas

"Where is she?" Antonia screams as she slaps me hard enough across the face to wake me from my unconsciousness.

I open my eyes to find her standing in front of me, an evil snarl on her face.

"What?" I ask, shaking my head to clear the fog.

"You know damn well what. Where is she?"

"Who?" I ask, wincing at a harsh throb in my temple.

What's the last thing I remember...

"Don't play stupid with me. Where is Amelia?"

"Amelia?" I ask, panic beginning to grip my body as the events of the last few hours—or days—run through my mind.

Amelia shifted. Pearl came and took her somewhere safe. Pearl also gave me two necklaces. I reach my hand down to my pocket, feeling the outlines of the stones and relief courses through me. I don't allow it to show, keeping the tension in my body.

"Yes. Our daughter, Amelia, who you corrupted."

"Corrupted?"

She nods. "You obviously did something to make her a shifter instead of a witch."

I scoff at her. "It doesn't work that way, and you know it."

"It doesn't matter. What does matter is that you tell me where she is." She lashes out with her magic, entangling me like a viper, restricting my movements and slowly squeezing me.

"I don't know," I grind out through clenched teeth.

"I. Don't. Believe. You," she says, her magic squeezing my throat once more. This time I welcome the blackness that overtakes me, as I slump to the ground with a thud.

"Dad?" A young male voice is somewhere nearby. Someone gently shakes my body. "Dad. Wake up."

I open my eyes. "Zach?"

"Dad? Are you okay?"

I shake my head lightly first, then wiggle my fingers and toes. My arms and legs are free, but my midsection is lashed to a thick pole.

"I think so," I answer. Like a bucket of cold water across my face, I am awake all at once when I see Zach in front of me. One of his eyes is swollen shut, his bottom lip is split, and I'm sure there are other bruises on his body somewhere. I bring my hands up to his face, and he winces.

"Are you okay?"

He nods, flinching away.

"Mom doesn't believe that I didn't know what Melia is or where she is." His eyes shine with unshed tears, and I wrap my arms around him, pulling him in for the first hug I've been able to give him in years.

It takes a minute, but the sobs come. I hold him close to me, rubbing his back, showing him the first bit of comfort, he's had in what probably feels like forever. I wish more than anything that I could sit with him and hold him in my arms like the child he is.

"If I could get us out of here, would you come with me?" I ask, and my ten-year-old son looks at me, his big brown eyes glassy and red from his tears.

"I...I..." He flounders, trying to think, but his eyes give him away. He's terrified of the thought.

"Listen to me." I place my hands on either side of his face. "If I had a way to keep us hidden from your mother and a safe place for us to go. Would you come with me?"

He pulls his head back, "There's no way to keep us hidden from the coven, she's too powerful."

"Let's say I did. Would you come?"

"When?"

"Now," I tell him, and his eyes begin to shine with hope for the first time in what feels like forever.

He thinks about it for a minute before he nods slightly.

"Once I undo my mother's bindings, she will know."

"Can you portal us somewhere quickly? It doesn't have to be far. Just somewhere with access to a vehicle"

"I think so," he says, standing up and beginning to pace.

"I need you to be sure."

He nods. "I'm sure."

"Okay, then. On the count of three, drop the binds and open the portal."

He looks at me with wide eyes.

"One..." I begin, and he raises his hands, his smoky magic pooling around me.

"Two." I feel his magic wrapping around the binds Antonia has around me, probing but not intruding.

"Three," I say and close my eyes as Zach's magic forcibly removes Antonia's bindings from around my middle, and I slide away from the pole. He takes a single breath before turning toward an empty spot, focusing his magic, and creating a smoky portal.

Not caring where it takes us, I lift him gently under my arm and leap through the portal. The second our feet touch solid ground, I slip my hand into my pocket, pull out the two necklaces, slip one around Zach's neck, and then my own. Once we are safe and the portal has closed behind us, I look around. We're in the middle of a parking lot.

"We did it!" I exclaim.

"Now what?" Zach asks, looking around like he's waiting for someone to jump out of the bushes.

"We take one of these cars to Parry Sound." I walk over to the cars and test each handle as I go. Of course, it's the last one in the row that opens, and, as if by some miracle, the keys are in the visor.

"Hop in," I tell Zach. He races around the car, opening the passenger side door, and climbing in.

When I start the car, the screen on the dashboard lights up. After a moment, an image of a map appears. I try to punch in " Parry Sound," but it wants an actual address. I just start driving south, hoping that I can follow the signs as we get closer.

The drive is long, but it's the best time I've had in such a long time. Just talking to Zach about his hopes, his dreams, and everything in between is incredible. I feel like he's never had the opportunity to speak so freely, and there's so much about him I'm ready to learn and know. We are in such a deep conversation that we almost miss the sign for Westwood Resort and Cottages. I slam on the brakes, making a fast right-hand turn on the long gravel driveway.

Zach gasps out.

"We just passed through a very powerful boundary."

"Then I guess we're in the right place," I say with a smile, looking over at Zach. He is nervous. I grab his hand. "It will be okay, buddy. I promise."

He nods, though the nervousness and fear still stay on his face.

It's my turn to be nervous when we get closer to the main area of the resort. I count four wolf shifters surrounding the car, only one of which is still in human form. I place the car in park, keeping my eyes on as many of the wolves now surrounding the car as I can.

"No matter what happens, stay in the car," I say to Zach, looking away from the threat and staring into his eyes. They're wide with fear, but he nods. "If something happens to me, you either portal yourself out of here and find your Ya-Ya, or you put this knob here next to the "D" and put your foot down on the right pedal until you're somewhere safe enough to portal."

"I thought you said this was somewhere safe," he says, looking around. Apprehension sets into his face; fear and panic infect his voice.

"It is. A good friend of mine told me to come here, These people will help us, but they don't know who we are yet. Just please stay in the car."

"I will," he agrees.

I give Zach one last look of what I hope is reassurance and step out of the car, pressing the lock button just before I close the door, locking him inside.

"Turn around, get back in the car, and leave," the man sneers.

I raise my arms, gesturing that I mean no harm.

"A friend told me to come here and ask for Aryn. I was told my son would be safe here."

"Mages are not welcome here," he scoffs, gesturing to Zach.

"He's not a mage," I pronounce loudly. "He's a ten-year-old boy with magic."

"Dark magic," he counters. As I glance around at the wolves, they're no longer snarling. Instead, they are looking between me and the car with curiosity.

"Matteo, maybe..." A female says, shifting back to human form.

He turns and growls at her, making her cower. My heart begins to beat hard in my chest. I know that look all too well. I turn back to the man—this Matteo—a snarl on my face at the way he treated that woman for trying to speak up.

"I said leave." He tries to put alpha authority behind his voice, but it falls flat. First, because I am stronger than him. Second, because he is not the alpha here.

"No," I declare. "I request an audience with your alpha."

Matteo steps closer to me. "What if I told you that I am the alpha?"

"Then I'd call you a liar," I respond, my chin raised high.

I see the fist coming, but I don't do anything to stop it. My priority is making sure these people know my son and I are no threat.

As his fist connects with my jaw, I hear a small voice call out right before the car door slams closed once more. I turn and see Zach, his smoky magic coiling out of his hands and down to the ground, ready to protect me.

"Zach, don't. It's okay," I tell him at the same time Matteo sneers.

"See. Dark magic. He's a mage. Get him." With those words, I turn and sprint toward my son, watching as if in slow motion as wolves surround him.

Come on, buddy. I know it's been a while, but I could really use you right now.

I call to my owl, who flaps his wings ready to fight. I jump in the air, shifting into my large brown owl. I push Zach so that his back is up against the car, and I'm in front of him.

I am no match for a pack of wolves, but I'm a lot larger than a regular owl. The top of my head is almost as tall as the car, and my wingspan almost covers its length.

I hiss and flap my wings at the wolves, most of whom seem to take the fact that I'm a shifter as a sign to back off.

The gray wolf with the drool dripping from his mouth continues to look almost feral. No, this wolf—who I assume is

Matteo—advances on me. I puff out my chest and claw at the ground, ready for the fight that I know is coming.

Matteo lunges, not going for me, but for Zach. That is his first mistake. I flap my wings raising up high enough to dig my long, sharp talons into his eyes, causing him to whimper. I leave myself open for an attack as he clenches his jaws around my wing, breaking several of the small bones and flinging me back toward Zach.

I don't stay down, I stand back up, spreading my wings as far as I can protectively in front of my son, hissing at Matteo to try again. He may have injured my wing, but I doubt he can see well right now if the blood pouring from his eyes is any indication.

Nonetheless, he gears up for another attack, and I ready myself to make the kill should I need to. My wing is injured, and this is my first shift in years; I need to end this fight as quickly as I can.

"Stop," an authoritative voice calls out as Matteo begins to charge. For a second, I think he's not going to stop, but the voice calls once more and Matteo skids to a stop. His head lowers to his alpha. From his bared teeth, I can tell he's not submitting by choice. It is his wolf's instinct that has made him bow.

"Olivia, get your mate out of here," the alpha says gently, gesturing to the woman who had shifted back earlier. "I'll deal with him later."

So that's his mate. I make a mental note to bring up how I believe she is being treated to her alpha.

Even once Matteo and Olivia walk away, I don't shift back. I do not trust the danger to be truly over.

The alpha walks closer to me, his hands spread at his side in the same gesture of peace I showed when I arrived.

"I am Aryn. Alpha of the Ironwood pack. Are you Loukas?"

My owl nods his head and Aryn looks around me.

"And you must be Zach?"

I don't remove my eyes from Aryn, but I feel Zach place both hands on my feathered back before he answers.

"Yes."

Aryn seems to breathe out a sigh of relief.

"I just got off the phone with Alaric. He said to expect you. I'm so very sorry about them." He gestures to the group behind him.

I look around, seeing only two shifters still in wolf form. The others have all shifted back and are looking at Zach and me apologetically. "I promise you are both safe here."

I search his face for a moment, hoping and praying that he's being honest. If I'm being truthful with myself, now that the adrenaline is beginning to wear off my strength is fading. I cry out as I shift back, the bones in the broken wing translating to a broken arm and fractured ribs as I fall in a heap at Zach's feet.

Aryn steps forward as if to help me, but Zach's magic coils around me protectively.

"It's okay, buddy," I tell him, grateful for the help his magic gives me to stand, and I place my hand on his shoulder.

Slowly, his magic recedes as he glares at Aryn.

"I wouldn't expect you to trust me yet," the alpha's eyes look truly sorry. "But please come inside. We can call Alaric and get you reunited with your family."

"Do you mean my sister? Is she here?" Zach asks, his voice laced with hope.

"She's not here, but I think she's with Alaric on the island," Aryn answers.

"If I were you, I would check on Olivia," I warn him, watching his face for any sign of compliance. Though I trust my mate, I don't know anything about her allies.

Aryn heaves out a sigh.

"My mate is with her now. Matteo won't touch her."

"Has he done that before?"

He stops walking, taking me in.

"Unfortunately. We haven't been able to convince her to leave him."

"Why is he still in your pack?" Aryn seems truly hurt by the violence, but I don't know if I want to put myself at the mercy of someone who would allow that to happen in their pack.

"If we banish him, she will go with him and…"

I nod in understanding, reading between the lines. "At least here you can protect her."

"Exactly," he agrees, leading Zach and me up to a large log cabin with a covered porch and a perfect view of the lake.

"We just finished dinner. There is still plenty on the stove. Help yourselves while I go find you some warmer clothes." He sizes up Zach and then me. "You're closer to my mate's size, so I'll grab you some of his."

I freeze in place at his words. "His?"

Aryn steels himself, raising his chin.

"The goddess blessed me with a true mate that is also a man. Is that a problem?"

"Not a problem at all," I tell him with a smile. "I watched men and women within my parliament struggle against the mate the goddess intended for them because most would not support them. It was unnecessary and painful to watch. Love is love."

Aryn was prepared to fight that battle, but he breathes out another sigh of relief.

"Thank you."

With that, he spins, heading up the stairs.

I follow Zach into the kitchen, where he's already piling a plate high with spaghetti and meatballs.

"Save some for me," I chuckle.

Chapter Fourteen

Pearl

"I'm going to go call Narissa from the beach and see if I can get an update," I whisper to Skarlyt as the rest of the village continues packing up their belongings.

"I talked to her yesterday; there was nothing new to report."

I give her a nod of thanks before looking around for Amelia. I spot her in the shadow of her Ya-Ya, talking animatedly about something. Knowing that she's safe, I turn, take the path through the rocks and back out onto the beach, and pull my phone out.

"Hello?" A voice answers.

"Kristle?" I ask, recognizing her voice.

"Pearl?" she asks almost excitedly.

"Yes. I wanted to check in."

"Thank the goddess," she says, breathing out in what I imagine is a sigh of relief.

"What's wrong?" Immediately, my hackles rise. She doesn't sound like she's underwater like I'd expect.

"I was just going to call you."

"Why? Did something happen?"

"Kind of. We were starving them out like we planned, but then the sea expelled them and pushed them onto shore."

"Where?" I ask. Wondering why, after ignoring their presence for almost three weeks, the goddess would choose to notice them now.

"I think we're still somewhere in Greece, but that's not the worst thing..."

"Spit it out, Kristle."

"We can hear Sky... I mean... we can hear his screams of pain. It's almost like they know we're here, and they're doing it to provoke us."

As she speaks, I hear the wobble in her voice.

"That's precisely what they're doing," I warn her. "They may not know exactly who's been starving them out, but they know someone is behind it. They *want* you to rush in so they can get more of us."

"Well, if something doesn't happen soon, that's exactly what's going to happen. Almost everyone, especially my mom, is ready to storm in and free him."

I cut her off quickly. "You can't let that happen."

She heaves out a heavy breath. "I know. The only thing stopping them is me and Mizu. Pearl..."

"Yes?"

"We could really use your help."

I glance back at the path to the village, even more torn than I was already.

"I know your mate is important, and I don't know that I would be able to choose anything other than Mizu to focus on if I were in your shoes but..."

"Shit," I whisper and begin pacing on the beach.

She needs help. My pod needs help. My kind needs help, but so does my mate. Can I really chance sacrificing either of them?

"Pearl?" Kristle's concerned voice halts my muttering under my breath and sparks a new idea.

"Okay, new plan. Send everyone except you and Mizu back to the island. Tomorrow, we attack."

"And me and Mizu?"

"You stay and monitor the situation, take as many pictures as you can, and send them to me. The more we know the better."

"Okay," she says, sounding a little more lighthearted than before.

"Pearl?" Skarlyt says, running up to meet me by the water.

"What is it?" I search her panicked face for answers. "What's wrong?"

"It's Loukas."

"Kristle, I have to go. Stick to the plan. Tell everyone I'll meet them on the island as soon as I can."

Kristle pauses, and I can sense her disbelief. She knows how important a mate is, and she thinks I'm going to only focus on Loukas and forget about her cousin.

"I will be there. I promise. See you tomorrow," I tell her, waiting to hear her exhale before hanging up.

"Now, what about Loukas?" I ask, turning to Skarlyt.

"He made it to the Ironwood pack, but..."

"What?"

She bites her lip, concern lining her features.

"He was attacked and..."

"Take me to him *now*," I demand, gripping her hand.

She doesn't waste time arguing with me, she simply grips my hand in her own and focuses for a moment before popping us up in front of the alpha house in Parry Sound.

I don't wait for Skarlyt. I simply stomp up the steps and let myself into the house. I don't know the new alpha pair well, but their house is familiar.

"Where is he?" I demand of Aryn as soon as I lay eyes upon him.

"Nice to see you too, Pearl." He chuckles and points to the kitchen.

I rush around him, catching a glimpse of my mate and launching myself into his arms. Immediately, my lips are on his and my hands are moving across his body. I feel him flinch under my touch. I pull away and hear him grunt in pain.

He's got marks on his face, and his arm is hanging limply at his side.

"Who did this to you?" I ask, my eyes going dark. My hands instantly light up with my green magic, and I begin healing him. It will take a few minutes for me to heal all his injuries. There are multiple cuts, broken bones, and bruised ribs, a lot more injuries than I anticipated. As my magic finishes with his injuries, his internal trauma tugs at my magic, wanting to be healed, but I pull back. Those wounds need permission before we can tackle them.

He places both hands on my cheeks. "*Agapi mou*, I'm fine."

"You may be fine now, but you weren't. Who did that to you?"

"Pearl..."

I spin, rounding on Aryn. "Who?"

"I don't—" he begins, holding his hands up.

"Who?" I growl again, stepping closer. "I sent my mate to you for safe haven, Aryn. Who did you let hurt him?"

Aryn shares a look with Loukas. I feel that my mate has stepped closer to me, but I don't take my eyes away from Aryn.

"It was Matteo."

"Matteo?" Skarlyt's voice is full of shock and disgust. "As in Olivia's Matteo?"

I turn to her.

"Olivia as in Lennox's—" I begin.

"Don't finish that sentence," Skarlyt warns.

"Where is he?" I demand, once again turning to Aryn.

"Now, wait for a second Pearl. There's more to this than..."

"He hurt my mate," I declare.

"Mate?" A small voice comes from behind Loukas, and I turn to find a boy who looks like a mini version of my mate. The first thing I notice is the black eye and split lip, and the growl that comes out of me is more animalistic than I've ever heard from myself.

He steps back toward the wall, and I internally curse myself for showing aggression. I know he's probably already afraid of everyone—especially every woman—he meets.

"No, no, please don't be scared," I plead, remaining in place. "I'm so very sorry. You must be Zach?" He nods his head. His eyes are wide with fear, but he's not looking at me. He's staring at Skarlyt.

"Hi, little guy," she says, but his eyes get even wider, and his body seems to vibrate in terror. Skarlyt sees this and, thankfully, decides to leave winning him over for another day. "I'll go get Alaric and come right back."

I didn't know that Zach's eyes could get any wider, but they do as Skarlyt disappears.

"Zach, this is Pearl. She is my mate," Loukas says.

Zach looks between me and his father. I reach out my hand to him. He stares at it for a few long moments before he finally reaches out and tentatively places his hand in mine.

My magic itches to reach out to him, to heal his injuries, but I hold it back.

"It's very nice to meet you, Zach."

"You too," he says quietly, slipping his hand from mine.

My eyes long to dart to Loukas, but I don't move them from Zach.

"Your sister will be so excited to see you."

That perks him up. "Melia?"

I nod. "She's with some friends of mine right now and your Ya-Ya."

A smile overtakes his face so big that he winces from the way his eyes squint.

I raise my hand and hover it in front of his face, but he looks at it in fear.

"May I heal you?" I ask.

He looks up at his dad, who I suspect nods, before returning his eyes to mine.

"Will it hurt?"

"Not at all," I tell him.

"It feels like you're drinking hot chocolate or warm tea. Instead of sliding down your throat it tingles all over, like a warm hug or a fresh towel out of the dryer," Loukas supplies.

"Okay," he agrees. Slowly and gently, I place my hand on the side of his face.

Just like Loukas, there are so many more injuries than I can see. There are bruised ribs and scraped knees, but it's his internal trauma that has me almost gasping.

So much pain and hurt inflicted on such a young boy. A growl threatens to slip from me at the thought of his mother—the monster who did this to her own son—but I swallow it down, not wanting to scare him again.

Just like with Loukas, I don't even try to heal his trauma. Even though it's hard to leave it all there, it's a discussion I need to have first with Loukas and then with Zach.

"Damn it, Skarlyt, I told you to stop doing that." Alaric's growl rings out from the front porch.

"Why would I stop when you make it so fun?"

"Fun for you." He growls again, and I can hear him stomping up the stairs.

"Exactly," Skarlyt says with a chuckle.

"Pearl," Alaric greets me as he walks in the door.

"Alaric," I say, dipping my chin in respect for the alpha. He may not be my alpha, but I respect him as a fellow leader. "I'd like to introduce you to my mate, Loukas, and his son Zach."

The two men stare at one another, seeming to have a battle of alpha strength. Neither of them blinks nor moves. My eyes flicker back and forth between them, shocked to see Alaric act anything less than welcoming to someone new.

"That's enough, you two," Skarlyt says, interrupting their staring contest. "You're both big, strong boys."

The two blink and look away at the same time.

"What was that?" I ask.

"I haven't met an alpha as strong as me who I haven't already considered family in a very long time," Alaric admits, stepping forward.

"Me either," Loukas agrees, and the two clasp forearms.

When they release, Alaric looks down at Zach.

"It's nice to meet you, Zach." He reaches out his forearm to Zach the same way he did for Loukas. Instead of clasping it, Zach's little hands tremble as smoky magic begins to bleed from him as he stares at Skarlyt.

"Zach, this is my friend Skarlyt," I say, stepping over to Skar and linking my arm with hers.

"She's a pain in the butt, but she'd never hurt you," Alaric finishes obviously seeing how scared he is.

"How do you do that?" Skarlyt asks in awe, staring at Zach's hands.

"What?" Loukas asks, confused.

"The smoke. His magic. It's like three of the elements are so strong and in such perfect harmony that they blend together," she says.

I can't decide if Skarlyt is more, or less frightening when she's curious, so I am not sure how Zach will respond to this change in topic.

Loukas' brows furrow. "What do you mean?"

"I mean. I can access all four elements, but I could never make mine blend like that." She holds up both her hands, creating a cyclone of water in one hand and a cyclone of earth in the other. She brings them closer together and I watch as she adds in her air.

Just like she said, she can't get them to blend into one substance—not the way Zach does. You can still see how the water droplets expel the earth and air.

Zach's eyes widen as he watches Skarlyt's magic. She adds in fire for good measure. Even though, theoretically, the water should be putting the fire out, it remains, slowly spinning in a circle around her other three elements.

"Can you separate them?" she asks, once more pulling her hands away from each other, keeping the fire and air in one and earth and water in the other.

Zach brings his hands up and creates a swirling vortex in his hands, his forehead scrunched up in concentration.

After a few tense minutes, he releases his magic and shakes his head. Skarlyt's magic evaporates.

"Maybe I can teach you, and you can teach me?" she asks Zach, stepping forward and crouching down in front of him. "Even without that, you can probably fly with your magic as it is."

"Fly?"

Skarlyt nods, pushing her hands down, and I feel the air gathering around her as her feet begin to lift off the ground, hovering there for a minute before setting back on the ground. "Plus, we have a really big school that will teach you all kinds of things."

"A school? With kids?" The fear in his eyes is slowly being replaced with curiosity. She nods with a big smile.

"My niece is about your age, and she goes to the school," I tell him.

"And both my son and daughter go there," Skarlyt adds.

"My children do too," Alaric supplies.

"Will I go there, Dad?" he asks, looking up at Loukas, his eyes pleading.

Loukas ruffles his hair, a smile on his face.

"Why don't we go see your sister first, and then maybe we can go on a tour."

"Okay," Zach says, sounding a little disappointed.

"Don't worry, I'm sure your dad will say yes when he sees it," Skarlyt tells him with a wink. "How do you want to do this?" She stands and directs this question to me.

"Take me and Zach first," I say, glancing over at Loukas who nods. "Then come back for the alphas. If that's okay with you, Zach."

He looks between Skarlyt and me, seeming to gulp in fear.

"It will be okay, buddy. Alaric and I will be right behind you," Loukas says before turning to me. "How and where are we going?"

"To the island," I answer at the same time Skarlyt says,

"We're going to teleport."

"Is teleporting like portalling?" Zach asks.

Skarlyt's forehead scrunches in confusion.

"It's similar. Portals usually require more than one witch to create, which is why we use teleporting."

"My mom's coven uses portals to go everywhere," Zach says, making Skarlyt's gaze slide back to him.

Her eyes alight with curiosity once more. "Really?"

"Now's not the time, Skar. Let's get back to the island," Alaric says. He glances at me, and I know what he means. Narissa's pod is probably making its way to the island as we speak, and we have more important things to worry about than Skarlyt wanting to learn some new magic.

"You're right," she admits, stepping closer to me and reaching a hand out to Zach.

He still looks at her with a little fear in his eyes, but he takes her hand anyway. Next thing you know, we're popping out in front of my home.

"I'll be right back," she says and is gone again.

"Where are we?" Zach asks, looking around with wide eyes. He does not seem unstable the way that some people are just after teleporting.

"Welcome to Supernatural Island and my home," I tell him, gesturing to the house in front of us.

"This is your home?"

I nod, but I don't get to say anything else before Alaric, Loukas, and Skarlyt are landing in front of me, all but the latter looking a little green.

"That was unpleasant," Loukas says, making Skarlyt chuckle.

"I'm going to go check in with Loukas' village," Skarlyt says, disappearing once more.

"So, this is the island?" Loukas asks, his eyes as wide and full of wonder as his sons were moments ago.

"It is," Alaric answers, and I watch as Loukas and Zach's eyes go even wider as the first people begin arriving via teleporting from his village, all looking just as green as he did.

"Daddy! Zachy!" A little girl's voice squeals, the three of us turning toward the sound. I watch with tears swimming in my eyes as Loukas and Zach take off, racing toward the little girl. The three of them wrap their arms around one another and sink to the ground.

The first tear falls as Loukas' mom joins the hug, then another person, and another, until almost all their village is joined in one hug.

Chapter Fifteen

Loukas

Holding both of my children while surrounded by the rest of my family and parliament is probably one of the most amazing feelings I've ever experienced and something that I thought would never happen. The only thing that would make this better is having Pearl here beside me.

I know that the kids are not ready for that kind of contact with her after all the damage their mother has caused them. Their trust in women is shaky at best. Especially with Pearl's friend Skarlyt since she has some similarities to Antonia. The long dark hair, blue eyes, and magic seem to be where the similarities end.

As people start to pull back, I stand. My mother pulls me in for one last squeeze.

"You're finally free."

"Not quite yet," I admit, knowing that the three of us won't truly be free until Antonia is taken care of for good. Whether that's death or imprisonment, I don't think it matters. The only thing that matters is that she's no longer free to hurt us.

"Who is your alpha?" Alaric asks, and I turn to search for my sister and her mate only to find everyone pointing at me.

"What? No. I'm not the alpha," I protest.

Nik walks over and takes a knee in front of me.

"You are our alpha; I was only holding the title until you were able."

I reach down and lift him to stand.

"No, brother. You deserve the title. You are the one who has kept them safe for all these years."

He shakes his head. "No. That was you."

"But—" I begin, but he continues.

"By placing yourself in harm's way day after day, you kept us safe. Without your sacrifice, we would all be dead or worse."

My sister, Cassia, agrees as she walks over to me.

"You are the alpha we need."

Once again, Nik lowers himself to his knee, this time followed by everyone within my parliament. I search the crowd, looking for someone to agree with me, but find only bowed heads except the residents of the island who are not in my parliament.

My eyes lock with Pearl's across the crowd. She has a big smile on her beautiful face, and I lift my hand, calling her over to me. She shakes her head, and I continue my waving until a woman with almost white hair zooms up next to her, picks her up, and deposits her at my side with superhuman strength.

"Breanne," Pearl growls.

"Don't you '*Breanne*' me. Your mate wanted you," the woman —Breanne—says before turning to me. "You're welcome by the way."

"Thank you," I tell her with a smile, sticking my hand out for her to shake.

She slaps it away. "You're going to be an uncle to my kids—that makes you family, and family doesn't shake hands," she says, throwing her arms around my neck and pulling me in for a hug.

"What is the meaning of this?" A man calls and I push

Breanne back, taking him in. He's a large man with blonde hair and black-rimmed glasses.

"Matt," Breanne warns, and he drops the angry facade letting out a soft chuckle.

"Sorry, I had to. I'm Matt."

Rather than a hug like with Breanne, Matt stretches his hand out for me to shake. But surprises me when he pulls me in for a man hug and whispers in my ear.

"Hurt her and they'll never find your body." I hear the hiss in his voice and even if Pearl hadn't told me about Breanne and Matt being vampires, I would still be afraid.

I gulp as he lets me go, looking first at Breanne who is grinning like the Cheshire cat, guessing that she heard that little comment and agrees one hundred percent. Pearl, on the other hand, is glaring at her friends.

"I won't," I declare, pulling Pearl to my side.

"So alpha, is there someone you want to delegate to handle housing for your parliament?" Alaric says walking over to our group.

"My sister, Cassia, and her mate have been the alpha pair for the past eleven years; they would know the needs better than me."

He nods, and I turn, gesturing for Cassia and Nik to join us.

"Cassia, Nik, this is Alaric, the alpha of the Westwood pack. This is Matt, Breanne, and my mate."

"Pearl," Cassia nods her head with a welcoming smile at my mate.

"Yes. I was hoping that you could help figure out temporary housing for our parliament."

"Of course, *Alpha*," Cassia snarks, and I chuckle. "Where should we set up?"

"We have more than enough room on my pod's land," Pearl offers.

"What if you find more mermaids?" Breanne asks, a smirk on her face.

"If and when we find more *sea nymphs,* we will figure it out," Pearl says.

"We would prefer to be in a forested area anyway," I tell them, placing a soft kiss on the side of Pearl's head.

"So around here?" Cassia asks, bringing the conversation back to the original topic.

"Yes, then tomorrow we can start carving out plans for more permanent homes," Alaric says, looking to me for approval which I give with a nod.

I feel a little tug on my hand and glance down to find my little pumpkin.

"Oh yes, Breanne, Matt, and Alaric, these are my children, Zach and Amelia."

"Hi, sweetie," Breanne says with a smile which both my children return, making my brows furrow. They're terrified of the witches but not of these two vampires?

"Nice to meet you," Matt says, giving Zach a fist bump and shaking Amelia's little hand.

No one gets to say more as two wolves come running up, one black and one rust-colored. Both shift back into men between Alaric and Skarlyt.

"I thought you were staying home with the kids?" Skarlyt says to the blonde man who was just the rust-colored wolf.

He places a kiss on her lips as he finishes pulling up a pair of shorts, giving me pause. I knew that cross-species mating occurred outside of our parliament. Hell, my mate is a sea nymph. I glance around, ready for someone to say something derogatory to them, to belittle their relationship. Thank the gods, it never comes. As I look around, all I see are happy smiling faces.

Maybe Pearl was right. Maybe this could be our home.

"Your mom has the kids," he explains, turning to our group.

"This is my mate, Lennox, and Alaric's brother, Darren." Skarlyt gestures to the men, though she doesn't need to tell me that Darren is Alaric's brother. The two look so similar I wouldn't be surprised if they are twins.

"This is Loukas, Zach, and Amelia." Pearl beams, still tucked into my side.

"Nice to meet you," I say as I reach out and clasp each man's forearm.

"Incoming," Darren says at the same time Amelia gasps.

I turn my attention to her, noticing her gaze on the sky.

"Daddy, look," she says, pointing up. I follow her finger and, not for the first time since arriving on this island, my jaw drops.

"A phoenix?" I say in awe. Like all supernatural creatures, I've heard of phoenixes but believed they were all gone from this earth. Much like dragons. But it seems this island holds all the secrets of the supernatural world.

As the beautiful flaming woman gets closer, a second one joins her and my jaw hangs open even further, the two performing an aerial dance with one another. Their deep red and bright orange flames blend in perfect harmony.

The dark red phoenix flies closer and drops something above Alaric.

"Catch me, Daddy!" A small voice yells, and I watch Alaric leisurely move over to catch the rapidly falling little girl with ease, nuzzling into her. "You and Mommy were supposed to stay home."

Her little lip begins to quiver, and I let out a chuckle, squeezing Amelia's hand, knowing that look all too well.

"I'm sorry, Daddy," she says.

"Don't do that," he growls, but it doesn't hold any anger, as he squeezes his daughter closer. No wonder Alaric is the unofficial leader of the island, with a phoenix for a mate.

"Okay," she says, sniffling.

"Come here, peanut," Darren scoops his niece up from his brother's arms with a pitying look. "Uncle Darren will protect you from the mean daddy."

"Yay." She giggles before yelling out, "Tidal wave, Mommy."

With those words, my gaze once again rises to the skies, and I watch as the two phoenixes continue their dance. This time, they clasp arms, letting out screeches so loud that a sort of sonic boom made of fire flows out from them. It doesn't seem to do any damage to the island other than pushing a warm breeze outward. Up in the sky, though, rings of fire push outward, one after another, in various shades of red and orange. It's a beautiful sight, and I have no doubt that it could cause a lot of damage if it were directed closer to the earth.

As the two phoenixes return to the ground, Darren places his niece on her feet and both he and Alaric spread their arms, catching now completely human women in their arms.

"You three were supposed to stay home," Alaric rumbles once again while Darren simply kisses the woman in his arms.

"Here, Pheebs," Skarlyt says, passing her a long dress. Darren accepts the one for the woman who I'm assuming is his mate.

"This is my mate..." Alaric begins, but he's cut off.

"She's a showoff is what she is," Skarlyt chuckles.

"I'm Phoebe, and this is my sister, Sophia." The now-clothed Phoebe pulls me in for a hug. "And this little munchkin is Aurora," she says, pulling Aurora closer to her.

"I'm Loukas, and this is Zach and Amelia."

I watch in awe as Aurora walks over to both of my children and throws her arms around them. The hug doesn't surprise me. I've been hugged more on this island than I was in the last eleven years combined. It's my children's faces that have me shocked. It's as if all the tension leaves their bodies as soon as this little angel touches them.

"We don't know why or what the cause is, but when Aurora is

able to soothe people when she touches them. If they're upset, they calm down. If they're afraid they have courage," Pearl whispers.

"It's been like that since the day she was born," Skarlyt adds.

"Incredible," I whisper back, still staring as this little girl begins talking animatedly to my children about all the fun things they're going to get to do on the island and how much fun they're going to have.

"Do you mind if we take them to the beach?" Phoebe asks, gesturing to herself and Sophia.

"Zach, Amelia, do you want to go to the beach with Aurora, her mom, and her aunt?"

Amelia's eyes light with excitement while Zach tries to keep it cool and simply nods his head, but I can see how excited he is. He looks like a kid again and it makes my heart happy. The girls take off running, but he remains, biting his lip.

"You will still be able to see our group from the beach behind my house," Pearl offers to Zach who no longer tries to hide his excitement. Instead, he runs to catch up with the girls.

"We will keep them safe," Sophia says.

"Thank you," I respond, looking at the two phoenixes, knowing without a doubt that they will keep them safe.

When Pearl was telling me about the island, I thought it sounded too good to be true, like there couldn't possibly be that many supernatural creatures living in harmony together. But as I look around, I see vampires, witches, sea nymphs, phoenixes, and shifters all laughing and joking with one another, helping strangers set up their homes, and keeping the kids occupied.

"It's a lot to take in at first," Breanne says.

"I think..." Alaric begins but is cut off by a group of people rushing toward us, each with brightly colored hair and pearlescent skin.

"Pearl," an older woman breathes.

"Narissa. I'm glad you could make it," Pearl says, her voice is colder and more detached than I've ever heard it before. Her posture has changed too. She was relaxing into my side, but now she is ramrod straight, her shoulders stiff, and her chin raised.

"This is my mate. Loukas."

I stick out my hand to shake hers.

"It's nice to meet—" But the older woman snarls at my hand, dismissing me and looking back to Pearl who steps in front of me baring her teeth.

"You will show my mate the respect he deserves."

"He deserves nothing until you keep your promise and help us," Narissa counters.

"Now wait a minute." Alaric tries to insert himself but is met with twin hisses, so he holds up his hands in surrender.

"Why do you think I called you back here?" Pearl challenges.

"I don't know. What I do know is that my daughter is currently sitting on some island listening to her cousin scream as those monsters torture him. All because you had to go save your mate."

Pearl steps up, right in Narissa's face, leaning forward so their faces are only inches apart.

"You will watch what you say about my mate. You are rightfully upset, but that does not give you the right to speak so brazenly about things you know *nothing* about."

"You're right. Of course. My mate is just upset," a man with hair the color of seafoam says, stepping up and wrapping his arm around Narissa.

She looks at him, her eyes still full of anger for a few beats before they soften.

"Taron is right," Narissa says with a sigh. "It's just been very hard hearing his screams."

I watch as my mate's posture relaxes.

"I know, and that's why I won't hold it against you. Come on, let's head inside to plan the rescue," Pearl says, spinning and walking toward her house, sliding her arm through mine as she goes, pulling me with her.

"Matt?" she calls out as we get inside, handing him a phone.

"Let me work my magic," he says, walking over to the TV on the wall, scoping up a laptop as he goes. By the time all the people are in the house and Matt is done with his clicking, photos of a large wooden ship on a beach in Greece are displayed on the screen.

"Everyone except Alaric, Skarlyt, Narissa, Taron, Matt, Breanne, and Loukas, if you wouldn't mind stepping outside. There are far too many people inside to plan properly," Pearl says, her voice easily traveling over everyone. The new sea nymphs mutter amongst themselves but eventually leave, followed by the rest of her friends, Lennox and Darren among them.

"This would be easier at the academy," Matt says. Pearl shakes her head, looking out the back patio doors.

"Amelia and Zach aren't ready to be that far from their father yet."

Everyone nods in understanding except me.

"Okay, I feel like I'm lost. What is going on?"

With that, Pearl launches into a quick rundown about how one of Narissa's pod, Sky, was taken and is being tortured by humans on this boat. The former I knew about already, but the latter, him being tortured and his cries for help being easily heard, is new.

"And you want to rescue him?" I ask, my gaze turning back to the photos, studying them closer.

"Yes."

"First thing we need to know is how many humans are armed on that boat," Skarlyt asks.

"We've counted close to one hundred, though they all wear the same outfits. It could be more, and it could be less," Taron says.

"But just based on the hair color and body shapes we know it's more than fifty," Narissa adds.

"And they're armed, with guns?" Alaric asks, and Narissa and Taron confirm with nods.

"I know this island," I say, walking closer to the screen that shows the pictures. "It's not far from Corfu. It's not large and you could easily surround them if you had the numbers." I look down at Matt. "Can you get an aerial view of Greece up on the screen?"

A few clicks later, and I'm looking at a map of Greece and pointing to a small island off the coast of Corfu.

"This is Ereikousa, and it's where I am almost positive that boat is. See how small the island is? The boat probably takes up most of the beach. If you could figure out a way to disable their weapons, you could easily take them out with a small team."

"Can you use a similar spell to what you used with the mages? Create barriers if we make multiple smaller teams with a witch in each?" Alaric asks Skarlyt.

"We should be able to," she confirms.

"And we should go at night so that you can use the vamps," Breanne adds.

With my geographical knowledge, Alaric's battle strategy, Skarlyt's magic, and Pearl's knowledge of the sea, a plan begins to form.

"Okay, I think we have a solid plan in place," Alaric says, looking around at the group. "Now we need to decide *when*."

"We have to make sure we get there at night," Pearl adds.

"Okay, Greece is six hours ahead of us right now," Matt says, glancing up from his computer.

"So, it's just before sunrise?" I ask.

Matt looks back down at his computer, giving me a nod of confirmation.

"Just enough time to sleep for a solid eight hours before we meet in the vamp wing of the basement to leave," Breanne says, clapping her hands together once as if it's been decided.

166

"Are you going to be able to sleep?" Pearl asks, concern lacing her words.

"I'll tire her out," Matt says with a wink, pulling his mate down on his lap.

Pearl rolls her eyes, and I chuckle because I have the same sort of ideas.

"You'll get Rayne to come with us?" Pearl asks, and Breanne scoffs.

"As if she'd miss it."

With the plan in place and the time set, Pearl ushers everyone out the back door where we find Zach and Amelia still playing in the sand with Aurora.

"Zach, Amelia, you guys ready for bed?" I call out before realizing that I have no idea where we're all going to sleep. As beautiful as Pearl's house is, there is only one spare room with a single bed.

"Want me to make a couple of quick adjustments?" Skarlyt asks Pearl.

"Temporary ones," my mate answers. "We will build once things settle."

Skarlyt skips back inside, leaving me wondering what kind of temporary adjustments she's making.

Chapter Sixteen

Pearl

As Loukas walks down to the water to gather Zach and Amelia, I stand rooted to my spot by the back door, not sure what to do. I desperately want to find my place beside Loukas, a part of his little family. But watching them together warms my heart. Watching from a close distance will have to be enough for now. Seeing Loukas chasing after them as they run away from him, laughing, and having fun makes me long to be included. I can almost picture it, the two of us chasing Zach and Amelia down the beach, all four of us falling in a heap. But until they get more comfortable with me, that's never going to happen. My thoughts stray momentarily... What if they *never* warm up to me? A sense of dread creeps in my stomach.

"All done," Skarlyt says, skipping back out of the house, thankfully interrupting my questioning.

"Thank you." I turn away from the beach to face her.

"I created an adjoining room to your spare room with a barn door separating them that way if Zach and Amelia want privacy from one another they can, but I suspect they're going to want to be close."

I nod. "Probably. Those kids have been through so much and I don't even know half of it."

She places a hand on my shoulder as I turn back to watch Loukas, and his children run and play.

"They'll be okay. Give them time."

Silently, I dip my chin in acknowledgement, feeling the walls that I've erected around myself beginning to crack. The traumatized woman that they pulled out of that facility begins poking through.

As the first tear falls, Skarlyt pulls me into her.

"You've been so strong for so long, it's okay to let others in and to be happy. You deserve every bit of happiness that man gives you."

"How did you..." I begin, the tears beginning to flow more freely now.

She pushes me back.

"You weren't around for the hell I went through, but I promise you that it will be okay."

I glance back at the beach, watching as Loukas walks back toward the house, holding both of his children's hands. I quickly wipe my face, trying to get rid of the evidence.

"It's okay to be vulnerable with him. He's your mate," Skar says, and I look over at her.

"Thank you for everything," I tell her, more tears slipping down my cheeks.

"I also soundproofed your room," she says with a wink. "You're welcome."

I can't help but laugh as I build my walls back up and put a smile on my face. I know Skarlyt is right, that Loukas is my mate and that I can be vulnerable with him, but the kids don't need to see that...yet.

"Anytime," she says, waving to Loukas and the kids before

rushing to catch up with Lennox who has been waiting down the beach.

"Hi guys," I greet them as they walk up the path.

"Everybody gone?" Loukas asks, looking around.

"Yup. Are you ready to see your rooms?" I ask, looking down at the kids.

"I get my own room?" Amelia asks and I keep my shock from showing outwardly.

"Of course. Zach's room is connected to it just in case you guys want to be close to one another," I tell them and watch as Zach visibly relaxes.

"Come on, Zachy, let's go find our rooms." Amelia squeals excitedly, rushing inside and pulling her brother with her.

"I'm excited to see *our* room," Loukas' husky voice whispers in my ear, his hot breath on my neck making shivers flow through my body.

"Skarlyt said she soundproofed *our* room," I whisper, and a growl slips out of his mouth as he begins placing soft kisses on my neck.

His hands roam my body, and a moan slips free.

"Let's go get them settled in, and then we can test that," he whispers, releasing me.

We step inside the house, finding the kids are already in their rooms. Skarlyt really pulled out all the stops. I smile as I walk into Amelia's beautiful room. There are large cherry blossom trees painted on the walls with a princess-style daybed with sweeping sheer material hanging from it.

My smile gets wider as I walk through the open sliding barn door into Zach's room, finding it representing what I know of him perfectly. The walls are painted gray and black, but his bed is covered in an olive-green bedspread, living ivy plants hanging from the ceiling with macrame nets.

"This is amazing," Loukas whispers as he watches his children explore Zach's room.

"Skarlyt's very good at knowing what people need."

"Obviously. This is almost exactly what I would've imagined for them," he admits.

"Daddy! Did you see?" Amelia exclaims, rushing and leaping into Loukas' arms.

"I did, Pumpkin," he says rubbing his nose playfully against hers.

"What do you think, Zach?" I ask, taking a step toward him but not entering his space. I want it to be a place he can claim as his own.

"You really did this for *us*?" he asks.

I shake my head. "No. Skarlyt did this for you both."

His eyes widen before narrowing. "Why?"

"Zach," Loukas berates.

I turn back toward my mate.

"It's okay. I want him to be honest." Loukas nods and heads back into Amelia's room, letting her lead him around the room.

"Can I come in?" I ask, still not taking that final step of entry until I get a nod from him. "You want to know why Skarlyt would make something like this for people she doesn't know?"

He nods, and I take a seat on his bed.

"I wondered the same thing when I first met her."

"I thought..."

"You thought that I've known her for a long time?"

"Yeah. I mean, you two seem close."

"We are. But I've only known her for just over five years. She and the other people you met earlier rescued me from a really bad situation. Just like you, I wondered why they seemed to go out of their way to help me when they didn't know anything about me. Do you want to know what I've learned?"

He seems to search my eyes before sitting on the bed beside

me, just out of arm's reach, still not trusting me not to hurt him. I try my hardest not to let it bother me, but it still stings a little. I know it's not truly me he's afraid of.

"I've learned that the people who live on this island are different from the ones you and I are used to."

"What do you mean?"

I look back into Amelia's room, watching Loukas lying on the bed with his daughter, tenderly rubbing her back before I turn back to Zach.

"I believed, probably much like you do, that everyone wants something from you. Nobody does something for nothing. Every act of kindness comes with a price that you must pay later."

"What do *you* know about everything costing something?" he asks, accusation clear in his tone.

"A lot more than you think. But that's a story for another time. When you're older," I add, not wanting to traumatize him even further by sharing my story of the hunters and other things that go bump in the night.

His biggest monster right now is his mother and her coven, and that is bad enough. He doesn't need any more to be afraid of.

"Back to the original question: the people who live on this island enjoy helping people. They want to see you succeed just because it will make you happy."

"That doesn't make any sense," he says, his brows furrowing in confusion.

"I thought the same thing. When I came here, I was broken, in a way. Maybe broken is a strong word for it. I felt small, like I couldn't make a difference, like it didn't matter what I said or did. Like *I* didn't matter. Do you know what I mean?"

"Yeah," he says, sullenly. "But you're not like that anymore."

"Sometimes I am," I admit. "But I've also had five years to let my friends—my family—help me. I've leaned on them even when it was hard for me to do. I've confided in them. And you know what?"

"What?"

"They've never asked me for anything in return."

"Never?" he asks, his eyes peeking up from his lap.

"Never." I shake my head. "I've helped them, but only ever because I wanted to."

"So, we're really safe here?" he asks, tears floating in his eyes.

"Yes. I can't promise that you'll never be in danger again because let's face it, the world is a dangerous place. But what I can promise is that no matter what happens, your dad and I will always do our best to keep you safe."

Zach flies off the bed and throws his arms around my neck, surprising me. "Thank you."

I rub his back, and he sinks into the hug, seeming more like a small child than the ten-year-old he actually is. "I will never expect you to thank me for keeping you safe. I may not be your..." I pause on the word, not wanting to bring her up.

"No, you're not, you're so much better," he whispers, squeezing me tighter.

"Amelia's asking for you," Loukas says from the doorway. Zach extracts himself from me, gets up, and walks to the door. Loukas places his hand on Zach's shoulder halting him. "She's asking for Pearl."

My eyes go wide, and I stand up.

"Me?" Loukas nods and places a soft kiss on the side of my head as I pass by. Butterflies dance in my stomach, nervousness overtaking my body as I walk into the room.

"Amelia?" I call out, walking close to the bed.

"Will you sing to me?" she asks politely, and my eyes go wide. "In all my story books, the mermaids had the most beautiful voices." Somehow even though she called me a mermaid, it doesn't bother me.

"Sure," I say, and she scoots over on her bed making room for me as I begin my song.

The moonlight guides the dance of the sea,
  A whispered story of eternity.
  From shore to shore, we ride the waves,
  In the ebb and flow, our hearts are saved.

Oh, the ebb and flow of the ocean's grace,
  A timeless waltz, in this boundless space.
  With every rise and fall, we find our way,
  In the ebb and flow, we're here to stay.

The waves, they sing a song, a haunting tune,
  A symphony of life, in the light of the moon.
  From the coral reefs to the deep abyss,
  In the ebb and flow, we find our bliss.

The moonlight guides the dance of the sea,
  A whispered story of eternity.
  From shore to shore, we ride the waves,
  In the ebb and flow our hearts are saved.

As I sing, Loukas and Zach walk into the room, and my eyes widen as Amelia snuggles into me to make room for them on the bed.

Oh, the ebb and flow of the ocean's grace,

A timeless waltz, in this boundless space,
With every rise and fall, we find our way,
In the ebb and flow, we're here to stay.

In the ebb, we learn to let things go,
    In the flow, we let our spirits grow,
    In the rhythm of the sea, we find our peace,
    In the ebb and flow, our love will never cease.

I gently brush Amelia's hair off her face with a smile as her little eyes flutter closed.

Oh, the ebb and flow of the ocean's grace,
    A timeless waltz, in this boundless space,
    With every rise and fall, we find our way,
    In the ebb and flow, we're here to stay.

I glance over at Loukas and smile, seeing that Zach has also fallen asleep next to his sister. I gently turn Amelia toward Zach as I get up and begin walking toward the door with Loukas.

As the tides will turn, and the world keeps spinning round,
    In the ebb and flow, our love is forever bound.
    With the ocean as our guide, we'll never lose our way,
    In the ebb and flow, we'll dance until the end of days.

. . .

"That was beautiful," Loukas says, as he gently closes the door to his sleeping children.

"Thank you. It's my niece's favorite."

"I can see why," he says, placing a soft kiss on my lips. I wrap my arms around his neck, pulling him in closer and deepening our kiss.

He grips my ass, lifting me, and I instantly wrap my legs around his waist, my hands roaming his body, trying to pull him closer. He begins to move, and I pull on his shirt, directing him. My lack of furniture has left a clear path to my room, so I don't have to remove my mouth from his.

I suck his bottom lip into my mouth, making him moan before moving to his ear and neck, sucking and nipping any skin I find in my path. I cling to him as he releases a hand to open the door, rubbing myself on him roughly, ready to claim my mate in every way.

The door closes softly behind him, and I look up to meet his eyes. His pupils are blown wide with lust.

"Do you trust me?" he asks. I nod instantly, surprising even myself.

I do trust him. One hundred percent.

"Good girl," he says, setting me down on the bed, pushing me back, and climbing up my body. I whimper as his mouth begins to play near my waistline and his fingers slowly slip inside the waistband of my pants, tugging them down inch by painful inch. He presses soft kisses down my leg, following the path of my pants.

I sit up, ready to help him pull them down faster, but he stops.

"Lay down." The forcefulness of his voice would normally have me bristling and gearing up for a fight, instead, it only turns me on more.

"That's my girl," he says, continuing to trail kisses until he reaches the bottom, slipping my pants off my feet and working the way back up the other leg.

My hand travels down as he reaches my center, threading my fingers through his hair. But as soon as I do, he stops once again.

"Can you be a good girl and keep your hands to yourself, or do I need to tie you up?" he asks with a knowing smirk.

"I'll be a good girl," I say, pulling my hands obediently back up above my head, desperate for him to continue. Once I do, he moves his mouth back to my center. As he slips his tongue out of his mouth, swiping it up along my lips and landing on my clit. I let out a gasp, my hands automatically drifting down again.

The second my fingertips reach his hair I regret it because he stops.

He doesn't say anything this time, just pins me with a hard look. I bite my lip and raise my hands back up. He follows the path of my hands, bringing my discarded pants with him. He looks into my eyes for a moment before wrapping the empty legs around each wrist and securing them to the headboard. They're loose enough that I could get free if I wanted, but they are tight enough that my hands don't slip free on their own.

He gives them a little tug. "Now you won't be tempted."

His mouth touches mine as he moves back down my body, and I slip my tongue out, licking the seam of his lips. He thrusts his tongue out to meet mine, and I let out a moan at the combined taste of his muskiness and my wetness.

There is something incredibly sexy about his commands and strength. Although I want him, all of him, desperately, it is somehow pleasant for him to tell me no.

He doesn't stay long, though, making his way back down, stopping to suck my pebbled nipple into his mouth. He tugs my left one with his teeth, and the mix of pleasure and pain has me crying out, arching my body off the mattress as I try to get closer to him.

"Patience," he whispers, and I wiggle, wanting him to make his way back to where I desperately need him to be.

This time, when he reaches my clit, there are no lazy circles.

He immediately sucks my clit into his mouth, flicking it back and forth with his tongue. It only takes a few seconds before I'm falling over the edge, screaming out my release.

"Can I have my hands now?" I ask, as he slowly makes his way back up.

"Do you still trust me?" he asks.

"Mmhmm," I hum.

He moves up my body, unbuttoning his pants as he does. I move my body so I'm sitting up more, my arms are still tied to the headboard behind my back. As I pull forward, I feel more strain on my arms, but I lean forward to run my tongue over his rock-hard cock the second he is close enough.

"Pearl," he growls out as I suck him into my mouth, hollowing my cheeks out. I bob my head as much as I can, but with my binds, it is extremely difficult.

"Fuck my face," I tell him, pulling back long enough to say the words.

He doesn't need any further encouragement. He begins to thrust in and out of my mouth. I use my tongue on the underside of his dick, massaging the deep vein there, wanting nothing more than to feel him come down my throat.

"Oh gods," he cries out, and I feel his legs start to shake with his impending release. "I don't want to come in your mouth," he says, trying to halt his movements. I increase my suction until he is crying out and his hot cum is squirting down my throat.

"Bad girl," he says, with a smile on his face. I lick my lips not wanting to waste a single drop of his taste.

"I'm not sorry," I tell him with a smirk.

"I can see that." He chuckles. "And if I'm telling the truth, I'm not sorry either," he admits. He softly unties my hands and looks solemnly into my eyes.

"Was that too much?"

"No. I actually think I liked it," I tell him honestly.

"Really?" he asks.

I tried so hard to rebuild myself after the facility, but people—even my friends—still treat me like I am breakable. To be handled roughly by my mate felt like being trusted, being believed.

I nod. "Really."

He kisses me hard on the mouth at my answer, instantly revving us both back up.

"Loukas," I breathe his name as he rotates his body so that his cock is lined up with my center.

Chapter Seventeen

Loukas

I line my member, already hard again, up with her wet heat using my hand, slowly pushing my way in. I don't think I've ever been this aroused before. With Antonia, she had full control all the time. Even if it seemed that I was in control, I wasn't, not really. The fact that Pearl cares enough to give herself over to me completely is the most amazing feeling.

"You're so tight," I whisper, using force to push my way in.

"Loukas," she cries out as I seat myself deep inside her. Her nails dig into my back as I slowly begin to pulse in and out.

"Harder," she grunts, planting her feet on the mattress and thrusting her body in time with mine.

"Not yet, *agapi mou*. Let me love you first," I tell her, sweeping down and capturing her lips in a soft, sensual kiss while keeping my movements slow and deliberate. I know she's not breakable, but a hard and fast fuck is all it ever was with Antonia. With Pearl, I want to make love to her. I want to show her with my actions, not just my words, how much of a difference she has already made in my life.

Her thrusts slow down, and she raises her hips, moaning

louder each time I hit that spot deep inside her. I grab a pillow, shoving it under her ass, keeping her raised up so that I can hit it every single time.

I hold my body up with one arm, running the other hand down the front of her body and using my thumb on her clit to bring her to the first climax. Her pussy pulses, squeezing my dick as she comes, and I wait until she's finished before I spin us around gently so that I'm on my back and she's riding me.

There's a moment of surprise, and I use that to tuck the pillow under my ass so that I can go exactly as deep as she wants.

I expect her to start fucking me, but to my surprise, she slowly raises herself up, caressing my chest with her hands and leaning forward.

"I've never wanted anyone as much as I want you," she whispers in my ear, pulling the lobe into her mouth.

"And I never thought I'd get lucky enough to find you," I whisper back, turning my head and capturing her lips with mine.

"Don't forget," she warns with a false sternness. "I am the one who found you."

Every raise of her body, she slams herself down on me, and her pussy begins to quiver with her impending release. I remove the pillow, hold her hips in place, and begin slamming into her from the bottom, taking the work away from her, and allowing her to enjoy every sensation.

"Fuck me, Loukas," she demands as soon as she catches her breath.

I don't need any more prompting. I flip her over and slam into her in one powerful thrust. She screams my name, her moans echoing around the room. I silently thank Skarlyt for having the forethought to soundproof it. My mate is definitely not quiet in the bedroom, and I am loving every second of it.

"I want you to come with me," she declares as she clutches at my back, lifting her hips in time with my thrusts.

"As you wish," I tell her, knowing that I wouldn't have been able to hold off much longer anyway.

Each thrust in and out pushes me closer to the edge, but when she can't hold her climax back any longer, her pussy milks me. I watch as her eyes widen and her teeth elongate, and I bare my neck to her, allowing her to sink her pointy teeth in, marking me for all to see as my owl comes to the surface, doing the same as we sink our beak into her neck.

The pain and pleasure of marking our mates and both of us pulsing in and around one another extends our orgasms for what seems like hours.

When the pulsing finally stops, I pull my mouth from her neck. My arms fail me, and I drop to the mattress. I roll, pulling her with me as I do to avoid crushing my beautiful mate.

Unlike what I'm sure the mating mark on my neck looks like— a bite from a supernatural creature—the mark on Pearl's neck is two large puncture holes on the front and back of her collarbone. My owl puffs out his chest with pride looking up at our gorgeous mate wearing our mark.

"Like what you see?" she asks with a giggle, sliding her long blue hair away from her neck.

"So much," I tell her, sitting up and peppering my mark with kisses.

"Shower with me?" she asks, rising off my already hardening cock and walking to the adjoining bathroom, swaying her hips like some sort of minx.

I watch her walk, enjoying the view. As she opens the door to the bathroom, I quickly sit up, rushing to join her. We have rounds two and three in the bathroom, and I hope and pray that Skarlyt worked her magic in here too because I had my mate screaming my name with my mouth, my fingers, and my dick more than once.

The fact that neither of the kids barges in to see what is happening is a good sign and by the time we dry off and climb into bed, I hardly have time to pull her close, wrapping my arms around her before we both fall asleep.

* * *

Bang. Bang. Bang.

I wake to a pounding on the front door.

"Open up. I know you're in there." A feminine voice calls out and for a moment I freeze, thinking it's Antonia.

"Go away, Aqua," Pearl grumbles, rolling over bringing my awareness back to where I am and who I'm with.

I roll over, wrapping my arms around her and tugging her into my chest as the next series of knocks come on the door.

"If you're not out here in five minutes, I'm coming in... Oh hello," The voice says, and I jump up and race to the bedroom door finding a woman with aquamarine hair having a mini standoff with both my children.

"Oh," she says, spinning as I walk past her and closer to my children. I should be concerned with having some random woman walking into Pearl's house while we were sleeping, but from the looks of her, this is Pearl's sister, Aqua. Her hair is a dead giveaway.

"Aqua, right?" I ask, turning to my children and placing soft kisses on the top of their heads. "Morning."

Aqua nods as she stands there, her mouth opening and closing, stunned into silence as Zach and Amelia, both give me hugs.

"I'm Loukas and these are my children, Amelia and Zach," I tell her, gesturing to each one. "This is Pearl's sister Aqua."

"Nice to meet you," Amelia speaks up while Zach remains stoic at my side.

"Uh... you too," Aqua says, looking from me to Pearl's bedroom and back. "I'm sorry. But who are you?"

"Loukas," I repeat, taking Amelia and Zach's hands and leading them into the kitchen.

Aqua shakes her head. "No, what I mean is *who* are you? Like who are you to my sister and what are you doing in her house."

"He's my mate," Pearl's voice comes out of the bedroom with a giggle.

"Mate?" she asks, her voice higher than before. "Since when do you have a mate? Last time I saw you, you said, and I quote, '*I think I found my mate and he's in trouble.*' What kind of person doesn't tell her own sister that she found her mate?" Aqua demands, rushing into the bedroom and leaving the door slightly ajar.

"I think we should make some breakfast, don't you?" I whisper to the kids as I hear the sisters talking in hushed tones through the open door.

"Won't Pearl be mad we're using her food?" Zach asks.

"I won't as long as you make me some too," Pearl calls from the bedroom, making Zach's eyes widen, he obviously thought he was quiet enough that she wouldn't hear him.

"You heard her, we best get to work," I tell him, bumping his shoulder.

When Pearl and Aqua emerge from the bedroom, the three of us are coated almost head to toe in flour and there is a sheet pan in the oven full of chocolate chip and blueberry pancakes.

"Mmm something smells good," Pearl says, coming over and placing a soft kiss on my lips.

"We made choco chip and blueberry," Amelia supplies, rising on her tiptoes to see over the kitchen island.

"My favorite is chocolate chip, but Aqua likes blueberry. What about you?" Pearl asks Amelia.

"I like choco chip too."

"And you, Zach?" His eyes widen like he didn't expect to be asked, and he clears his throat.

"I don't know," he replies honestly, another reminder of all the time that was stripped from us. We should've been in the kitchen together every Sunday, making breakfast for our family. Instead, he wasn't allowed to look at me or talk to me after he started showing real magic at the age of five. Only on very rare occurrences was he able to spend time with me and never alone. The food the coven liked to make was never fun. If there were pancakes, they were plain.

"That's okay. You'll just have to try them both and see," Pearl says, and I give her a soft smile of thanks.

"And next time we could try and make a bunch of different ones just to be sure," I tell him, reaching into the oven and flipping over the pancakes.

"My dad makes really good banana pancakes," Aqua says, coming into the kitchen and grabbing five plates to set the table.

"He really does," Pearl agrees, grabbing the silverware and passing the forks to Zach. "Would you mind putting these on the table for me?"

"Sure," he says, spinning on his heel and marching over to the table, placing a fork next to each plate as he goes.

"Knock. Knock." Another feminine voice calls out from the front door, and I turn seeing both Skarlyt and Phoebe standing there with another petite blonde woman and a large, towering man.

"Andres!" Amelia exclaims, rushing to the screen door, throwing it open, and launching herself into the big burly man's arms.

"Should I be worried about that?" I whisper to Pearl, who chuckles and shakes her head.

"That's Andres," she responds.

"The dragon?" I ask, looking back at the big man in a new light. I don't know how I didn't realize it; Amelia couldn't stop talking about him last night.

"I had some of Ryker and Riley's old clothes put away and Drusilla had some of River's old clothes as well. They might be a little big, but Sarah is already making Amelia some nice dresses," Phoebe says, and I notice for the first time that all three women are carrying in at least two garbage bags.

"You didn..." I begin, but Pearl cuts me off.

"Thank you."

I clear my throat. "Yes. Thank you."

Phoebe holds out the two bags in her hand to Zach.

"These are for you." He looks from the bag to her face and then to Pearl who nods before he reaches out and grabs the bags from her.

"Thank you."

"You're very welcome. The blue bag in Skarlyt's hand is also for you but I think they might be a little big yet."

Zach reaches out and grabs the third bag as I walk up, taking the bags from the small blonde and the last bag from Skarlyt but she holds hers back. "Is it okay if Drusilla tries taking Amelia to put away her new clothes?"

"Why?" I ask, narrowing my eyes in suspicion.

"Let's just say I have experience helping little girls work through their trauma," Drusilla, the blonde woman, supplies, and, in her eyes, I can see that is the truth. I nod, mentally filing that away as something to ask Pearl about.

"How about it, little one, do you want my mate to help you put away your new clothes?" Andres rumbles.

"You come too?" she asks, sweetly.

"Not this time. Next time, okay?"

"Can daddy come too?" she asks, and my heart just about melts at the pleading in her eyes. I look between Drusilla, Andres, and Amelia.

"I have to check on the pancakes, Pumpkin. I'll be in as soon as they're ready."

"Okay," she says as Andres puts her down.

"Come on, Amelia. I think Sarah might have finished a princess dress for you already," Drusilla says with a wink, taking all three bags and following a hyped-up Amelia to her room. I should feel concerned rather than relaxed at perfect strangers walking away with Amelia, but I don't. It's like there's a part of me that already completely trusts these people despite meeting them for the first time.

Safe, my owl says to me before preening his feathers and falling asleep.

"What did she mean she has experience with helping little girls through their trauma?" I ask once she's left the room.

"Drusilla was taken as a child by hunters," Andres provides, looking at the doorway his mate just went through with love shining in his eyes. "And then my niece River was found and rescued from the same group of hunters." I suck in a breath. "Drusilla was able to help her through her trauma and recover because she understands what she went through. Amelia may not have been taken by hunters..." Andres growls.

"She was abused by her own mother," I supply.

"And that might be worse," Andres adds, reaching out his forearm to clasp mine. "I'm sure you're already aware, but I am Andres."

I nod, clasping his arm. "Loukas."

"I haven't met another avian alpha as strong as you in a very long time," he says as he releases me.

Not knowing what to say, I turn back toward the kitchen.

"We were just about to have breakfast; would you like to join us?"

"No. Thank you for the invite, but we already ate this morning."

"Another time?" I ask.

"Sure," Andres agrees.

I grab out the first batch of pancakes and place them on the table "Everyone hungry?"

A round of cheers barely precede the sound of little feet as Amelia speeds out of her new room with Drusilla behind her. I smile as I take in my sweet daughter wearing a beautiful pink puffy princess dress and the enormous smile on her face and thank the gods that we're here.

I turn back to the kitchen and scoop out another batch of pancakes onto the baking sheet when I feel a presence behind me.

"She'll be okay, Loukas," Drusilla's small voice says, and I spin looking at her.

I glance over at the table, watching Amelia talk to everyone animatedly, even Skarlyt.

"She will?"

"Yeah, she's such a strong little girl. But I would like her to come work with me and my niece River on some meditation techniques. It might not be a bad idea for Zach either."

"I don't know how open he'd be to that," I admit.

"You might be surprised," she says, turning back to the group.

It's a good thing that I made multiple batches of the pancakes because, despite Andres saying they had already eaten, both he and Skarlyt couldn't help themselves before leaving.

"So, what's on the agenda for today?" I ask Pearl, walking into the kitchen and wrapping my arms around her middle.

"I need to get ready to leave for Greece."

"You mean *we* have to get ready to leave for Greece," I supply.

She looks up at me, her aquamarine eyes shining with something I can't decipher.

"No. I don't."

"But..." I go to protest.

She puts her finger on my lips. "You guys just got here. The kids need to meet friends and take a tour of the school. Your entire parliament recognized you as their alpha last night. You have a lot to do here."

"What if something happens to you?"

She places both her hands on my face.

"Nothing will happen to me. I have a lot of people coming with me."

"And one more wouldn't hurt," I tell her, pulling her close and placing a kiss on her lips.

"The kids need you here," she says, pulling back.

As much as I want to argue with her, I know she's right. She knows I know. I let out a heavy sigh. "As long as I can help with the planning."

"I don't see how that's going to be an issue," she says with a smile, merging her lips with mine.

"Are we going to see the school, Daddy?" Amelia interrupts before the kiss can get too hot and heavy.

"We are, Pumpkin. Why don't you and Zach get ready? Pearl has to go to the academy anyway."

With that, both Zach and Amelia rush off while Pearl and I head into the bedroom, getting ready ourselves.

Chapter Eighteen

Pearl

I hated having to convince Loukas not to come with me, I don't want to leave him here as much as he doesn't want me to go without him. But we both know that Amelia and Zach need to come first and him coming with me, rushing headfirst into danger, is not what's best for them.

"Are you sure I shouldn't come? What if I am the lookout?" he asks, his voice full of concern.

I take his face between my hands and place a soft kiss on his lips. "We both know you won't be able to sit out if there's a chance I could get hurt."

A growl rumbles in his throat. "You're not allowed to get hurt."

I raise my brow at his choice of words. "I know we don't know each other all that well, but I expected you to know that you cannot tell me if I'm *allowed* to do anything."

He lets out a sigh. "You're right. That was a poor choice of wording." He pulls me into his chest, and I go willingly, melting into him as he wraps his arms around me. "I just can't stand the thought of you being hurt and me not being there."

"I know," I whisper, soaking in his warmth, not wanting to

leave him either. "I won't be alone. Besides, they're just humans, what can they do against the team we've assembled?"

"You're right. I know you are, and up here," He points to his head. "Is on board with the plan. But here," He pulls my hand with his, covering his heart. "Is not ready to leave your side."

"I'll always come back to you," I whisper, going up on my tip toes and merging my mouth with his. What was meant to be a sweet kiss turns heated in an instant as he slips his tongue into my mouth. I bring my hands up, running them through his thick hair, tugging it, and pulling him closer to me.

"Dad?" Zach says through the door, and I pull away from Loukas, breathless.

Loukas clears his throat "Yeah buddy?"

"Melia and I are ready."

I step back as Loukas lets out a groan and adjusts himself in his jeans.

"We will be right there," he answers, and I chuckle, turning to grab some yoga pants and a tank top. I know that Breanne is going to have me wear a pair of her fighting leathers since the chances of me needing to shift are slim.

"Little cock blockers," Loukas whispers against my ear as I raise my hands to slip on my shirt.

"Cherish this time, they won't always want you around," I tell him, leaning back into him.

He places a soft kiss on my neck, I expect him to keep going, instead, he lets out a heavy breath. "You're right."

"Plus, we can have all the alone time we want when they start at the academy." I chuckle as I nuzzle into his neck.

"And once we get all of our enemies out of the way," he says.

"We will never be able to get rid of all our enemies. Not until this stupid prophecy is done," I say, pulling the shirt over my head.

"What prophecy?" he asks and I turn to him.

"I didn't tell you?" I ask. "I was sure that I did." My brows furrow as I go over all the conversations we've had since we met and I realize that although we've talked about a lot of things, as I continue looking back, I realize we didn't talk about what's going on in the world, the vengeful goddess, or the prophecy.

"Not that I remember," he admits.

"I'll tell you on our walk," I tell him, slipping my feet into my flip-flops. I prefer to be barefoot, but, if I wear shoes, my toes cannot be covered.

"Ready, little ones?" I ask, as I open the door, finding both Zach and Amelia standing there, vibrating with excitement. Amelia is dressed in a blue princess dress, meaning she's already changed out of the pink one this morning.

"Can I fly there?" Amelia asks, looking from her dad and back to me.

"It's okay with me," Loukas whispers in my ear, letting me answer her.

"Sure."

"Me too?" Zach asks.

"How?" I ask, keeping my tone light.

"Skarlyt said that I should be able to fly with my magic and I'd like to try."

I nod my head, remembering Skarlyt's display.

"Then absolutely," I tell him, and he beams at me, gripping his sisters and hand rushing out of the house.

"Well, that works, now they can fly, and we can talk," Loukas says, reaching out and threading his fingers with mine.

When we get outside, Amelia has already shifted, leaving her dress and shoes in a pile on the ground. I reach down and scoop them up, tucking it under my arm for the walk, and watch as Zach hovers a few inches off the ground, his smoky magic surrounding him. He wobbles as he looks at us before returning his concentration to his magic and evening out.

"Amelia, fly above the trees and look for a big castle," I shout, watching as Amelia does as I say, her little wings flapping. She hoots when she sees it and takes off toward it.

Zach, seeing this, does the same, albeit a little slower as Loukas and I begin to walk.

"So, this prophecy..."

"I don't even know where to begin," I admit.

"Does it have anything to do with everything that's going on in the world? The infertility issues, the ocean spitting out all the garbage?"

"Yes," I say. "Thousands of years ago, there was a prophecy foretold:

When the daughter of the storm and the son of the moon become one;

A hunter and her prey put aside their differences;

The lost daughter of air mates the first son born of magic and fire;

A son and daughter of fire join together;

The dual natured son and the dawn cement their bond;

A new age arrives where Supernatural beings will need to come out of the shadows as a new enemy awakens.

"The daughter of the storm and the son of the moon are Sarah and Sebastyn. A hunter and her prey are Rayne and Drake."

"So, parts of the prophecy have already begun," he says, no question in his tone.

"Yes. That's why everything has been happening. The 'new enemy that awakens' is Gaia, the mother of all goddesses. From what we can figure, she awoke and saw what had happened to her earth and decided to retaliate. The first wave was infertility."

He nods. "Amelia was born two days before. Three other

witches were with child, all three lost them at the same time. We thought it was a magical attack or something but then as more time passed and no one got pregnant, it seemed less likely to be a targeted attack, then we heard about how the rest of the world suffered as well and knew it had to be something more..."

"All the original members of the Westwood pack and surrounding supernatural factions were saved from that attack by Artemis."

"So, they've had children?" he asks, hope shining in his eyes. "We could have children?"

"I wasn't part of that original group. Artemis and Demeter have strengthened the barrier surrounding this island, hoping to combat the spell. Breanne was not one of the original members, but they have Erik, who is six months old now."

He stops walking, turning to look at me. "But there's a chance that if we want to have children, we could?"

"It's possible. But..."

He picks me up, hugs me tightly, and spins me around. "This is the best news I've ever heard."

"There's no guarantee," I tell him.

"But there's a chance, and that's more hope than I had yesterday," he says with a smile which I return, allowing myself hope for a minute. I know that Artie says Demeter's gift to Breanne was a one-time thing, but I also know that the reason she had Demeter strengthen the wards around the island was because she was hoping it would lessen the effects of Gaia's attack. Even with that knowledge, I didn't allow myself to hope of having children myself. I needed a mate for that and was beginning to lose hope for that.

"There is," I admit, as he sets me down, intertwining our fingers once more.

"And the rest of the couples in the prophecy?"

"The lost daughter of air and the first-born son of fire and magic is River and Riley. Alaric and Phoebe, along with River's mom Andrea, have asked that they wait to cement their mating bond until we know more, but the closer they get to eighteen, the harder it's going to be. They are hoping that if they wait to mate the attacks will cease or stay the same, but we still don't know who the rest of the couples in the prophecy are and the attacks haven't stopped..."

"And what happens when all the couples are together?" he asks.

I watch as Zach finally finds his groove. He and Amelia are flying circles around each other, both giggling like the children they are.

"Andres asked that question to the oracle who gave the prophecy apparently. The answer was that should the couples within the prophecy not come together, all hope would be lost. It's not necessarily the couples themselves, but some of their offspring that will lead us into a new era. One where supernaturals and humans work together."

"I find that hard to believe."

"Me too. I can't imagine a world where humans wouldn't be a danger to us if they knew the truth," I tell him honestly. "But we've had a long time to look at this prophecy, all of us have our own opinions of what will happen. But the one constant is that we don't think we will be able to stay hidden from *all* humans forever."

"Like we only need to expose ourselves to some—not all."

"Exactly. Alaric believes that if we can set up meetings with the world leaders individually and explain what's happening, we will have a better chance at survival."

"But what is it Gaia wants?"

"We really don't know. But Artie seems to think that the humans destroying the earth is her main issue."

"But most supernaturals respect nature."

"We do, you're right. But we're also not doing anything to stop them. In her mind, we're just as bad and deserve to be punished."

He opens his mouth to respond as a naked, giggling little girl runs up to us, making him release my hand in time to catch her.

"We're almost there, Daddy," she exclaims, and he spins her around like he did with me earlier.

"That's fantastic, Pumpkin," he says, and I pull out her clothes as he sets her down, sliding the dress over her head and running my fingers through her now tangled hair.

"Wait until you see it, Dad. It's humongous," Zach says, landing softly in front of us.

"It looks like a castle," Amelia says giddily.

"Then it's the perfect place for you, princess," Loukas says, lifting her up and peppering her with kisses.

"Pearl?" Zach's little voice says, looking up at me.

"Yes?"

"Will there be other kids my age? Witches like me?"

I mentally go over the people that I know. "I'm sure there will be. I know my niece Makayla is your age, but she's a vampire."

"Your niece is a vampire?" he asks, looking at me in confusion.

"Her mom is my best friend, we're as close as sisters so her kids call me 'Aunty Pearl.' But I'm sure that there are lots of kids your age."

"What if they don't like me? All the kids in my mom's coven hated me."

"Zach..." Loukas says, placing Amelia on the ground. I crouch down in front of Zach, nodding for Loukas and Amelia to keep going.

I reach out my hands, holding them palm up, letting him decide whether he wants to take them or not.

"First of all, they were probably just jealous of you. Even then, it's their loss. I happen to think you're pretty amazing, and anyone would be lucky to be your friend. I hope one day you'll consider me your friend."

He searches my eyes for what feels like forever before he places his hands in mine.

"I'd like that."

"Come on, let's catch up to your dad and sister," I tell him, not wanting to say what I'm thinking. That if some little kid wants to be mean to him, I'll deal with it. I can't imagine after his mother, that he would be receptive to that. Still, though, it doesn't change the fact that if one of the kids tries to be mean to him, then they'll have to deal with me, and they won't like the outcome. If I know Makayla, which I'd like to believe I do pretty well by now, she's going to be the same.

Surprisingly, Zach doesn't release my hand as we walk. I look down at him as we break through the trees. I wonder what he might be thinking, but I relish in the fact that he never wavers from my gentle grip, as if in this moment we're forming our own little bond. As we catch the first glimpse of the towering academy, I watch as his mouth drops open in awe.

"Hey guys," Phoebe says, walking up to us. Aurora quickly rushes toward Amelia, the two of them squealing. Kayne watches Loukas, a scowl on his face and his arms crossed, clearly in protective mode.

"Kayne, I'd like you to meet Zach." Skarlyt's son is a few years younger than Zach, but he is a good stepping stone.

Zach looks at Kayne warily, trying to interpret the look the younger boy is giving Loukas.

"Kayne is Skarlyt's son." At the mention of his mother, Kayne finally tears his eyes away from Loukas and takes in Zach.

"Hi, I'm Kayne," he says, stepping up and taking charge, just like an alpha would. It's not surprising considering who his parents are.

"Zach," he responds, removing his hand from mine and clasping Kayne's little one.

"Are you new here?" Kayne asks and, with that, they begin a conversation about magic and what the school is like while Phoebe and I step back and watch them. Both of us let out a relieved breath.

"I was hoping the age difference wouldn't be too much. It was either him or Ryker," Phoebe says.

"I think either one would've been good. But Kayne is not a normal six-year-old either," I supply.

She chuckles. "He is too much of an alpha for his own good."

I dip my chin in agreement. "So where should we start with the tour?"

"I was going to let them play out here for a bit. The other kids will be out on their first recess soon. I figured Aurora and Kayne could introduce them to some."

"That's a great idea, Phoebe. Thank you," Loukas says, out of breath from running after the girls.

I snuggle into his side.

"Did the girls wear you out?" I ask, hiding my chuckle.

"Those two are like little balls of energy," he responds, putting his arm around me.

Over the next couple of hours, we watch from a safe distance as both kids make some new friends and take a tour of the academy. Despite still obviously being wary of the entire situation, even Zach makes friends with a couple of boys his age.

One's a shifter from Axel's sleuth, and the other is a witch. They fall into an easy conversation. Zach glances over at me, and I give him a little wave, happy that he's beginning to enjoy himself.

"Who's that?" I hear one of the boys ask, and I hold my breath. I am not sure how he will answer.

"She's my dad's mate, Pearl. She's pretty cool," Zach answers simply, and my smile gets even bigger. At least it was nothing negative.

Knowing that Zach is on the right path, I turn and glance back at Loukas, chuckling as he holds both Aurora and Amelia's hands while they talk his ear off. I didn't need to be worried about that one. I don't know if it's because of Aurora's presence or because she's so young, but I don't think she's going to have very many issues adjusting.

"They're waiting for you in Bree and Matt's office," Phoebe says as we approach the vampire section of the academy which is easily identified by the lack of natural light and the windows covered in metal panels.

I stop and turn.

"Zach, did you want to come with us, or did you want to go to class with your new friends?"

He looks between me and his new friends, biting his lip.

"Why don't you go to class with them? Jake knows the way back here if you want to come join us later," Phoebe supplies and I send her a grateful smile.

"Are you sure it's okay?" he asks.

"Of course," I respond, looking over at Loukas.

"Aurora and Kayne are going to take your sister to class too," Loukas says. "I'm sure you guys can all walk together."

Amelia doesn't wait, letting go of Loukas' hand, grabbing Aurora and Kayne, and skipping back in the direction we came from. Zach follows behind quickly, ready to protect his sister should she need it.

"Won't they be in different classes? Amelia and Aurora, I mean," Loukas asks Phoebe.

"Not normally, no. For the most part, they will still be in the same classes, learning the basics, but since Amelia has already shifted, she's going to have to be in some of the more advanced shifter classes so she can get control over her shifts," Phoebe says.

"Would it be better for her if she had another avian shifter as a teacher?"

Loukas furrows his brows. "Probably. Do you have any avian shifter teachers?"

She shakes her head. "I was hoping that someone from your parliament would be interested."

"I'm sure I can find someone," he says with a smile, and I tug his hand toward Matt and Bree's office now that the kids have disappeared down another hallway.

Chapter Nineteen

Pearl

"Oh good. You're here," Alaric says as we walk into the office. Neither Breanne nor Matt is in here, but that's not surprising since it's still daytime and they're most likely trying to get as much sleep as they can. "We were just going over the plan."

Loukas and I walk over to the large table surrounded by my friends. "We were just giving the kids a tour of the grounds."

"How'd they do?" Sebastyn asks.

"Really well, I think. Kayne and Aurora took to Amelia immediately and Zach made some friends too," Loukas says with a proud grin on his face.

"That's great. I'm Sebastyn by the way, Skarlyt's brother," he says reaching over and clasping Loukas' hand. With that, the others who haven't officially met Loukas yet do the same before we turn back to the map on the table.

"Matt was able to get some satellite images of the ship for us," Darren says, tapping on a screen and pulling up at least a dozen images, all featuring the ship sitting on the beach over the last few days if the timestamps on the pictures can be trusted.

"We were thinking of having a dozen vampires go in first to take out any easy targets," Drake says.

"And we'd have a dozen or so witches surrounding the boat ready with a barrier so that no one escapes," Rayne adds.

"We also have recent graduates who joined the supernatural enforcement agency ready to join us. So, there are about thirty more, a mix of shifters, vampires, and witches," Darren says.

"Supernatural Enforcement Agency?" Loukas asks.

"It's a new thing," I whisper before Darren can begin.

"Five years ago, we started a supernatural 911 network to help supernaturals in need across the globe. It started with four teams of four, but we all have families now and decided that we would add an extra two-year program at the academy for graduates who would be interested in joining the agency. This is the first graduating class."

"Seriously dude, you sound like an infomercial," Sebastyn snarks, earning a glare from Darren.

"So, they've never been in the field so to speak?" Loukas asks apprehensively.

"The ones we've invited to come with us have. It's part of their training. Each one has to attend at least fifty 'calls for service' with a full team before they are permitted to join a team of their own. That's why there are only thirty. We had one hundred and six graduates in this class."

"That's a lot," I say, not expecting that big of a number, though I should have. When they decided to offer it as a class, there was a buzz all over the island about it.

"We allowed mature adults to join the program as well. Some of the graduates are in their thirties, a couple are even in their fifties," Darren says with a smirk.

"Empty-nesters who want to help out," Alaric explains.

"That's incredible," Loukas says, his smile wide.

"Okay, so what do you want the sea nymphs to do while you're all fighting?" I say, going back to the original discussion.

"Well..." Sebastyn begins, looking around.

"They didn't think you guys would want to fight because it's not in the water and you're all healers by nature, so they were going to have you on the sidelines to heal anyone who gets hurt," Rayne blurts out.

I clamp my mouth closed, taking a couple of deep breaths through my nose.

"It's just that we..." Alaric begins, but I cut him off with a raised hand.

"I appreciate that you were looking out for my pod, but this is our fight more than it is any of yours," I begin.

"Pearl..." Sebastyn tries to cut in.

"But," I say, cutting him off. "It is a member of my pod—*my kind*—that is being held captive on that boat. You are correct. We do not normally enjoy violence, but this is something we *need* to do." I finish, looking around, catching a smirking Rayne.

If I had to guess, she knew what my reaction was going to be to their plan. The question is if she tried to explain it or didn't say anything just to see it. I wouldn't be surprised if she was recording it to show Breanne later too.

I almost glance around looking for the hidden camera but then remember we are standing in Matt and Breanne's office, there are probably a dozen or more hidden around the room.

"Okay. So how many of your pod should we include in the plan?" Alaric asks.

"Skarlyt, can you go get Narissa and bring her here? This is a conversation she should be included in," I say as Skarlyt walks through the door, a cookie halfway to her mouth.

"But I..." she begins, her mouth opening and closing, no doubt wanting to argue that she just got here. Instead, she shoves the entire cookie in her mouth, scowling at me before vanishing and popping back in with a wide-eyed Narissa.

"What is the meaning of this?" she demands.

"Skarlyt. You could've at least told her why you wanted her," I say and Alaric snorts knowing his best friend.

"You asked me to go get her, not explain why. Besides, how was I supposed to explain with a mouth full of cookie?" Skarlyt says with a shrug, walking over to her brother.

I narrow my eyes at her before turning to Narissa.

"Sorry about that, some witches need a lesson in manners." I send a pointed look at Skarlyt who places a hand on her chest in mock innocence. "But we were going over the plan for tonight and wanted to get your input."

Narissa's eyes are still wide after the short exchange between Skarlyt and me, but she clears her throat.

"I appreciate that, Pearl."

"You're welcome," I tell her, placing my hand on her elbow and guiding her back to the table. "We need to know how many in your pod are comfortable fighting on land and how many would rather wait and be ready to heal anyone who is injured."

"Who is going to fight if not us?" she asks, anger in her voice.

"We are," Drake and Rayne say at the same time.

"And us," Skarlyt says, gesturing to herself and her brother.

"Us too," Darren says nodding at Alaric.

"Why? Why would you all fight for people you don't know?" Narissa asks.

"Because Pearl is their family," Loukas says, stepping back up from somewhere behind me and placing his hand on the small of my back. "I haven't been on this island long, but I've learned that the people here genuinely care for other supernaturals."

Narissa scoffs. "What do you want in exchange?"

"Nothing. They...We want nothing in exchange except for your pod to be safe," I tell her.

"But we're sea nymphs, not witches or vampires or shifters."

"And that doesn't matter," Skarlyt says. "Maybe once upon a time, all supernatural factions were separated by their bigotry, their purist beliefs, but no more. If that were the case, my mate wouldn't be a wolf."

"And mine wouldn't be a hunter," Drake adds.

"Nor would ours be phoenixes," Alaric says, tipping his head toward his brother who nods.

"I don't understand," she says, looking at me and then at Loukas and around the rest of the table.

"You will," I assure her.

"How can you trust that they will fight as hard as we would?"

"They won't," I say with a soft smile. "They'll fight harder and better because every single person in this room has fought before and train in combat regularly."

I search Narissa's eyes and see that she's not going to believe me unless she sees it.

"Can you show her some of the 911 missions?" I ask Sebastyn, knowing that out of everyone in this room, he knows the system the best. Still not as good as Matt, but he's the second-best option.

Sebastyn nods, leading Narissa over to the wall of computer screens, Loukas following behind. I watch with a smile on my face as they both watch, eyes wide, glancing at each person around the room.

Her face still has a surprised look on it when they rejoin us at the table.

"See, this is what they do. They help those in need," I say.

"We," Rayne corrects. "Don't forget you are also on one of the teams."

"Not recently."

"Only because your team took a break when Erik was born, and you didn't want to go to another one," Sebastyn says, sending a pointed look my way.

I wave my hand dismissively not wanting to get into this whole song and dance again. When Erik was born, both Breanne and Matt took time off and because I didn't want to go with another team, so did I. It's been a very boring six months.

"So how many?"

"Oh," Narissa says, realizing that I'm talking to her. "I think that four men plus Kristle will want to fight and won't be a hindrance. The rest of us will stay on shore and heal those in need."

I nod. "Okay, so that's five plus Mizu, Caspian, and myself for fighters."

"You're going to fight?" Narissa asks, disbelief clear in her tone.

I don't get the chance to defend myself, Rayne taking the liberty of doing it for me.

"Pearl can kick the ass of most people on this island. Especially when she has a spear in her hand."

Narissa still has an unreadable look on her face as we continue to discuss logistics.

After that is sorted, it's literally just a waiting game and not a very long one because of the time difference. Still, Loukas and I sneak off to check on the kids.

"Are you sure you don't want me to come?" he asks, as we walk hand in hand down the hallway.

I stop. "Of course, I want you to come. But you heard the plan, it's a sure thing. And as much as I want you by my side, the kids need you more."

"But you just said it's a sure thing, so we can leave the kids with my mom and..." I place my finger on his lip, stopping him from talking.

"They need *you* to be here."

"And *I* need *you*," he says.

"I need you too. But I'll only be gone a few hours," I tell him, merging my mouth with his hard and fast, pushing him up against a wall.

When we finally come up for air, I glance around, spotting a closet and dragging him toward it.

"Now where were we?" I ask, once the door closes, I wrap my arms around him and pull him close.

We fumble with our clothes like a couple of teenagers, and I curse myself for choosing yoga pants rather than a dress. All thoughts of my clothes are forgotten as he spins me around, securing both my hands in one of his and pressing them above my head, using his other hand to guide himself inside me.

"Sorry, *agapi mou*. I can't do foreplay right now." He grunts, and I moan as he seats himself fully inside me.

I arch my back as he slams into me, pushing my ass out, meeting him thrust for thrust. His hand moves from my hip to my clit.

"I'm not going to last much longer," he says as he begins to rub my little nub, bringing me quickly to the brink.

Far too soon, but just soon enough, the two of us are falling over the edge together, and I press my mouth into my shoulder, hoping to muffle the sound. I spin as he slips from me, merging my mouth with his. Both of us are still fully dressed above the waist, so we only need to pull our pants back on. His is a lot easier than mine since he had simply allowed his jeans to fall to the floor in a pool at his feet rather than pulling them off as I had to.

I quickly shimmy up my pants.

"Let's go see how the kids are making out," I tell him, reaching for the door. He pulls me back, merging his mouth with mine.

"You're going to come back to me, right?" he asks, his voice pleading.

"Always," I assure him, placing one last soft kiss on his lips before turning the handle on the door and stepping out.

"Oh. Hello, Val," I say as I stumble out of the door, Loukas behind me, landing in front of Valerie, Rayne's mom.

She raises a brow at me with a knowing smirk. "Pearl." She dips her chin in acknowledgement.

"This is Loukas. My mate," I say, pulling him up beside me. "Loukas, this is Valerie, Rayne's mom."

"It's nice to meet you," he says, sticking out his hand smoothly for hers as if we didn't just come stumbling out of a janitor's closet.

"Valerie doesn't..." I begin, wanting to tell him that she doesn't usually shake the hands of new people. Even though Opal is the oracle of this generation, it doesn't mean that Valerie's gifts simply vanished. But my words stop, and my mouth drops open as she clasps his hand, covering it with her other hand.

Her eyes go wide, white overtaking both her iris and pupils. Loukas goes to pull his hand free.

"Don't," I whisper, placing my hand on his arm.

"What's happening?" he whispers, his head leaning toward me but his eyes never leaving Val.

"She's having a vision. Valerie is an oracle," I whisper back, and he nods, though I can see from the pinch between his eyebrows that he doesn't truly understand, and it makes me wonder how little he knows about other supernaturals despite being one himself.

We stand there for a few moments in silence, waiting for Valerie to complete her vision. She comes out of it with a gasp, pulling Loukas in for a hug.

"You are so strong," she whispers to him, stepping back and looking at me. "You were blessed with a strong mate."

I tuck myself into Loukas' side, looking up at him.

"I know," I tell her with a smile.

"What did you see?" Loukas asks but both Val and I shake our heads.

"She can't tell you."

"Can't or won't?" he asks.

"Both," Valerie answers. "To tell you what I saw would be to change what is to come and believe me, the future is bright for you despite the challenges you will face."

"But..." he begins, but I cut him off.

"Thank you, Val. We have to go check on the children. But we will come visit soon."

"Bring them with you when you come," she tells me as she turns and continues to make her way down the hallway.

"What was that all about?" Loukas asks as I tug on his hand and stop at the first classroom, peeking inside, watching as Amelia sits and colors with Aurora.

"Wait until you meet Opal. It's even weirder," I tell him with a smirk.

Checking on both kids doesn't take as long as I expected but by the time we make it back to the vampire portion of the academy, Breanne, Matt, and the kids are waiting for us.

"Aunty Pearl!" The girls exclaim, running toward me. I let go of Loukas' hand, crouching in time to wrap my arms around both of them.

I hear Nora sniffle and I push them back, wiping her tears.

"Hey now. What are those for?"

"I missed you," she says, wrapping her arms around me and nuzzling into my neck.

"What about you? Are you too big to have missed your aunt?" I ask Mak.

"Never," Makayla says, but instead of snuggling into me like her little sister, she remains standing.

"And what about you?" I ask, looking at little Erik in Bree's arms, lifting Nora as I stand and walking toward them.

"Oh, he missed you all right. So much so that I think he needs a full day of Aunty Pearl," Bree says with a smirk.

"He's not sleeping?" I ask, placing Nora on her feet and reaching out, taking Erik from Bree's arms.

"He's cutting teeth again," Matt says, and I place my forehead against Erik's, my magic seeping out of me a little and soothing his newly formed teeth.

A throat clears behind me, and I turn to find Loukas standing behind me.

"Girls, I would like you to meet Loukas, my mate." Both girls have wide eyes, surprise evident. "You didn't tell them?" I ask Bree and Mark.

"No, I thought you'd like to tell them."

"Hi, girls. It's nice to meet you," he says, shaking each girl's hand.

"Are you a mermaid too?" Nora asks while Makayla nudges her with her elbow.

"Sea nymphs."

"Oh right," Nora says with a nod. "Are you a sea nymph too?"

"Nope, I am a shifter," Loukas supplies.

"What kind?" Nora asks and once again her sister nudges her. "That's rude."

Loukas chuckles. "It's okay. I'm an owl shifter."

"That's so cool," They both say.

"All right. Give me my grandbabies," Deb says, walking up and scooping Erik out of my arms.

"Baby stealer," I accuse with a smile on my face.

"Proudly," she declares, snuggling into Erik. "Come girls."

"Wait. Deb, I'd like you to meet my mate, Loukas," I say, stepping back into Loukas' arms.

"Well, it's about time," she says with a smile. "It's very nice to meet you, Loukas. Make sure you take care of our girl, or you'll have a gang of pissed-off supernaturals ready to take you out."

"Mom," Matt warns.

"It's true. We're very fond of Pearl," she says, placing her free hand on the side of my face.

"Aw, Deb, I'm fond of you too. But have no fear, Loukas is a good man."

"He better be," she warns, ushering the girls out the door. "But it is very nice to meet you, Loukas."

"I suppose this is where I say goodbye to you too," Loukas says, turning to me.

I dip my chin in acknowledgement. "It is." I glance around seeing everyone gathered and ready to go.

He pulls me in and merges his lips with mine and I wrap my arms around his neck, pulling him in closer.

"Come home to me."

"Always," I whisper against his mouth.

"I'll take you to the kids and back to the house," Skarlyt says, stepping closer to us. "A few of your parliament have been asking for you."

Loukas nods, stepping back next to Skarlyt. "I love you, Pearl."

"And I you," I tell him and watch as he and Skarlyt disappear.

After getting changed into the leathers that Breanne had waiting for me, I go stand with my assigned group, each of us leaving the office and landing on the sandy beach.

As we approach the abandoned pier where the boat is beached, the rhythmic creaking of the wood beneath our feet seems to echo the tension in the air. The moonlit waves whisper secrets of the impending battle.

The large wooden ship, an ominous silhouette against the night sky, is pushed up onto the sandy beach. Its sails billow in the breeze, an eerie dance that seems to mock the confrontation in our midst. Our group exchange knowing glances, a silent acknowledgment of the dangers that lay ahead.

Despite my argument that the nymphs need to be involved in this rescue, I know they are not the battle-hardened warriors from the other factions. Still, they deserve the opportunity to be part of the rescue. I don't expect bloodshed from any of the nymphs, but I wouldn't be surprised if their hearts had been hardened by the kidnapping of one of their own.

I can hear the soft padding of the wolf shifters' footsteps beside me as we move forward, each step resonating with the collective determination of our motley crew. Sebastyn and the rest of the witches trail behind us, their eyes focused and hands tingling with magical energy.

As we approach the pier's edge, the ship's crew become aware of our presence. Shadows shift on the deck, and the murmur of voices carry across the water. The moment for stealth is over.

"Prepare yourselves," Drake commands in a hushed yet author-itative tone. "We move as one."

The vampires descend upon the ship like shadows. The first cries are heard, and my small group of sea nymphs and shifters make our way toward the ship, our movements coordinated with supernatural precision. A wolf shifter leaps onto the deck, his claws glinting in the moonlight.

As I follow in his wake, I notice that the battle ahead of me already rages on, a symphony of clashes, roars, and incantations that reverberate through the night. The ship's crew, though armed with technology and weapons, are no match for the supernatural might against them.

I slip down below, searching for the location where they are keeping Sky. I slip around the corner and find myself face to face with the man I assume is the ship's captain, a grizzled man with a cruel glint in his eyes. He grips a menacing gun in one hand, and the other is wrapped around Breanne's neck.

"One more step and I blow her brains out," he warns, and I raise my hands in surrender. I catch Breanne's eyes. She gives me a wink, and I keep my face stoic though I want to smile. That's the thing about Breanne, she is a tiny little blonde girl who you would expect to be weak rather than the lethal killing machine she is.

"We just want the man," I tell him.

"The monster, you mean?" he asks, still snarling.

"You would know about monsters, wouldn't you?" I ask with a snarl of my own.

He grips Breanne tighter, and she cries out, though I know it's a jest, still I take a step forward out of instinct.

Because of this, he pushes the gun tighter to Breanne's head.

"Stop moving—"

He doesn't get to finish. Breanne spins with her supernatural speed, snapping his neck in one quick movement.

"Gods, he stinks," Breanne says, wiping off her hands as if she can wipe the stench of him off her.

"You okay?" I ask, stepping up and pulling my magic to my hands, healing the minor bruises she got from his grubby little hands. Of course, they would have healed on their own in time. But now we don't have to wait the hour or so it would take.

"Never better," she responds with a smile, taking my hand and leading us deeper into the boat. When we reach the lowest level of the ship, we are met with a chilling sight—a makeshift holding area where a captive sea nymph languishes in a saltwater-filled tank. His silvery scales with a bright red outline glow faintly in the dim light, and his eyes, filled with a mixture of fear and hope, meet mine.

"Stand back," Breanne commands, and Sky swims back up against the far wall of the tank, slowly, his face contorting in pain with each flick of his tail. Bree's hand snakes out, shattering the glass front of the tank and freeing Sky from his watery prison. Sky, weakened but alive, lands on the ground, his tail slowly separating into two legs. The shift was the most painful thing I've ever seen.

"We're here to help," I reassure him, my voice a soothing melody. "You're safe now."

I reach down, my hands already glowing with my healing magic, and I push it into him. His eyes flutter closed in relief. I push as much of my healing magic into him as I can but it's not enough. Sky falls into unconsciousness, and I slump to the ground, my magic completely depleted.

"Breanne?" Matt calls out just as everything goes black. I realize too late that I gave too much magic.

Chapter Twenty

Loukas

Neither of the kids wants to leave the academy, both preferring to stay and play with their new friends. I don't want to take them away either, but they reluctantly agree with the promise that they can come back tomorrow.

"Where's Pearl?" Zach asks.

"She had to stay and do some stuff for her friends," I respond, and they both nod.

"Daddy. Rora says I can have a sleepover at her house sometime soon," Amelia says excitedly as we make our way back to Pearl's home through the forest.

"Well, I will need to talk to Aurora's parents first," I tell her and smile at the normality of that statement. Never had I dared to hope to be able to have a conversation like this with her. I didn't think that we'd ever be free to live our own lives, let alone for her to make friends.

"What about you Zach? Did you make some friends?"

He nods. "I did. The kids there are really nice."

"I'm glad. What about the classes?" I wait with bated breath as he thinks about his answer.

"To be honest they were a little boring. The things they were teaching I've known for years."

"Not me. I learned all kinds of stuff. And we got to color pictures," Amelia says.

"That's awesome, Pumpkin. And Zach, what if we got you a private teacher for the magic stuff so you can learn new magic."

"Can I still stay in the same class with my new friends?"

"Of course. We may have to talk to the teachers to be sure, but the way it was explained to me, it seems like magic is only a *part* of the schooling."

"That's what Miss. Opal said earlier."

"Opal?" I ask, racking my brain trying to remember where I heard that name before. It was definitely from Pearl. But what did she say?

"She was my teacher for the history of magic. She wears gloves all the time because she said she gets visions when she touches things." That's where I've heard that name. Pearl told me I'd stop thinking Valerie was so strange once I met Opal.

"And did you learn something in her class?"

"Kind of," he says sheepishly.

"What is it?"

"Well, some of the things she taught I have heard before but not in the same way."

"What do you mean?" I ask.

"I know what he means," Amelia says, and I turn to her in question, wondering how she can. "He means when we learned the same things with Mommy's coven, they told the stories different."

"Different how?"

"For starters, the people here pray to the goddess of the moon..." Zach begins.

"So does Ya-Ya and her parliament," I supply, and he nods.

"I know, but when the Daughters of Eris told us stories about her, they were always about how she was such a bad goddess, how she didn't care about any of us and that's why they pray to Eris instead. But the way Opal talks about the Goddess of the Moon, it's like she's a completely different person than what we've been told."

I stop walking, turning to face both my children, crouching down to their level. "You know that most of the things you've learned at your mother's coven aren't..." I struggle to find the words. I know that their mother is a monster. At the end of the day, though, she is still their mother. Despite my feelings about her, I refuse to talk trash about her to her children.

"We know, Dad," Zach says.

"Mommy is not a good person," Amelia says, her voice quiet and shy.

I nod my head. "But she's still your mother."

"I wish she wasn't," Zach mutters under his breath and my heart breaks a little that he feels that way.

I clear my throat, choking down the emotion threatening to spill out at the atrocities committed against my children by their own mother. Maybe it's not the right thing to do, to ignore his statement, but I do, easily changing the subject. "I heard that your Ya-Ya was looking for us."

With thoughts of their mother behind us, I stand, holding out my hands to each of them, which they each take and the three of us continue our walk.

"I like it here, Daddy," Amelia says after a few moments of silence, and I chuckle. That was probably the longest she was able to stand the silence.

"I'm glad," I tell her, squeezing her hand.

"Me too, Dad. I like Pearl too," Zach adds, and I look down at my son, giving his hand a squeeze as well.

"Yeah, Pearl is nice and really pretty. Can I have hair like Pearl when I grow up?" Amelia asks.

"I heard some of the older girls talking about a spell to change their hair color. I can ask Skarlyt to teach me," Zach says, a smile on his face as he looks at his baby sister, I raise my eyebrows in surprise. Of all the things I thought he could possibly say, him offering to learn something from Skarlyt was definitely not one of them.

"Really, Zachy?" Amelia says and he nods. She lets go of my hand and starts clapping excitedly.

"It's not permanent, is it?" I ask.

"I don't think so, the one girl said she changes her hair every week." And with that, Zach starts talking about the other spells he heard kids talking about today, Amelia joining in, telling me about the different things she learned. Despite saying the classes were boring, it seems he learned some things from the other kids. I allow myself a minute to imagine that this is how our life always has been. That we've walked home from school each day, talking about what they've learned. That their days were full of laughter and love. When the first homes come into view, I let go of their hands and wipe the tears from my cheeks.

"Ya-Ya!" Amelia exclaims, releasing my hand and running into my mother's open arms.

I glance down at Zach. "You're not too old to still want a hug from your Ya-Ya, are you?" He looks up at me, biting his lower lip but only for a moment before he releases my hand and runs to his Ya-Ya, creating an Amelia sandwich. The sight in front of me makes tears threaten to spill out once more but I blink them back.

"And where have you guys been?" she asks them as she looks behind me. "And where's Pearl?"

"Nice to see you too, Ma," I tell her. She pins me with her 'are you kidding' look making me chuckle. "Pearl and I took these two munchkins to tour the academy and then she had to go," I tell her with a look trying to convey that I'll explain it away from the kids. I know that they know a little of the situation just from being around, but I still don't need them worrying right now.

"All right then. Guess we'll go check in with the parliament. You two run along," she says, shooing the kids off ahead of us. "Now tell me what's going on?"

"A member of Pearl's pod was captured by humans." She sucks in a breath, her hand going to her chest. "So, she, along with a large number of other supernaturals that live here, have gone on a rescue mission."

"And you didn't go with her?" she asks, a little accusatory.

"We agreed that because we just got here, and with everything that's happened, it would be best if I stayed with the kids."

She dips her chin in understanding, linking her arm with mine. "You know, when Pearl showed up to convince us to come here, I thought for sure it was a trick. I mean when was the last time you met anyone who cared about someone other than themselves? And then, seeing Amelia with her and the King of Dragons."

"Andres," I supply.

"Andres, I still thought that it was too good to be true. Sure, they might take us to a safe island, but they had to expect something from us. But then, we got here, and not only is it beautiful and safe, but the amount of people who have been coming and offering us assistance in getting settled is astounding." As she talks, I glance around recognizing members of our parliament working on building homes for us, but not only them. Mixed in with the familiar faces are new ones. People I've never met, people my family and friends have never met, are walking around, swinging hammers, lifting beams, handing out food. And as I catch the eyes of my parliament, each one bows their head slightly in submission.

"Why did they want me in charge? I've been gone for so long..."

She stops, pulling me to stop in front of her, this little slip of a woman with the same hair and eyes as my own. "You were only gone to protect us. Everyone knows that."

"But if it wasn't for me, Dad..." I begin, never having the courage to bring it up to my mother. I never wanted to put a damper on the limited time we had together.

She takes my face in her hands. "Your dad would be so proud of you and the man you've become. He would've willingly given his life to see this day come to pass. Don't for a second blame yourself. The blame lies solely with that monster."

"But ma, that's the thing," I begin, placing my hands on hers and holding them out in front of us, "That monster wouldn't have known anything about us or where we lived if it wasn't for me."

My mother opens her mouth to say something, probably to tell me once more how the entire situation is not my fault, but she doesn't get the chance.

"Loukas," Skarlyt calls out, running over to us.

"Skarlyt? What's wrong? Is it Pearl?"

She shakes her head. "No. It's the Daughters of Eris."

My mom hisses out a breath at the name of Antonia's coven, hating them as much as I do.

"What about them?"

"They're attacking the pack in Parry Sound where we found you," she says, the words coming out rushed.

"But how?" I ask, looking around as if Antonia is going to jump out from behind a tree and take me back.

"I don't know, but she's saying you're the only person she'll talk to..." I look at my mother and back to Skarlyt. I am ready to tell her that I would die a happy man if I never had to see that woman again, but she isn't done. "Loukas—I'm sorry—"

"What is it?"

"She has hostages."

That one word changes everything; I turn to my mom.

"Take care of the kids, I have to go."

My mom grips my hands tighter as if she can keep me here. "Let someone else go. Please," she begs, placing her hands on my face, tears streaming down her own. "I just got you back. If you go to her again, I'll lose you forever, I just know it."

"Ma. I can't just leave them to clean up my mess," I tell her, gently removing her hands from my face and reaching up to wipe the tears from her cheeks. "Please take care of the kids." I don't wait for her to answer, letting go of her hands and reaching out to Skarlyt.

Just like the first time I teleported, when we arrive, I'm a little woozy, but it passes quickly. "She grabbed two children on their way home from school before they crossed the boundary," Skarlyt begins to fill me in as we walk. "She can't get onto pack lands because of that boundary, and despite having the children hostage, they're not tied into the spell so they can't act as a bridge between the two."

"Why doesn't the pack here live on the island with you?" I ask, keeping up with her, the faint sounds of snarls beginning to float through the air.

"The people here are the ones who didn't want to leave society and Aryn and Lucien have graciously agreed to be the go-between. It's become sort of a waypoint for supernaturals in need of rescue. Besides, it's our main source of income. The humans rent out cabins at the three resorts surrounding pack land yearly and pay very well."

"Wait," A blonde woman says, materializing in front of the two of us.

"Opal? What are you doing here?" Skarlyt asks, stepping closer to her.

Opal leans over whispering something in Skarlyt's ear, the latter sneaking looks of concern at me as she does before stepping back and letting Opal walk closer to me.

"I know you and I have never met, but I need you to listen to me."

"Okay..."

She closes her blue eyes and takes a deep breath. When she speaks, her voice takes on a more ethereal air.

"Beware the siren's call that echoes through the labyrinth of compromise. Shadows may whisper the allure of sacrifice, but within the dance of negotiation, guard the sacred ember of self. For in the hostage's ransom, the true cost might be your own liberation."

She doesn't wait for a response, disappearing before my eyes, leaving me standing in the middle of an unfamiliar forest wondering what the fuck she was talking about.

"Did you understand any of that?" I ask Skarlyt.

"You'll know what she meant when the time is right."

"How will I know when the time is right?" I question, as she begins to walk toward the snarls once more, following behind her.

"Trust me. You'll know," she says, giving me a pointed look that tells me she definitely knows more than what she's saying.

"Just send the children back to us and leave. No one needs to get hurt." I recognize Aryn's voice.

"I already told you. I will only speak with Loukas. I know he's here. That you're harboring him," Antonia sneers.

"I'm here," I call out, making my way through the trees, stopping short when I see Antonia, along with a good portion of her coven spread out around her. It's the two children, both close to Zach's age, that Anthony and Roman have restrained with their magic that make my heart race. Their eyes are wide with fear, tears streaming down their faces. "Let them go."

"There you are, my pet," Antonia purrs, walking close to where I'm assuming the barrier is but not crossing. "I'll let them go when you and my children are back where you belong."

I place one foot in front of the other, a tremble in my step at the memories of what this monster has done to me in the past. What she's done to our children, but still, I keep placing one foot in front of the other, raising my chin in defiance until I am close enough that I don't need to shout.

"You will never see *my* children again."

My owl flaps his wings, begging to be let out, to take out the demon that's haunted us for years.

"Then I guess I don't need these children anymore," she says, looking over at her brother and mate.

"Stop," I demand, stepping even closer as the children begin to thrash against the magic. "What do you want?"

"You already know what I want, pet," she says, raising her hand to stop the two men from injuring the kids further.

"I will never give Zach or Amelia to you," I spit.

She waves her hand dismissively. "Amelia is of no use to me now that she's proved to be unworthy of magic and Zach..." The way she says his name lets me know exactly what she truly thinks of him. "Despite his unique magic, he has the wrong anatomy to be useful to me."

"But you said..." I begin and she smiles that evil smile, rotating her wrist slowly, merging her magic with that of Anthony's, the bigger of the boys thrashing wildly. "Stop. I'll give you anything. Anything except Zach and Amelia."

Her hand freezes once more, turning that smile on me. She's got me exactly where she wants me.

"You will come with me."

I look back at Skarlyt, then over to the kids.

"I'm sorry, Pearl," I whisper lightly, hoping that the sound travels on the wind to her, wherever she may be. "Okay."

"Don't do this," Skarlyt says, walking up to me.

I turn and whisper in her ear. "She won't want me once she learns I'm mated to Pearl. Just get the kids to safety."

"But..." she begins but stops herself when she sees my resolve and disappears, leaving me standing alone.

"Beware the siren's call that echoes through the labyrinth of compromise. Shadows may whisper the allure of sacrifice, but within the dance of negotiation, guard the sacred ember of self. For in the hostage's ransom, the true cost might be your own liberation."

When I try to recall Opal's words, they come back with shocking clarity. As I repeat the words, I can admit that it could mean Antonia doesn't plan on keeping her side of the bargain. Even then...I turn and look back at the two children who are stranded on the unprotected side of the pack's barrier and then over to the two couples who must be their parents. All four parents are being held back by their friends and family. I know full well that if I was one of those parents, I would want anyone with a chance to save them to try.

"Come now, pet, or have you replaced me so quickly?" Antonia sneers, "Though you could've at least traded up, not down." The insult is meant for Skarlyt, but she's already long gone.

"Let them go, and I'll cross," I tell her, stepping closer to the barrier.

"How do I know you will actually cross?"

"I swear to the Goddess of the Moon, that I will cross this barrier to you at the same moment the children do."

Antonia raises an eyebrow at my mention of Mother Moon, but nods her head, looking over at her brother and mate who slowly release their hold on the children.

Chapter Twenty-One

Pearl

"Pearl!" A voice shouts and a stinging pain in my cheek makes my eyes fly open.

"Skar?"

"We have to go," she says, but for some reason, she's not just teleporting me away.

"Go where? What happened? Is everyone all right?"

"Everyone here is fine."

"Loukas? Amelia? Zach?" I ask.

"Zach and Amelia are fine," she replies, and I place my hands on the ground beside me, pushing myself up, or trying to, my arms are weak.

"You used too much magic trying to heal Sky," Breanne says from behind me, and I whip my head around to look at her, cursing myself for doing so as it begins to swim.

"That's why I haven't teleported us yet. I need you to be at full strength when we get there."

"Get where?" I ask, sitting back down and putting my head in my hands.

I look up in time to see Skarlyt and Breanne share a look.

"What? What happened?"

"Antonia attacked Aryn and Lucien's pack, taking two of their children. Loukas was going to sacrifice himself for them when I left. That's why I need you. I need you to convince him not to."

Panic begins to set in at her words and despite my wooziness, I stand. "Take me now."

Skarlyt shakes her head. "I don't think you have enough magic just yet."

I spin and look at Breanne. "Give me some of your blood."

"What?" she asks, horror on her face. She's offered me blood what must be hundreds of times when I was injured in battle because of its healing properties. But each time I turned her down, explaining the addictiveness that vampire blood has on sea nymphs. Because we are healers by nature and the main thing that vampire blood does for other supernaturals is heal, sea nymphs are extremely susceptible to becoming addicted.

"I need it," I plead, walking closer to her.

"I'll give you some," Rayne supplies, stepping closer to us.

"No," Both Breanne and I exclaim at the same time, making Rayne's eyes widen and step back.

"No offense, Rayne. But vampire blood is already addictive to my kind. If I had vampire blood laced with that of a goddess..." I let the possibilities hang in the air. She raises her hands and steps back.

"Are you sure?" Breanne asks, already pulling out one of her blades.

"I am. He's my mate and he needs me. Just promise me never again."

"I can't promise you that," she says, staying her knife. "If you truly need it, you know I won't be able to say no. What if you are dying and it's the only way to save you?"

I let out a sigh. "Fine. Only in life-or-death situations."

"Deal," she says, sliding the knife down her wrist and holding it up to my mouth. My gums ache, my teeth shifting into razor-sharp points as the smell of her sweet blood taints the air. I latch on quickly, the coppery taste of her sliding down my throat, filling me up, the power spreading through every nerve ending in my body until I feel like I can take on the world. But even then, I don't stop gulping.

Not when she tells me that's enough.

Not when Matt tries to pry me away.

It's not until Rayne slices my leg with a blade of her own that I release Breanne's arm, spinning to hiss at Rayne.

"Yeah, you're angry," Skarlyt says. "Use that."

She grips both Rayne and me by the arms and teleports us away. I'm still hissing and snarling at Rayne when we land in the middle of a familiar forest.

"Pearl. Loukas is over there."

At the mention of his name, some of the fog lifts from my brain. All thoughts of getting some more of Breanne's blood fade as I swing my gaze toward my mate. With my extra little boost in power, I notice a few things very quickly.

First is that my mate is walking away from everyone and toward who I can only assume is Antonia and her cronies. The wicked smile on her red-painted lips tells me she's getting exactly what she wants while everyone else behind him is just letting him go.

Next, there are two small children running full tilt toward the barrier and the pack. I wait until their little feet are firmly on our side before calling out.

"Stop!" I command, my attention going right back to Loukas.

He spins, his eyes going wide as I begin to walk forward.

"Pearl," he whispers.

"A deal is a deal, pet. You swore an oath to your goddess. What would she think of you breaking it now?" Antonia sneers.

"I wouldn't worry about her," Rayne says, waving off the monster of a woman.

"And who are you?" Antonia asks, focusing her attention on the snarky hunter and me.

"Who am I?" Rayne asks, going into performance mode. I'd roll my eyes if I wasn't going to enjoy this. "I am the granddaughter of Artemis, the Goddess of the Moon you were just talking about. I'm also a vampire and a hell of a fighter, but it's not me you should be worried about."

A few gasps go around Antonia's coven, but surprisingly she keeps her cool.

"I'm not *worried* about anyone," she declares loudly. "Who exactly do you believe I should be *worried* about?"

"She means me," I declare.

"You?" Antonia says, mocking in her tone, and a smile on her face as she looks me up and down.

I nod my head. I am not the showman Rayne is. I have nothing to prove to this woman.

"Why would I be concerned about you? You're nothing but a *mermaid*. What are you going to do? Sing me to death? I don't see any water around here for you to fight me in." She laughs as she talks, the rest of her coven joining in. "Come now, pet," she coos to Loukas, reaching out a hand for him.

"If you lay one finger on my *mate*, it'll be the last thing you ever do." I step forward, nuzzling into Loukas' side as I finally reach him.

"Mate?" she questions, looking back and forth between the two of us.

"Antonia. I'd like you to meet my mate, Pearl. My *true mate* that is," Loukas says, finally getting over the shock of me showing up here.

"What? How?" she sputters before ending in a deep scowl.

"This is a farce," she says, pointing her bony finger at me. "He knows he's mine!"

A tall man walks over to her, rubbing her arms up and down, obviously trying to soothe her.

"Looks like you have a mate of your own to worry about. Why don't you go obsess over him and leave mine alone," I tell her, still feeling like I could take on the world and win.

"Why, you little," she says through clenched teeth. She flings herself toward me but is stopped by the pack's barrier. "I'll get him one way or another. He was mine first and always will be mine. I can wait forever. I can take as many children as I need until he decides to come back to me, and he *will* come back to me."

I don't get the chance to say anything. The next thing I know, a blur races past me. Before I can make out the form of Rayne running a blade through Antonia's throat, she's already coming back to stand beside me.

I glance over at Rayne as she wipes the blood off her knife.

"What? She just threatened to kidnap as many children as she wanted to get him back. You should be thanking me."

I look back at Antonia, watching as she desperately tries to stop the blood flowing out of her throat. What surprises me is that not a single person, except a man who I assume is her brother, rushes toward her.

"Come on. Help her. She's your high priestess," he cries, his magic rising to try and heal her, but it doesn't work like that.

"He's also going to hold a grudge," Loukas whispers to Rayne, and I shoot him a pointed look. "What? If he is alive, he will always want revenge. We will have to look over our shoulders for the rest of our lives."

I glance over at Rayne who raises a brow in question before looking at Antonia and her brother. Anthony is glaring at Loukas and me with blind rage in his eyes.

"Do it," I tell Rayne.

She doesn't wait, just blurs forward, sliding the blade of her knife across his neck as well, leaving them both bleeding to death in front of us.

"You all are free to leave as long as you make a vow to leave us in peace," Loukas says, stepping forward.

"Our fight was never with you, Loukas. We were just following the orders of our high priestess," One of the women says, stepping forward.

"Then I suggest you get a new high priestess," Skarlyt says. "And like Loukas said, you are free to leave. But first I need you each to make a magical vow that you will not get revenge for the death of your high priestess or her brother."

Murmurs go around through the members of Antonia's coven, but one by one, they all step up, clasping Skarlyt's arm and vowing never to take revenge.

The more time that goes by, the more my magic replenishes itself, until it begins fighting against the vampire blood, absorbing it from my body. As the seconds pass by, my gums begin to ache, my body begins to shake and sweat starts to pour down my face. I glance around, not understanding what's happening to me, but when my gaze lands on Rayne, it's like a switch goes off in my brain telling me that she has what I need to feel better.

I rush toward her with a speed that I know I don't possess, opening my mouth wide, my teeth already having shifted, ready to take a bite out of her. Luckily, being the trained warrior that she is, Rayne is able to grasp me by the neck and slam me down on my back, straddling my legs. And still, I snap my teeth at her, trying to get a drop of that golden blood. I feel like I'm having an out-of-body experience. I know that what I'm doing is certifiably insane, but I am powerless to stop it. Nothing will stop it except some of Rayne's blood.

"What's wrong with her?" Loukas asks, his voice full of concern. I want to reach out to him and reassure him that I'm fine.

That everything is going to be okay, but I can't even make my eyes move from the slow pulsing in Rayne's neck like a siren's song, calling to me.

"I don't know," Rayne responds, the little veins in her neck pulsing harder as she moves her mouth. "It looks like bloodlust."

I buck my hips upward trying to dislodge her, but she holds firm.

"It can't be. Right?" Skarlyt asks, looking around.

Rayne looks down at me, now pinning my hands to my chest with one arm and still squeezing my throat with the other. "Come back to us Pearl," she says, her voice pleading in a way I've never heard before. I desperately want to listen to her, to open my mouth and not want to eat her face off. But I can't. Every fiber of my being wants to devour Rayne and not in a sexy way either.

"Pearl? Baby?" Loukas says, moving into view but I ignore him, my eyes on my prize and not willing to look anywhere else.

"Breanne is going to be so pissed," Rayne mutters under her breath, stealing a look of pity with me. Just from those words alone, I want to stop behaving this way. If I hurt someone, she is going to blame herself for giving me her blood no matter if I asked her for it or not.

"Artemis!" Rayne yells as I thrash harder, faster, stronger than I was before knowing that if she is successful in calling the goddess, the chances of me getting the sweet nectar are gone. "Hold her legs," Rayne says to someone as I kick hard enough to raise both Rayne and me off the ground, twisting my body and almost gaining my freedom.

"Artemis! Get down here, you old bag."

"Who are you calling old, Spawn?" Artemis says with a snarl, obviously expecting the normally witty banter that she and Rayne love so much yet pretend to hate.

"Oh, what happened?" she asks, rushing over and placing a glowing hand on my forehead.

The red haze burning in my veins lessens a bit, and I watch as Artemis looks at her granddaughter with the most fury I've ever seen.

"Who?" she demands, her voice no longer soft and melodic, but hard and powerful.

"Don't blame her," I say through clenched teeth, strong enough to keep the urges at bay. Rayne, seeing that I am semi-lucid, loosens her grip but I shake my head. "Don't let go."

"I don't understand. I didn't know this would happen," Rayne says, her voice the smallest I've ever heard. Normally she's the larger-than-life, kick-ass, takes-no-shit hunter, but right now she seems so small.

"Did she drink from you?" Artemis asks, looking at Rayne who shakes her head. "Good." Artie follows up with a heavy sigh of relief.

"Can. You. Fix. Me?" I ask, the words getting harder to force out, the *need* ramping up once more.

"How much did she drink?" Ignoring me, Artemis pins Rayne with her stare.

"A lot." Is all she says, never taking her eyes from mine.

"Nobody touch her except Rayne," she says and I feel Loukas and Skarlyt remove their hands from my body as the haze ramps up, my body beginning to thrash involuntarily. "This is going to hurt, my sweet girl." That's the only warning I get as she moves above my head and places glowing orbs for hands on each of my temples.

I scream out, my back arching off the ground, pain like I've never felt before rushing through my body. It feels like my blood is on fire. Both my magic and the vampire blood are stripped as her magic spreads.

"Almost there, sweetling. Just a little more," Artemis coos. Instead of feeling relief, the burning seems to get worse for a few beats. It builds to so much pain that I can't even scream out anymore.

As if by magic—and I guess it was—the pain disappears instantly along with all my magic that had been replenished. I panic for a moment, worried that along with the vampire blood, she burned up all my magic, but when I search inside me for that green well, I find it deep in my chest, flickering lightly, dormant, almost asleep.

"She's okay now. You can let her go," Artemis says and I feel the pressure fall off my throat.

"Thank you," I manage to croak out, my voice hoarse and throat dry. I guess I was screaming more than I thought.

"You're welcome, sweetling. But promise me you will *never* give in to temptation again. Thanks to my granddaughter, you didn't hurt anyone *this time*. If she wasn't here..."

I nod my head.

"I don't understand. What just happened?" Loukas says, stepping up behind Rayne and helping her up while Artemis slowly lifts my back off the hard ground, sitting me up.

"I depleted my magic saving Sky after we got him free, and I passed out."

"What?" Loukas demands, moving forward and pulling me up into his arms.

I ignore his question and keep going because the reality of what I did, of what I witnessed. Of what I allowed to—asked to—happen here begins to set in.

"I woke to Skarlyt telling me that you were going to trade yourself to Antonia and I knew I couldn't let that happen, so I drank from Breanne."

His brows furrow. "I don't understand. Why is that a bad thing? Vampire blood has healing properties, doesn't it? Shouldn't it have helped?" he asks, looking around.

Luckily, Artemis takes pity and answers for me.

"In all supernaturals and humans, yes, that's correct. A drop of vampire blood can speed up the healing process, even help magic manifest faster, well all supernaturals except sea nymphs." Loukas looks at me, pulling me into his chest. "Because sea nymphs, in their natural form, are blood drinkers already, eating fresh, uncooked meat directly from the source, vampire blood has a different reaction..."

"It causes a bloodlust?" Rayne asks.

"Of a sort," Her grandmother answers, coming over and running her hand over my hair, pulling it off my face where it's sticking from the sweat. "When they initially drink, they're fine. Better than fine. They're stronger, faster, and their magic replenishes quickly. But once their magic well is full once more, it tries to get rid of the invading blood, creating a war of sorts inside their bodies."

"What?" Rayne asks in horror, looking at me. I try to plead with my eyes that I didn't know. "But Pearl said it was just addictive."

Artemis nods. "It is. Because her magic and the vampire blood were at war with one another inside her body, it depleted both just as quickly as she received it and the only way her body knew how to replace it quickly was to get more. The more she ingested, the more she would need the next time and the next time. Always searching for her next meal. Becoming the vampires of legends that destroyed entire villages in a single night. Always thirsty and never satisfied, much like a human with an addiction, always chasing a high."

"Oh shit," Skarlyt says.

"My sentiments exactly. Fortunately, I was able to burn all of the toxins from Pearl's blood. She will be weak for a few days and sleep a lot, but she will recover."

"What about the addictiveness?" Loukas asks.

"She shouldn't crave any vampire blood now. But it might be

best to keep Bree and the kids away from her for a little while."
Artemis gives me a look of sympathy.

A sob breaks free from my throat at the knowledge that I could
possibly hurt any of them. "I just want to go home." I cry into
Loukas' chest not wanting to hear any more.

"You'll be okay, sweetling. I'll come to check on you in a
couple of days," Artemis says, placing a soft kiss on my head, and
the next thing I know I'm laying on something soft with Loukas'
strong arms surrounding me.

"I'm so sorry," I cry, all the walls I built up over the last five
years crumbling to the ground with a bang as I let in the visions of
what happened while I had Breanne's blood running through my
veins.

*Antonia lying on the ground, covering her throat with her
hands, thick red blood pouring out from between her fingers.*

Looking at Rayne and encouraging her to kill Anthony.

*Watching with a satisfied feeling as he falls to his knees, blood
pooling on the ground beneath him as he reaches for his sister,
falling just short of touching her.*

Attacking Rayne. Wanting nothing more than to drain her dry.

I cry on Loukas' chest until I fall asleep, and even then, the
visions haunt me.

Chapter Twenty-Two

Loukas

This is not how I thought tonight was going to go.

I was resigned to my fate. Resigned to give myself up to Antonia in exchange for those children. When Pearl showed up, I let out the breath I was holding, knowing that with her by my side, there is nothing we can't accomplish together. Luckily, Antonia kept her word and let the kids go, allowing them to reunite with their parents before Pearl showed up, probably thinking that I would never go back on my word. Because normally I wouldn't, not when there was the possibility that she could simply lie in wait for the next opportunity to grab a hostage.

But I have to say, defeating both Antonia and Anthony seemed almost too easy. Like their quick deaths were too good for them, but the feeling of finally being free was exquisite. Until it wasn't...

Until I watched the woman I love try to kill one of her friends for a drop of blood, and then watched, helpless, as she writhed in pain on the dirt-covered ground. And again, as a literal goddess descended from the heavens to come to her aide.

I'm still in shock at that. I believed Pearl when she told me she'd met Artemis. I did. But there was still a part of me that didn't truly *believe* until I saw her with my own two eyes.

Pearl whimpers in her sleep, and I tug her petite frame into me, rubbing soothing circles on her back. I should've noticed something was wrong when she readily agreed to killing Anthony. My mate being the sweet, gentle woman that she is, would've tried to find another way. But at the time, I was only thinking of myself and of the revenge I could get on my tormentors. Not of the consequences. Not even just with Pearl. But with Zach and Amelia too.

How am I supposed to tell them that their mother is dead? That she was killed trying to take me back? That I watched with a smile on my face as the blood was freed from her body and the light in her eyes went out?

Loukas? My mom surprises me by speaking through our mental link.

I'm here, I tell her, feeling her getting closer to the house.

Skarlyt came and explained. The kids want to grab a few things and are going to sleep at my place tonight.

She doesn't phrase it as a question. Instead, she is stating a fact, giving me no room for argument. As much as I want my children under the same roof as me—especially after today—I know that Pearl needs to come first right now, though she'd disagree.

Do they know about... I begin, unable to say that monster's name.

No. That will be a conversation that you can have with them when Pearl is better.

I breathe out a sigh of relief. I wouldn't think that I would feel relieved to have to be the one to tell them about Antonia, but the fact that they don't know yet is what relieves me. At least for tonight, they can pretend that all is right in their world.

Thank you. I'll come and meet you at the door. I place a soft kiss on Pearl's head and nudge her over gently.

She hiccups in her sleep, the aftershocks of crying so hard and for so long. I pull the covers up, tucking her in before heading out the door.

I step out onto the porch in time for a little girl to come flying up the stairs and launch herself at me.

"Daddy!"

I wrap my arms around her, pulling her tight and then reaching out and pulling Zach in as well when he gets closer.

I hug them to me tightly, not realizing how much I needed to feel them safe in my arms.

"Are you okay, Dad?" Zach asks, trying to pull back, but I don't let him. He tenses up for only a moment before he seems to realize that I just need to hold them. Even Amelia isn't trying to talk up a storm, instead, snuggling her head into my chest.

I look up at my mom, tears streaking down my cheeks. Not at the fact that Antonia is dead. But at the thought of having to break my children's hearts. She may have been a monster and a horrible mother. But she was still that... Their mother. And no matter how horrible she may have been, they still loved her as much as they could have. And I'm sure she loved them... in her own way.

My mom walks over to me, wiping the tears from my eyes.

It will be okay, my boy, she promises through our link.

How do you know?

She crouches down, putting her finger under my chin.

Because the three of you are here. You are free and you are safe.

But what if they hate me for letting their mother die? I ask.

My boy. Feel the way they cling to you. The way their hearts beat in time with yours. You see them, but you do not truly see. She wipes more tears from my cheeks. *They could never hate you.*

A sob escapes me at her words. "Daddy?" Amelia's soft voice calls to me, leaning her little head back to get a look at my face. "Don't cry. We won't sleep at Ya-Ya's if it's going to make you cry."

"I'm not crying because you're sleeping at Ya-Ya's. I think it's great that you get to spend time with her," I tell her, forcing a smile on my face as I look at them both.

"Then why are you crying, Daddy?"

"Because we're safe. Because we're together. Because I love you both so much it hurts sometimes," I tell her, pulling her back into my arms. Zach, who sees entirely too much isn't convinced by my words, I can tell by the look on his face. But he also doesn't say anything. Choosing to remain silent and trusting me to tell him when the time is right. Or at least I hope that's the reason.

"Where's Pearl?" he asks, looking inside the house over my shoulder.

"She's sleeping. She got hurt earlier so she needs to sleep and heal for a little while."

"She's okay, right?" he asks, making my smile wider and more real at his concern.

"She will be. Now come on, you guys need to at least grab some pj's if you're going to sleep at Ya-Ya's." The four of us walk through the house in relative silence, both kids shooting concerned glances toward the closed bedroom door that Pearl is sleeping behind.

After gathering some of their clothes, I walk them to the door. "You two be good for your Ya-Ya and I'll see you in the morning. I'll make pancakes."

"Can we try different kinds tomorrow too?" Zach asks, seeming to see that I need normal conversation.

"If we have the ingredients," I agree.

"We will bring some stuff when we come back in the morning," My mom says, earning a smile from both the kids.

Amelia jumps up, wrapping her arms around my neck. "Good night, Daddy."

"Good night, Pumpkin. I love you," I tell her, setting her down and turning to Zach. "You too, my little man."

Surprisingly, he rushes forward, wraps his little arms around my waist, and buries his face in my chest. "Love you, Dad."

"And I love you." He lingers with his arms around my waist, and I squeeze him tighter. I love both my children equally, but I've been separated from Zach for much longer than I was Amelia, and I don't want to take a second of his love for granted. Especially not with what I have to tell him.

"All right, *mikrés agápes*. Time to go," my mother says, and I place one last kiss on the top of each of their heads, watching as they walk hand in hand with my mother to her new home.

Thank you, I link to my mom. She glances back.

It's my pleasure.

Knowing that they're safe for the night, I walk back inside, climb into bed, and pull a mewling Pearl into my arms. She lets out a relaxing breath as I do, snuggling deeper into me and I follow her into sleep, hoping that her dreams are better than mine.

* * *

I wake to a small body trying to escape my grip, and I crack an eye open.

"Good morning, *agapi mou*."

She blinks up at me, her eyes widening when she sees me looking down at her but only for a moment. She dips her head down, trying to hide her face from me.

"Hey. Don't do that," I tell her, placing my finger under her chin. Her eyes still don't meet mine. "Talk to me," I plead.

Her big, aquamarine eyes finally rise up to greet mine.

"I'm sorry." The words are barely out of her mouth as the tears start flowing and sobs begin to wrack her body.

I pull her close, rubbing her back and letting her cry.

"Pearl?" I say and wait until she pulls back, using her shirt to wipe the tears from her eyes.

"I'll understand if you want to reject me." She sniffles.

"Reject you?" I say, leaning back. "Why would I ever do that?"

"Because I drank vampire blood. Because I got the mother of your children killed. Because instead of choosing mercy, I chose more bloodshed. Because I tried to kill one of my best friends for a single drop of her blood. Because I am now a danger to..." A sob cuts her off and I lean in to comfort her, but she puts her hand up, stopping me. "Because I am now a danger to some of the people that I love most in the entire world." She grips my shirt. "I can't hurt them," she begs. "Please don't let me hurt them."

"Shh," I say, pulling her to me despite her protests. "First of all, you drank the vampire blood to save me. If you hadn't, I don't know whether I would've been able to hug my children again or see your beautiful face." I place a soft kiss on each of her cheeks. "Second, and this is very important." I wait until she looks up at my eyes so that she can see the truth. "If Antonia lived, she would never stop hunting us. We would have to look over our shoulders for the rest of our lives. Zach and Amelia would never be safe."

"But her brother didn't..."

"Yes, he did. Who do you think gave Zach that black eye?" I ask, and she sucks in a breath. "He was Antonia's weapon. He carried out her every whim because he enjoyed it. He got off on inflicting pain on others. If he had lived, he would hunt us just the same, wanting revenge for his sister."

"But..."

"No. It's the truth. And you didn't know how the vampire blood was going to affect you. I believe that if you had, you wouldn't have taken that chance."

"That's the thing." She sniffs, whipping her nose on the sleeve of her arm. "I want to say that I wouldn't. That I would've found another way. But if the choice was to allow her to take you or become a mindless beast." She doesn't finish, she doesn't need to.

"You have to know I wouldn't want that."

She nods, "I do. But I also know that I wouldn't be able to stand the thought of what she..."

"I know, *agapi mou*," I say, pulling her back into me. "You sacrificed so much for my freedom, and for that I'll be eternally grateful."

"You don't want to reject me?"

"Never," I declare; there is no hesitation.

"What if I hurt Br..."

"You won't," I proclaim. "You would never hurt them and until you're sure of that yourself, I'll be right beside you."

"How can you be sure?"

"Because I know how much you love those kids, even if you felt the urge, you'd remove yourself from the situation before you could hurt them." She opens her mouth to protest, but I place my hand on her lips. "Besides, I'll be with you every step of the way."

"I feel like I'm no longer the person I've strived to be over the last five years. The person I've made myself be, someone who is strong. Someone who is not broken..."

"You are not broken," I say with a growl. "You're the strongest woman I know. You've survived so much, yet you still have a heart of gold."

"But I just stood there as Rayne killed them."

"If she didn't. I would have," I state adamantly. She looks at me and I worry for a minute that she's going to look at me differently because of that. Instead, she wipes off her face and merges her lips with mine. It's a sweet kiss, full of love.

"Come on, let's get you cleaned up, the kids will be back soon." At my mention of the kids, her eyes go wide with fear.

"What if they hate me?"

"Now you listen to me," I say taking her face in my hands and taking a page out of my mom's book. "They won't hate you. I'm not going to lie and say that I'm not worried about what they are going to think when we tell them, but I trust that the relief of being free is going to outweigh the fact that their mom is gone."

I don't give her any room to argue, instead, I pick her up in my arms and lead her into the tub. I groan internally at the sight of her naked body, wanting nothing more than to ravage her and spend the day worshiping her like the goddess that she is, but that's not what she needs from me right now. What she needs is for me to be strong and to take care of her, so that's what I do. I gently wash her hair first, taking care to rinse all the shampoo and conditioner out before taking the loofah and washing all the dirt from her body. As I start to notice her body relax, I take this moment to scoot out and grab some clothes.

"Daddy?" I hear Amelia's little voice call out as I pull up my pants.

"Be right out, Pumpkin," I say, turning to look at Pearl as she steps out of the bathroom and stares at her clothes laid out on the bed, with a faraway look on her face.

"I'm going to go start breakfast, take your time," I tell her, lifting her face and placing a soft kiss on her lips. I wait until she nods before heading out of the bedroom and into the main area of the house.

I stop short at seeing Rayne sitting at the breakfast bar with both Zach and Amelia. She stands walking to me. "How is she?"

"She'll be okay," I respond, knowing that it's the truth. "What are you doing here?" I say but then realize how rude that sounds so quickly add, "Not that you're not welcome it's just..."

"I wanted to check on Pearl and I thought I should be here when you tell them," she says, glancing back at Zach and Amelia.

I dip my chin in thanks, squeezing her arm. "What about Pearl? Artemis said..." I begin but she cuts me off.

"If I know Pearl, she's going to need me here. Plus, I don't agree with Artemis. I think that in order to overcome it, Pearl needs to be near vampires otherwise she will never be in the same room as one again out of fear that she will hurt one of us and that wouldn't only destroy her, but Breanne and the kids as well." I don't disagree with her logic despite not enjoying going against the wishes of a literal goddess. "Besides, I can handle Pearl," she says with a wink.

"If you're sure," I say glancing back at the room.

"I am," she declares, the two of us walking over to the living room.

"Zach? Amelia? Can you two come sit down for a minute?" I ask. They both glance at each other, then at my mom, and then at me before coming to sit down. Zach sneaks wary glances at Rayne.

"Is everything okay?" he asks, and I shake my head. I look back at the door, wishing Pearl could be here for this conversation, but feeling that it might not be what's best for her right now. I don't want her to have to pretend to be okay for them. I want her to be able to take the time she needs and forcing her here for this conversation definitely won't allow that.

"It's about your mother," I state, and both of their eyes widen with fear, Zach placing an arm around a shaking Amelia and pulling her close.

"We don't have to go back there, right Daddy?" she asks, her voice trembling.

"No. She's..." I pause, looking up at my mom, unsure how to proceed.

Don't drag it out. Rip it off like a Band-Aid.

I nod at her words through our link.

"She's dead."

Amelia's little shoulders release the tension she was holding but begin to shake as tears stream down her face.

"How?" Zach asks, his face void of much emotion.

Once again, I look up at my mom, this time she just gives me a nod of encouragement.

"She was killed because she was trying to get us back."

"Who killed her?" he asks, and I don't get the chance to respond.

"I did," Rayne declares. "And her brother."

Zach sucks in a breath, and Amelia's tears flow faster.

"Good," he says, though a lone tear slips down his face.

Rayne walks around and sits on the coffee table facing them. Neither of them pulls away as she approaches.

"I'm not sorry for killing them, but I am sorry for the pain it's causing you."

"It's not causing me pain," Zach declares, his eyes hard but filling up with tears.

"Yes, it is," Rayne says, her tenderness surprising me. "Even if it's just that it hurts to watch your little sister be sad."

Zach looks down at Amelia, his eyes softening as she cries.

"I know mommy was mean ..." Amelia begins.

"It's okay to miss someone who was cruel to you. Even though she wasn't a nice person, she was still your mother and you loved her," Rayne says and Zach scoffs.

"Rayne's right," I add.

"My dad was a bad man," Rayne admits. "He did horrible things to people I love. When he died, at first, I felt nothing. I thought the world was a better place without him in it. It wasn't until much later that I gave myself permission to mourn him. He was awful, but he was still the one who taught me everything I know. He might not have told me he loved me all the time, but he was also the one who put food on the table, taught me how to fight, and made sure I had clothes. Those things don't make him a saint by any means, but it still showed me that he cared. I'm sure your mom did that for you too." My eyes widen at Rayne's words, the emotion behind them something I wasn't expecting from the rough and tough hunter-vampire. "If you ever want to talk about it, I'll be around."

Zach surprises me by shooting up to his feet and wrapping his arms around Rayne's neck.

"Thank you for setting us free," he whispers.

Her body tenses up momentarily before softening into the hug. She seems to be surprising herself with this moment of affection, allowing her guard to come down.

"Come on, Pumpkin," I say to Amelia, reaching out a hand and leading her and my mom to the kitchen, giving Zach and Rayne some space to talk. The fact that he is willingly touching her is enough proof that in time he's going to be okay.

Chapter Twenty-Three

Pearl

I stand and stare at the clothes laid out on the bed for so long that my eyes blur. I hear voices on the other side of the door, and I want to go out and join them, but I can't tear my eyes away from the bed.

I feel like I'm back to being the girl they pulled from that facility so many years ago. The one that I tried desperately to bury.

Broken. That's what I feel like.

I shake my head, sliding my mask back on, trying desperately to rebuild the walls with the crumbling ruins surrounding them. I reach down, my body moving on autopilot as I step each leg into the yoga pants and tug the shirt over my head.

"Are you okay?" Rayne's voice startles me from the door. I'm so lost in my head that I didn't even hear her come in.

For a moment, seeing her face sends relief through my body. I need a friend. Not that Loukas isn't the perfect mate, but having someone who saw me at my worst and helped me through the trauma is a welcomed sight until I remember...

"You can't be in here," I whisper, my body moving backward like having the bed between us will make the difference.

"Pearl," Rayne says, her voice sounding pained.

"I don't want to hurt you," I whisper again, tears filling my eyes.

She blurs closer to me, using her speed and taking my face in her hands.

"You would never hurt me."

"I almost..." I choke down a sob, visions of yesterday flashing by.

"Look at me," she demands, and I raise my eyes to hers. "Yesterday was not your fault. Plus, you didn't hurt me. See." She lowers a hand, gesturing to herself.

"I could have."

She lets out a chuckle. "Babe. I am a highly trained hunter. The only time you would hurt me is if I let you. Unless I know I deserve it, I won't." A small smile graces my lips at her words, knowing they're the truth. She may have been right when she admitted that I can beat a lot of people on this island in a fight, but she is not one of them. "There she is."

"What about Bree and the kids?" I ask. "Did you tell them?"

"I told Bree," she says, stepping back. "But like me, She doesn't believe for a second that you will hurt any of us."

"I wouldn't mean to."

"Do something for me," she says ignoring my previous statement and I dip my chin in agreement. "Search inside you. Right now, do you feel like you want to bite me? Like you want my blood."

My eyes widen, but she pins me with a stare, so I close my eyes and do as she asks. She steps closer, I feel her body brushing against mine, hear the slow rhythmic beating of her heart, the warmth of her skin, but unlike yesterday when all I could think of was getting one little drop of her blood, I feel nothing but safe with my friend beside me. There is a small part of me that remembers how it felt at first but...

"No," I say, my eyes opening to see Rayne smiling. "I mean there is a little thing in my brain telling me that I can be powerful if I were to drink from you but it's something I can ignore."

"And your magic?" she asks and once again I close my eyes, searching for that spark inside me. The green well where my magic resides.

"It's small but there."

"See. You're not a danger to us. You're stronger than you give yourself credit for."

"Thank you," I tell her, flinging my arms around her neck, unafraid that I will hurt her and trusting that she can handle me if I do. For the first time this morning, I feel like my life will actually be okay.

I know Loukas tried to convince me of that, and I desperately wanted to believe him, but I didn't. Not really.

"It's what family does. I was only the first option. If it didn't work with me, Drusilla and Andres were up next. Breanne was not willing to accept what Artemis said."

"No, I can't imagine she would be." I let out a giggle. I glance at the door. "How are things out there?"

Rayne lets out a sigh and sits on the bed. "Loukas told the kids about Antonia, and I admitted to the part I played."

I suck in a breath. "How did that go?"

"Better than I expected, but I do think Zach is going to need an outlet. He is conflicted. On one side he's happy that he's free and doesn't need to worry about her hurting them ever again. On the other hand—which he doesn't want to admit to yet—he's sad because she was..."

"His mother," I finish with a nod.

"Exactly. And I know how he feels, I felt the same about my father when he died. To me, he was cold and distant but made sure I was happy, safe, and healthy. At the same time, he was able to do horrible things to Drusilla and then to River. It was hard to come to terms that I was allowed to mourn who my father was to me and hate the monster he showed the world."

"So, they don't hate me?"

"Hate you? Why would they hate you?"

"Because I stood there and watched as you killed them," I tell her, and now that I have a little clearer head, I can see how that might seem a silly thing to say.

"If they were going to hate anyone, it would be me. And as for right now, I think they feel more relief than anything. Come on. Come see for yourself," she says, standing up and reaching for my hand.

The two of us walk out of the bedroom, finding a house full of our friends and families. There's a moment where I look for Breanne, Matt, and the kids, not seeing them anywhere, and feel a little hurt. I wonder if they're afraid of me now until I register that the sun is out. I find Loukas' eyes and see the relief in them at seeing me standing here.

"Pearl," Amelia's little voice calls out moments before I'm tackled by a little blur with chestnut hair.

"Hi, sweetheart. Are you okay?" I ask, crouching down and wiping the tears from her cheeks.

She nods but says, "My mommy's dead."

"I know, sweet pea, and I'm sorry," I tell her, brushing her hair off of her face.

"Zachy says we're safe now, that her being dead means she's not a threat to us anymore." The words coming out of her little mouth shock me, but she's not done. "But then Rayne said it's okay to still be sad because she was my mommy."

"I never thought I'd say this," I mutter under my breath looking up at the sassy vampire who smirks at me. "But Rayne is right. It's okay for you to be sad. And even though I never want to see you cry, I will give you all the hugs and snuggles you need until all your tears dry up."

She wraps her arms around me, snuggling into my neck and I hug her back tightly, closing my eyes.

"Pearl?" Zach's voice says softly from behind Amelia, and I straighten up.

"Mmmhm?"

"Come on, munchkin, I think your dad could use some help with those pancakes," Rayne says to Amelia, reaching out a hand and leading her back to the kitchen.

"I just wanted to say thank you for going back for my dad." My mouth drops open in shock at his words, not realizing they told him the entire story. "Rayne said…"

"Of course, she did," I mutter under my breath once more, glaring at the vampire, making sure to soften my gaze as I look back at Zach.

"Rayne said that my mom…Antonia was trying to take my dad and that you made sure she didn't."

"It was a little more complicated than that," I tell him.

"Still, because of you,"

"And Rayne," I supply, and he nods.

"And Rayne, my dad is here with us, and we are safe. We don't need to run or worry that she's going to find us tomorrow or next week."

"She never would have gotten you guys back. I wouldn't let her have you," I declare, my strength coming back to me easier in defense of these beautiful children.

"I know you wouldn't. Still, I wanted to thank you."

"You know you are far too mature for a kid your age; anyone ever tell you that?" I ask with a smile.

"Dad and Ya-Ya do."

"Well, they're right." I take a risk, placing my hands on his upper arms. "You don't have to thank me. Your dad is my mate, that makes you my family. In this family, we protect one another."

"So, you don't want Dad to send us away?" he asks, his voice small.

"Now why would I do a thing like that?"

"In the coven, if someone met their mate and they already had children with someone else, they would send them away,"

My heart breaks for this little boy standing in front of me. He's probably been worried sick about what is going to happen to him.

"I will *never* send either of you away."

"What if you and my dad have other kids, won't you love them more?"

"Never," I declare. "If your dad and I are blessed with more children, my heart will just have to grow to fit you all inside. You and your sister may not be mine by blood, but I've claimed you as my own with every fiber of my being."

"You have?" he asks.

"Of course, I have," I tell him, and he wastes no time launching himself into my arms. I feel small wet droplets on my shoulder, hoping and praying that they are happy tears as I hug him back.

I wait for his tears to dry up before pulling back and wiping the evidence of them off his face, walking with him into the kitchen where I kiss my mate and hug our children to me.

One week later...

The moon hangs low in the ink-black sky, casting a soft, silvery glow over the secluded beach behind my house—sorry—*our* house.

The gentle rhythm of the waves plays a soothing nocturne, a prelude to the mystical union that is about to unfold. My heart flutters with a mix of anticipation and nervous excitement as I swim just off the shore, the cool night breeze carrying the scent of salt and the faint fragrance of exotic flowers adorning the makeshift altar. Tonight is the night I will unite my life with the extraordinary being who has captured my heart—Loukas. The owl shifter who the goddess deemed my perfect match.

Emerging from the inky depths, my scales shimmer in the moonlight, and the sea nymphs who accompany me hum a melodic tune, creating an enchanting atmosphere around the ceremony.

My long, flowing hair, the color of the aquamarine seas, cascades down my shoulders as I glide toward the shore.

Loukas' eyes, reflecting the shimmering moon, meet mine, and in that silent exchange, I feel a profound connection—tonight is the night we will bridge the gap between our worlds. This will be the first mating ceremony anyone other than sea nymphs has been to, and I'm both nervous and excited about it.

Loukas stands there, waiting, wearing white linen pants and a shirt with the top buttons undone, his expression a mix of awe and love. Both Narissa and Alaric stand on a raised platform on the beach, ready to officiate the ceremony. Together, they represent our two worlds. My fins turn to legs and Breanne raises up the simple white flowing dress, slipping it over my head as I walk barefoot along the beach toward my mate.

"Under the watchful gaze of the moon and the whispers of the ocean, we gather to witness the union of two souls, bound by the threads of love and destiny," Narissa proclaims, her words resonating with a deep, mystical energy. "The sea nymph and the shifter, two worlds entwined in a dance of eternal connection."

As she speaks, the elements respond in harmony. The night breeze carries the scent of salt, and the waves rise and fall in sync with the beating of our hearts, as if nature itself acknowledges and celebrates our union under the moonlit sky.

"As is our custom in pods, the mates will now pledge themselves to one another," Narissa says and I turn back toward Loukas, gesturing for him to go first.

"*Agapi mou*, I pledge to be your anchor in the stormy seas. To love and cherish the gift that you are for the rest of my days."

"I vow to be your guiding light in the darkest nights. I promise to love you fiercely. To protect you and...." I reach down, tugging both Amelia and Zach over to stand with us looking down at them. "And I also vow to you both to love and cherish you as if you were my own children. To be an ear to listen, a shoulder to cry on, a friend in your times of need."

Even Zach has a small tear trailing down his cheek, and I pull them both in for a hug, Loukas wrapping his arms around the three of us. Loukas and I didn't talk about including the kids in the ceremony, but it just felt right.

"This is a little different from most mating ceremonies I've officiated, particularly because we are not only here witnessing the joining of true mates, but also welcoming two new groups to our little slice of heaven," Alaric calls out as we step back. "Do you Loukas take Pearl as your bonded mate, taking your rightful place amongst her pod and she with your parliament?"

"I do."

"Do you promise to guide and protect all members of the pod and parliament from this day forward until your dying breath?"

"I do."

He then turns to me, "Do you Pearl, pod mother, take Loukas as your bonded mate and accept his place at your side and you at his?"

"I do," I reply.

"Not that I need to ask, after knowing you for so long..." Alaric begins. "But do you promise to guide and protect all members of the pod and parliament from this day forward, until your dying breath?"

I look out at the large crowd on land, seeing not only my friends and family from all the supernatural factions but also everyone from Loukas' parliament as well. Then I look to the sea, seeing all the members of my and Narissa's pod swimming, humming the tune of our people.

"I do," I declare.

"With Mother Moon as our witness, I declare Loukas and Pearl bonded mates and the alpha pair of both the Luminara Sea Nymphs and the Greek Parliament."

The sea nymphs just off shore join in a harmonious chorus, a symphony of underwater voices that adds a magical layer to the nighttime ceremony.

As husband and wife, Loukas and I seal our union with a kiss that speaks volumes—a kiss that tastes of salt and dreams, of passion and promises, beneath the silvery gaze of the moon. Everyone erupts in joyous cheers, and the beach seems to come alive with the celebration of a love that defies convention under the night sky.

The celebration continues into the night, with a feast of exotic fruits and seafood that seems to appear magically. The sea nymphs, vampires, and shifters dance under the moonlit sky, their laughter mingling with the rhythmic crash of the waves. It is a joyous affirmation of love's ability to transcend the boundaries of the known and embrace the magic that lies within the heart.

As Loukas and I stand on the beach, surrounded by those who have witnessed our union, I can't help but reflect on the extraordinary journey that has brought us to this moment.

Love, it seems, is the most potent magic of all, capable of bridging the vast expanse between land and sea, between different worlds and realms, even under the enchanting veil of the night. Our union marks a harmonious convergence of two beings who, against all odds, find solace and completion in each other. The island, now bathed in the soft glow of the moon, seems to bear witness to a love that will echo through the ages—the love between a sea nymph and a shifter, bound by a nighttime ceremony that defies the ordinary and embraces the extraordinary.

We make our way back to our little home, soon to be bigger home as we've already discussed the extension plans with Axel.

I'm a ball of nerves as we enter, not sure how he's going to feel about my mating gift.

I take a deep breath as I hand him the box I'd hidden under the bed.

"What's this?" he asks, and I gesture for him to open it. I watch as he tenderly pulls apart the ribbon. A combination of excitement and anticipation overwhelms me. I hold my breath as he takes the top off the box. His eyes go wide as he realizes its contents. He looks up at me with a mixture of curiosity and lust. "Are you sure... Is this really what you want?".

I gaze back at him with so much love and adoration.

"Loukas, you've given me so much already, I just wanted to give you something no one else could, pure control... I want you to do whatever your heart desires, any fantasy you have, I want to be a part of it. I trust you".

He drops the box and takes me in his arms. He kisses me fiercely, as if every ounce of his desire had been bottled and is now overflowing. The taste of his lips sends my body into a frenzy as fireworks start spreading throughout my veins. There's a passion in him that I feel I will never get enough of, leaving me hungry for every touch, every caress. I want it all, always.

He picks me up and leads me over to the edge of the bed. He whispers in my ear, "You're sure of this."

I nod and all I can squeak out is, "Yes, please."

My words falter as the anticipation consumes me. He gently sits me down on the satin sheets. He looks at me with fierceness in his eyes.

"I want you to pick a safe word."

I unexpectedly giggle, until I realize the seriousness of what he's saying. I struggle to come up with something witty on the spot.

"Red light," I blurt out, feeling the apprehensiveness behind my words.

He pulls the blindfold out of the box and crawls up on the bed behind me. He places it softly over my eyes and leans into my ear as he tightens it behind my head, gently he whispers, "If you're uncomfortable at any time, you say the safe word."

I shiver as his breath hits my neck.

All my other senses heighten with the sudden loss of my vision. I nod as every word now escapes me and my only thoughts are of his touch.

"That's my good girl," with an undertone of longing in his voice. I unexpectedly melt at the sound of his praise.

"Arms up." I obey as he slides my dress over my head, feeling a rush of cool air on my bare skin. He pauses for a moment, "My gods you are so beautiful."

I blush, knowing he's examining every inch of my naked body. I feel a rope pass over my chest. He slides it over my skin at such a slow pace, up and over my arms like a snake entangling its prey. He lightly kisses the side of my neck as I feel new knots being tightened all down the front of me.

There's something so soft and beautiful in the way he binds me with the ropes he's pulled from the box as he tenderly caresses my skin with his lips after every new knot is tied, as if he's wrapping up a delicate flower into a pretty little package.

I feel safe in this type of surrender, giving everything to him at this moment. Every sensation brings about something new, unexplored. I've never been more excited or turned on. My arms, now bound behind my back, restrict my ability to move. He pulls my body right to the end of the bed in a sitting position and pulls my legs apart. I feel my heart racing as he traces the inside of my thigh with his finger inching his way higher, stopping just short of where I need him. I try to slide myself over so he's hitting where I want, but as I do I feel him get off the bed. Suddenly, his head is right between my thighs.

"Is this what you're searching for?" he asks as I feel his fingers slide inside me.

"Yes." I moan as electricity courses through me.

"Or maybe it was this?" he asks as he slides his tongue up my leg straight to my clit. I cry out, begging for more.

The restriction of the ropes and the blindfold cutting off my sight leave me with nothing to do but enjoy the sensations.

"Please..." I beg. "Loukas, you're going to make me..."

He pulls away, cutting me off short of my release. He stands me up and flips me over, pushing my torso into the bed.

"You're not allowed to cum until I say so, understand?" The assertiveness in his tone almost sends me over the edge.

"Yes, sir." I giggle as he lightly smacks my ass, knowing full well I don't think I can last much longer. He strips down and pauses at my back, with a feathered touch he traces his fingers around my thighs.

"Are you ready?"

"Please, Loukas." He slides inside me as he grips my waist a little harder with each thrust. Each plunge brings me that much closer, propelling us both to the brink of pure bliss.

I don't know if it is the bindings, the blindfold, or simply giving Loukas full control over everything and being able to shut off my brain, but I find myself having the biggest orgasm of my life, pulling him over the edge with me.

"I love you, Pearl," he whispers as he finds his release.

"And I love you, Loukas. Now and always," I respond, for the first time secretly hoping that Demeter's magic being added to the barrier will allow us to expand our little family.

I snuggle deeper into my mate, letting sleep take me, for the first time in a very long time excited about what the future has in store.

Epilogue

Meredith–Present Day

"Meredith?" Samara calls from the side of the sparring ring where I am currently getting my ass kicked. By choice, in case you were wondering.

Sometimes the new recruits need to get their asses kicked, and sometimes they need to kick some ass. It's important to be able to tell the difference.

This is the latter. Camille is in her first year of the Supernatural Enforcement Program, and she has been making amazing headway. She's strong, fast, and smart. She's so great, in fact, that she's been sparring with the third-year students for the last month, and it's been affecting her self-esteem. I decided to hop in the ring with her. I'm sure she knows that I'm letting her, but I also can tell she's enjoying it.

"Time," I tell Camille who stops, her fist raised.

"Aw, Mer. I was just about to finish it," she whines, though she still has a smile on her face, so I know she's not really upset.

"I know you were, Cammie." I pat her on the shoulder before climbing out of the ring, grabbing my towel, and wrapping it around the back of my neck.

"Hey, Alpha," I say to Samara, taking a big drink of my water bottle.

It's hard work getting your ass kicked.

She wrinkles her nose. "I told you to call me Sam."

"I'm just being respectful and calling you by your title."

"Yes, well, I think it's more respectful to call people what they ask to be called," she retorts, and I chuckle.

"You'd think after almost a decade of being the alpha of the feline shifters on the island, that you would be used to the title."

"You'd think," she says with a smirk, wrapping her arm around my shoulder, leading me over to the chairs, and gesturing for me to take a seat.

"You wanted to talk?" I ask after a moment or two of silence.

She nods. "I wanted to talk to you about joining a team."

I shake my head, cutting her off.

"We've talked about this. I don't want to join a team, I'm happy teaching."

"I know, and I heard you. I want you to join my team."

My mouth drops open. "Your team?"

"My team," she agrees.

"And what exactly will *your* team be doing?"

"Does that mean you're interested?" she asks, raising an eyebrow.

"Let's say that I am," I tell her with a smile.

"I thought you might be." She smirks. "As you know, the other leaders and I have been reaching out to the human leaders for the past four years."

I nod because I did know that. "Okay..."

"Well, finally, after numerous Zoom calls, teleconferences, and phone calls, the Canadian Government has agreed to a private, in-person meeting."

My eyes widen.

"Really?" I ask, excitement coursing through me. With the

threat of the prophecy hanging over our heads and then with River leaving four years ago, we've redoubled our efforts to get the human government to listen.

The sooner we get them on board, the sooner River can come home. The sooner that Riley will be whole again. They may be a few years younger than me, but their being the next couple in the prophecy makes them pretty much celebrities. Even a blind person can see how much River leaving has destroyed Riley, and only a monster would want to drag that out.

"Yes. And we're making a small team of trusted enforcers to accompany us and watch our backs."

"When you say our, who exactly do you mean?" I ask.

"Right now, it's Alaric, Darren, Sebastyn, Loukas, and me who plan to attend."

"What about the others? Axel? Drake?" I don't ask about Rayne or Skarlyt because I know them well enough to know they aren't prepared for diplomacy.

"We decided as a group that these individuals had the best chance of communicating. Axel and Andres are far too large and intimidating. Skarlyt and Pearl will automatically not be taken seriously, and we need to be taken seriously."

I nod, understanding. "And Drake?"

She chuckles. "Where Drake goes, his mate goes."

"Understood," I agree. "And who else is on this team?"

"Each leader has chosen one person to accompany us, to be their personal bodyguard."

"And I'm yours?" I ask, "Surely you can find someone older and more experienced to choose."

"There are people who have more experience like you say," she agrees. "But I don't trust them as much as I trust you." My tiger preens at the praise from our alpha.

Simmer down before you embarrass us, I mentally berate her.

"Thank you. That means a lot coming from you."

"Does that mean you'll join us?"

I pretend to think it over, but the truth is that she had me the second she said she wanted me on her team.

"Of course. When do we leave?"

"The meeting is set for next week, but you and I will be leaving tomorrow and staying in a hotel close by so we can scout out the place. We will try to find any weak spots and follow the human politicians to make sure they're not up to anything."

"And gather any dirt we can at the same time?"

She nods at my guess.

"Well, then. I better go pack," I tell her, both of us standing at the same time and heading toward the door.

"I'm glad you agreed to come with me," she says softly.

"Just out of curiosity, who was your second choice?"

"I didn't have one," she chuckles. "I trusted that you would have my back."

I can't tell whether she is lying or not, but both my tiger and I are inclined to believe her. After all, I was trained by the best. I was trained by her.

As I make my way home, excitement flows through me at the idea that I will finally be able to make a difference in the supernatural world. Trepidation sinks in when I realize I have to tell my mom and brother about my mission.

I know they will both worry. That's the real reason I have never accepted Samara's offer to join a team. My mother fears losing me like she lost my father. My baby brother—though he's only a couple of years younger than me—fears he will be left behind... Again.

That is one of the biggest regrets of my life. Though I was only a child myself, my parents gave themselves up to ensure our safety. I kept him safe for a while. But that was all it was. A while.

Trace, my little brother, has never held it against me, but I see the looks he gets sometimes. Like everyone else who was rescued from one of the facilities, he has trauma.

Sometimes he gets a far-off look in his eyes or flinches at the sound of a door closing. His flashbacks have become less frequent now, thankfully, but the fact that he has them at all hurts. Especially knowing that it's all my fault.

If I hadn't fallen asleep. If I had found us a safer place to stay. If I had made sure that he stayed within arm's reach at all times.

If. If. If.

I've spent hours with Charleigh going over how it wasn't my fault. How there was nothing I could've done. How I was just a child myself. Most days I believe her.

Our little house comes into view, and I stop, taking a deep, steadying breath and readying myself for this hard conversation.

"Mom? Trace?" I call out as I walk into the house.

"In the kitchen," My mom responds, and I slip off my shoes and make my way into the kitchen.

"Hi, Ma," I say, walking closer to her and pressing a kiss to her cheek before I ruffle Trace's hair. "Little bro."

He grunts, standing to his full height, almost a foot taller than me. "Not so little anymore."

"You may be bigger than me, but you'll always be my baby brother," I tease.

"You seem happy," My mother surmises as she takes the loaf of bread out of the oven.

"I am," I admit, taking a piece of cheese off the counter and popping it in my mouth.

"Oh, do tell," my mother says, raising a brow.

"Samara has asked me to accompany her and the other leaders to a meeting with the human government."

"You're going on a mission?" My mom says, placing the hot loaf pan on top of the stove, her voice wavering.

"Mom," I say, stepping closer to her, and placing my hand on her shoulder. "It's not the kind of mission that puts me in danger. I won't be going straight into the lion's den so to speak."

"No, you'll just be meeting with humans," she snarls.

"Mom," I plead.

"You know what they do," she challenges.

"Not all humans are the same," I retort, looking into her eyes.

"No, perhaps not. But a lot are. What they did to your brother and me should be evidence enough."

"Those were hunters."

"They were humans who chose a dark path," she scolds.

The room falls quiet, the weight of our shared history hanging in the air. My mother's experiences with hunters have left scars that run deeper than any physical wound. I understand her fear; it is etched into her every word and gesture. Trace, who has been silent throughout our exchange, finally speaks up.

"Mom, Meredith's not going out there alone. She's with Samara and others who can protect her," he interjects, his voice firm but gentle.

My mother's gaze softens as she looks at Trace, the worry in her eyes fading into resignation. "I know, Trace. It's just... I can't help but worry. You both mean everything to me."

"I promise, Mom, I'll be careful," I assure her, feeling a pang of guilt for causing her distress. "And I'll make sure I keep in touch, okay?"

She nods, the lines on her face softening. "I trust you, Meredith. It's just... hard."

"I know," I say softly, pulling her into a tight hug. "But I'll be back before you know it."

Trace steps forward, joining our embrace. "We'll take care of each other, Mom. Meredith's got this."

Reluctantly, she lets go, wiping away a tear that escaped. "I know you do. Just... promise me you'll be safe."

"I promise," I say firmly, exchanging a glance with Trace, silently reaffirming our commitment to each other's well-being.

As I begin packing for the impending journey, I can't shake the mix of emotions swirling within me. Excitement for the opportunity to make a difference mingled with the weight of my family's worries. As I look at the few belongings I need to take, I know I am ready to face whatever lies ahead, bolstered by the support and love of my family.

The next morning, I leave a note on the kitchen table, assuring my mother and Trace that I'll be in touch regularly. As I step out of the house, I can't help but feel the gravity of the task ahead. Still, I square my shoulders, determined to make my family proud and contribute to a better future for all supernaturals.

The next week flies by with Samara and I scoping out the meeting place in Alberta. Rather than meeting in a government building, the human politicians felt it would be safer if we were to meet in a hotel conference room. So, we checked into the same hotel, booked the conference room, and set up some hidden cameras according to Matt's specifications so that we could livestream the meeting back to the rest of the alphas on the island. Because we know the humans will likely check for them, we had Sebastyn teleport in and use magic to conceal them.

I'm sure that the meeting would go downhill pretty fast if they were to find out that we were recording it. But, like Samara said, even though we're only bringing a small number of the leaders, the rest aren't any less important and deserve a seat at the table.

Despite our best efforts, none of the politicians came early, so getting dirt—well more dirt than Matt was able to find online—isn't an option. We just have to hope that it's enough to sway them should we need leverage.

"I think we're ready," Samara says, walking back toward me and the door after triple-checking that all the cameras are in working order.

I nod in agreement knowing that there isn't an inch of the room that isn't visible from one camera or another as well as microphones to catch even the slightest sound. "So, what's the plan?"

She looks over at me with a smile. "We go downstairs, have some breakfast, and wait for everyone else to show up."

"And give the humans time to check out the space while hoping and praying that they don't find any of our cameras."

"They won't," she declares, her faith in Sebastyn and Matt unwavering.

"Let's hope," I whisper, following her out into the hallway, down the stairs, and into the attached dining area of the hotel.

When we walk in, we find the rest of our group already seated and enjoying their meal, all the alphas dressed in suits and ties at one table and their chosen enforcers, dressed in black tactical gear at another. I join the latter while Samara joins the former.

Unlike the others in our group, I can't eat. My tiger is restless inside me, pacing back and forth as if she's caged—which I guess she is. Still, it's uncharacteristic of her. Normally she's very passive unless needed. Now, it feels like she knows something I don't. Like she knows something big is going to happen. And I guess if I go by the feeling in my gut, I do too. I just don't know if it's going to be a good thing or a bad thing.

"Mer?" Riley says, touching my hand.

"Hmm?" I ask, snapping out of the trance I seemed to be in.

"I asked if you're okay. I've been talking to you for the past five minutes," he says, keeping his voice low.

"Oh yeah. I'm fine. Just zoned out there for a minute," I respond, placing a confident smile on my face even though I don't feel confident at all.

"Good. You had me worried," he says, his blue eyes glinting in the lights, though they don't light up anymore on their own—not since River left. He tries to put his best foot forward. To be happy.

But anyone who really knows him can tell that he's struggling. The longer she's gone, the harder it is for him.

I place my hand on his shoulder.

"You're a good friend, Riley."

"You are too, Mer," he says with a wink, shoulder-checking me.

"All right everyone, show time," Alaric says, his eyes following a group of humans and what must be their bodyguards as they move through the hotel toward the conference room. Rather than tactical gear like us, they're all wearing suits. The only giveaway is the guns on their hips and tiny earbuds in their ears.

As one, the group of enforcers stands, moving to join our assigned person. Me with Samara, Riley with Alaric, Nik with Loukas, Lennox with Darren, and Zander with Sebastyn. Not that any of them need us to protect them. Not really. They are all more than capable of taking care of themselves, but Rayne said it would make the humans feel less threatened by them if they acted like they needed guards. Not two or three per person like the politicians we're following, but one apiece would do the trick.

As we walk, my tiger's pacing increases and my nostrils flare as I catch the scent of something amazing. I inhale deeply, the citrusy scent getting stronger the closer we get to the room.

"Riley and Zander will join us inside. The rest of you, find positions outside the door but within earshot," Alaric says, and my tiger roars inside my head.

What's wrong? I ask her.

She doesn't answer. Instead, she just claws at me from the inside until I'm moving forward toward the door. The closer I get, the more she calms, and I furrow my brows in confusion. I take a spot next to the door, nonetheless. As soon as I turn my back to the door, my tiger redoubles her efforts at clawing her way out, and I gasp.

Are you okay? Samara asks through our link.

I look at her.

I don't think so. I think I need to be in that room.

Are you sensing danger?

I don't know what it is, I admit. It's *my tiger; she's going crazy. She wants—no—needs to be in that room.*

I'm going to pull Alaric into our link, she warns, and I give her a nod.

Samara and I have a bond because she is the alpha of my pride and, despite his reluctance to accept the results of the recent election, Alaric is now the Alpha-King or King Alpha. Because of this, he now shares a mind-link with every alpha on the island. It's also why Darren is now the alpha of the Westwood pack and no longer Alaric's beta.

You're sure that your tiger wants you in that room? Alaric's deep voice filters through the link.

My eyes dart to his, and I do another quick check-in with my tiger.

I'm sure.

Okay, he says through the link.

"Change of plans. Riley and Meredith will join us in the room. Zander, you stay out here and be ready."

Zander's eyes widen in surprise and then curiosity, but he dips his chin in agreement.

Thank you, I tell them both, taking Zander's place in the formation while he takes my spot by the door.

I scan the room as I walk in, steps in front of Samara. I stop short as my eyes land on a tall man with white-blonde hair and bright green eyes.

My tiger roars in my mind.

Mate.

His eyes widen as they meet mine, and I take an involuntary step forward only to be stopped by Samara.

My tiger begins to let out a growl at her, how dare she keep us from our mate?

I look back at him, and he gives a subtle shake of his head.

I swallow my anger, confusion flowing through me.

"Meredith, are you okay?" Samara asks, her hand moving to my shoulder.

I shake my head; my tiger is just as confused as I am.

Why has our mate not stepped forward to claim us? Why is he standing on that side of the table with a bunch of humans?

"I don't know," I respond, searching my mate's eyes for some sort of explanation.

About the Author

F.D. Fair is the author of the Westwood Pack Series. As an avid reader of Paranormal Romance Novels for the past 20 years, she turned her love of everything paranormal into steamy True Mate novels with a twist.

F.D. Fair lives and works in southern Ontario, Canada and

spends her time when she is not working or writing with the loves of her life—Her husband and 3 boys.

She is as weird as they come but is proud of it. Embracing her weirdness makes for some great stories.

Sign up for FD Fair's Newsletter:
https://dashboard.mailerlite.com/forms/76323/
58096238431569310/share

Make sure to stalk her...

Instagram:
https://www.instagram.com/f.d.fairauthor

Facebook:
https://www.facebook.com/profile.php?id=100071688648516

Goodreads:
https://www.goodreads.com/author/show/21734156.F_D_Fair

Twitter:
https://twitter.com/FdFair

Bookbub:
https://www.bookbub.com/authors/f-d-fair

More from Foundations
Rhiannon's Revenge

www.FoundationsBooks.net

Rhiannon's Circle by Emily Bex

GET IT HERE: https://www.emilybex.com/the-bohannon-witches-duology/

"Readers seeking occult fiction that excels in mystery, romance, and family struggle will welcome Rhiannon's Circle's powerful, compelling saga." **- D. Donovan, Sr. Reviewer, Midwest Book Review**

On Goodreads' "Best Books with Witches" and "Best Adult Vampire Books" Lists!

Eilish Bohannon is the witch destined to lead the coven, but only if her older sister doesn't kill her first.

Set in Charleston, SC, the Bohannons lead a coven whose legendary powers date back to ancient Ireland. In each generation, one witch is destined to rise to High Priestess. Oldest sister, Seraphina, is certain the role is hers and will do anything to ensure Eilish doesn't interfere with her plans.

Even if it means getting rid of her baby sister for good.

If Eilish is to survive and claim her rightful role, she'll need the support of her middle sister, Anya, and a lot of help in the form of a vampire named Ian Cross...who was seemingly placed right in her path by the goddess Rhiannon. Their attraction to each other is immediate. Searing. And, ultimately, *forbidden*, since no coven will follow a Priestess who has bonded with his kind.

On their quest to find the answers needed to stop Seraphina, they consult with one of the oldest members of the coven, a crone named Henwen, who presents them with another problem – a Bohannon grimoire exists and has been purposefully hidden. Eilish and Anya will need to find the book if they have any chance of survival...

...as it holds the power of the Bohannon coven and can only be controlled by the witch destined to own it.

This dark and imaginative paranormal story by International Bestselling Author Emily Bex has romance as hot as a steamy Charleston summer with a pinch of Wiccan magic, a little mystery, and a lot of murder.

More from Foundations
Vengeance Marked

www.FoundationsBooks.net

Vengeance Marked by S.J. Pierce

GET IT HERE: https://www.sjpiercebooks.com/full-width-page-2/

International Bestselling Author SJ Pierce brings a "heart-pounding" and "electric" story to the Paranormal Romance genre that's interlaced with twists, turns, HEAT, and thrilling suspense. This one's a must-read...

Complete series available now!

When the woman of your dreams looks like a

demon...that's never a good sign.

Isaac doesn't know it, but his dreams of a woman with black eyes are actually a premonition. So, when he meets her in real life, sans demon-eyes, he knows something isn't quite right. But he also has a hard time staying away. What do these dreams mean? And why, despite their sizzling chemistry, can't he shake the feeling it will all end in catastrophe?

Probably because he also knows she's hiding something.

When the man you crave is also the man you've been sent to kidnap...things get messy.

The ones who created Alyx are watching her every move, which includes her forbidden meetings with the man she's been sent to spy on: Isaac...who also doesn't know who or *what* she is. So, when her creators finally summon to fulfill her purpose and capture him, she knows they're not the only ones she'll have to answer to. When all of mankind hangs in the balance, there is no room for error, and her draw to Isaac had her stumbling from the start. It's only a matter of time before things start going to hell.

Literally.

If only she'd followed the rules...

Fans of Gena Showalter and Christine Feehan will devour this EPIC end of the world, FORBIDDEN ROMANCE series. One-click today to get your binge-read on!

If you like **PARANORMAL ROMANCE** *books, or supernatural, you will love this.* - **Michelle's Paranormal Vault of Books ★★★★★**

WOW! *What an awesome beginning to a new series!* - **Nomi's Paranormal Palace ★★★★**

A **CAPTIVATING BOOK** *right from the start.* - **Mandy, Goodreads ★★★★★**

Foundations Book Publishing

Our mission is to exceed the expectations of our authors and the reading community with an uncompromising commitment to quality, individualism and personal pride. We measure our success one book at a time.

You can find more great works in multiple genres including Romance, Literary Fictions, Thrillers, Suspense, Young Adult, and more!

Visit us at FoundationsBooks.net

www.ingramcontent.com/pod-product-compliance
Lightning Source LLC
Chambersburg PA
CBHW050355260626
47156CB00003B/742